Charlotte Hobson's first book, *Black Earth City*, won a Somerset Maugham Award and was shortlisted for the Duff Cooper Prize and the Thomas Cook Travel Book Award. She lives in Cornwall with her husband, the writer Philip Marsden, and their two children.

Further praise for *The Vanishing Futurist*:

'The book's strength is its portrayal of the Russian avant-garde scene, with its futurist performances and poetry, seen through the eyes of a newcomer.' *Spectator*

'A rapturous, carnival-like ride into political disorder, heady romance and absurdity as one societal infrastructure is dismantled and replaced with another . . . What is conveyed most affectingly, with all the reviving powers of a shot of Armenian brandy, is the exhilaration and promise of a dream, an exceptional historical moment that continues to reverberate today.' *Guardian*

'The tale ping-pongs between the conservative and the absurd, and the style has shades of Mikhail Bulgakov's *The Master and Margarita* . . . A very accomplished first novel.' *Scotland on Sunday*

'Hobson has a wonderful gift for writing about Russia with a deeply Russi~~an tenderness that makes me~~ go week at the kn~~ees. Rus~~ ~~~~ ~~~~ so very intimate, and she writes about it from the inside . . . Heart-breaking, funny and brilliant.' Rosamund Bartlett, author of *Tolstoy: A Russian Life*

'Hilary Mantel once said of Elizabeth Jane Howard that "She reminds us of what novels are for." While I yield to no one in my admiration for Ms Mantel, I feel that this statement is far more applicable to *The Vanishing Futurist*. It is wonderful – in its ambition, its insistence on the truth, its refusal to be daunted.' Artemis Cooper

'Like her futurist's revolutionary schemes, Charlotte Hobson's novel is a marvel: a beautiful lament for doomed dreams and innocents crushed by history's brutality, an expedition on the hazy border between victimhood and guilt – and, at the same time, an ingenious, vivid, mesmerising story. I loved it.' A. D. Miller

'An extraordinary novel which captures the mixture of tragedy and idealism that has characterised Russia's modern history.' Marcel Theroux

'Deftly pulls you into the exhilarating vortex of revolution, and leaves you weeping yet somehow full of wonder on the other side. That rare case of a profound book being unputdownable.' Peter Pomerantsev

The Vanishing Futurist

CHARLOTTE HOBSON

FABER & FABER

First published in 2016
by Faber & Faber Limited
Bloomsbury House, 74–77 Great Russell Street
London WC1B 3DA
This paperback edition first published in 2017

Typeset by Faber & Faber Ltd
Printed and bound by CPI Group (UK) Ltd, Croydon, CR0 4YY

Excerpt from Trotsky's *Sochineniia*, XXI: 110–12, from *A People's Tragedy: The
Russian Revolution 1891–1924*, published by Jonathan Cape. Reproduced by
permission of the Random House Group Ltd.
'Incantation by Laughter', Velemir Khlebnikov, translated by Gary Kern, from
The Chatto Book of Nonsense Poetry, edited by Hugh Haughton and published by
Chatto & Windus. Reproduced by permission of the Random House Group Ltd.
Excerpt from 'Trumpet of the Martians', Velemir Khlebnikov, in *Russian
Futurism through Its Manifestos*, translated by Anna Lawton and Herbert Eagle,
Cornell University Press, 1988
Excerpt from 'The Twelve', Aleksandr Blok, translated by Jon Stallworthy and
Peter France in *Selected Poems*, Carcanet, 2000. Reprinted with permission.

Every effort has been made to trace or contact all copyright holders. The
publishers would be pleased to rectify any omissions or errors brought to their
notice at the earliest opportunity.

A CIP record for this book
is available from the British Library

ISBN 978-0-571-23487-5

2 4 6 8 10 9 7 5 3 1

For Clio and Arthur

What is man? He is by no means a finished or harmonious being. No, he is still a highly awkward creature. Man, as an animal, has not evolved by plan but spontaneously, and has accumulated many contradictions ... To produce a new, 'improved' version of man – that is the future task of Communism. Man must look at himself and see himself as a raw material, or at best as a semi-manufactured product, and say: 'At last, my dear homo sapiens, I will work on you.'

LEON TROTSKY

There are things which a man is afraid to tell even to himself, and every decent man has a number of such things stored away in his mind.

FYODOR DOSTOEVSKY

ON THE NIGHT of 21 January 1919, the Russian inventor, physicist and polymath Nikita Slavkin vanished.

In the months and years that followed, the Soviet press reported that the Socialisation Capsule, Slavkin's latest invention, represented an extraordinary advance in human knowledge. Slavkin, building on the theories of his hero Einstein, had revolutionised our understanding of the universe. What's more, his disappearance was proof that his theories had a practical application: he had found a means of subverting time itself. 'The Vanishing Futurist', as he was dubbed, became a Soviet icon. Monuments and streets were named after him, biographies written, children's books, portraits, films. No word has been heard from him since that day. Yet the idea persists, based on Slavkin's own remarks, that one day he will reappear; that if his Socialisation Capsule can distort our perception of temporal reality, then it can equally reinstate it.

In the 1950s, the film *The Vanishing Futurist* showed Slavkin climbing into his Capsule and fading away. It ended with one of the characters saying dreamily, as the camera panned over a scene of empty, sunny countryside, 'Who knows? Perhaps Nikita will come back for us one of these days. "Come on, jump in, comrades," he'll say. "Don't you want to see Communism for yourselves?"'

1

In May 1914, much against the advice of my parents, I took up the post of governess to the Kobelev family, of No. 7, Gagarinsky Lane, Moscow. My new house was a large, ramshackle building, in need of a good coat of paint; it was reddish-brown, with a hefty, slightly sagging façade of white columns and pediment. On the other three sides leaned a mass of shabby outbuildings: coach house, stables, laundry, kitchens, bath house, servants' accommodation, a courtyard full of poultry and an overgrown lilac hedge. As I put my head out of the carriage, my first impression was of the dizzying scent of lilac and the heavy branches of pale, wet blossom gleaming in the half-light. My second was of a surprisingly deep and oily puddle, into which I immediately stepped.

I include these details because, now that I sit down to piece together these memoirs, it strikes me that they give a rather accurate shorthand of my life with the Kobelevs. Before I left my home in Cornwall, my parents and their friends had informed me at length of the mistake I was making. Several girls of our acquaintance had gone off to France or Italy to work as governesses, while Jenifer Trevargo was in Austria and, so we heard, skiing like a demon, but Russia was generally held to be a country of wild Cossacks, bears, anarchists and so forth. My father, a solicitor in Truro who had no natural inclination towards adventure, would never have given his permission if it had not been for the fact that the introduction came through the redoubtable Miss Clegg. Miss Clegg was born and bred in Truro, a solid, leathery woman as dependably stuffed with good Chapel values as a pasty is with potato, despite the fact that she'd been working as a governess in Moscow for almost a decade. Nonetheless, my mother wept when I told her I wanted to go.

'Oh, you are unfeeling! Aren't there enough children needing to be taught in . . . in Devon, or somewhere?'

But I was a bookish, scrawny girl, a spinster in the making; argumentative and contrary to my father (as he often said) and disappointingly serious to my mother, who wanted to gossip with me about clothes. Reading Tolstoy had made me long to visit this country full of peasant women in birch-bark sandals, young officers as fresh as cucumbers, forests filled with unheard-of berries. In any case I'd spent four years since leaving school underoccupied and at home. I taught a little, I assisted with the Sunday school, I helped my mother with the house. No suitors appeared to ask for my hand, if one discounts James Andrews, who had walked me home from Chapel a few times, talking gloomily about marine insurance. My parents had made it clear that not much could be expected of me, but still I hoped for a little more than this.

Nonetheless, in my first weeks it was unsettling to discover that my relatives' warnings – particularly those made from a position of absolute ignorance and prejudice – proved remarkably accurate. The food *was* rich and indigestible, the climate lowering, the arrangements chaotic, and the house not terribly clean. The servants – of whom there were an astonishing number, perhaps forty – were constantly travelling up and down from the Kobelevs' country estate at Mikhailovka, south of Moscow, so it was months before I learnt their names, let alone their duties, which in some cases seemed absurdly specific: a pickling chef, and two large, liveried footmen who brushed the hats. When they weren't brushing hats they were usually asleep on the front doorstep, and one had to step over their legs to get in or out. The family was further swollen by all sorts of hangers-on, retired employees such as Mrs Kobelev's aged French governess Mamzelle, Mr Kobelev's old aunt Anna Vladimirovna, and friends or relations who seemed to drift in, staying for a meal, a day or a week as the fancy took them.

On the other hand, however – and the longer I stayed in Moscow, the more it seemed to me that this was the only hand that mattered at all – from that first auspicious whiff of lilac, there was something irresistible about the Kobelev household. The front door swung open to reveal a large, dusty, red-papered hall and the colossal rear view of a footman in brown-and-gold livery. Without looking round, he held the door open with one hand and with the other cupped his mouth so that his voice would carry further.

'*Priekhala Mees!*' he bellowed. 'The Miss has arrived!'

Immediately the servants began to appear in the hall,

as if they had been hiding behind doors in anticipation. Several young maids cannoned into each other as they arrived at a run. People clustered on the stairs to peer at me through the banisters. A hum of interested conversation arose, as though nothing so exciting had happened for weeks – although I later discovered that almost any arrival, even the clock-winder's weekly visit, was greeted with equal enthusiasm.

A plump young woman with her hair in a turban, a little younger than myself, arrived, frowning. 'Miss Freely? I'm Sonya Kobelev. Welcome.' She gave me her hand with a limp, regal air that confused me: as I shook it, it occurred to me that perhaps she had expected it to be kissed. 'This is my younger brother, Pasha—'

'How do you do, Miss Freely.' A young man with a conspicuously well-tended moustache came up behind her, smiling. 'Pleased to welcome you to our abode.' He spoke with an accent that hovered somewhere between Russian and lowland Scots. 'As you can perhaps tell, I have already completed my schools certificate in English, thanks to a Miss Edie Campbell from Melrose.'

'She must have been an excellent teacher.'

'I hate to correct you, but you probably mean, "She's done a grand job", don't you?'

'Oh, for goodness' sake, Pasha, don't start teasing her already,' snapped Sonya. 'Ah, here come your charges, Miss Freely – my youngest brother and sister, Dima and Liza—'

They arrived panting and grinning – a solid, fair-haired boy and a taller, skinny girl with plaits.

'Hello, miss. Do you speak Russian?' the girl asked.

'No, not yet—'

'Then I say to you what servants are saying,' she told me. 'They are saying, in England all ladies ride bareback like monkeys. Is it true? I want to ride bareback.'

'Liza!' hissed Sonya. 'Miss Freely, do come this way. My father is looking forward to meeting you.'

Dima put his hand in mine. 'I am waiting and waiting for you, miss,' he said sweetly. 'Papa says you will teach me Rugby football.'

In the study Mr Kobelev, a tall, slight man with a grey-streaked beard, came forward to greet me. 'Welcome, welcome, my dear Miss Freely – sit down with us, drink some tea. You must be tired.'

I took a seat. As the room was painted dark green, full of smoke, and unlit, I could barely see who was opposite me. At last I made out two ancient ladies – the old governess Mamzelle and Mr Kobelev's aunt – behind a large brass samovar, bobbing their heads and smiling at me. I bobbed and smiled back, and they waggled their heads all the more energetically.

Pasha came to my rescue, murmuring at me to stop first. 'Otherwise you could be nodding at each other for days.'

'Is that why the last governess left?'

'Yes, a very sad business. In the end her head fell off.'

'Is she ill?' the aunt said loudly to Mr Kobelev, in French. 'She's making barbaric noises.'

'No, no, Aunt, *soyez tranquille.*' He leant across to talk to me. 'So, my dear, you have met the children already.' He was in his late fifties, I supposed, but seemed younger, with the same dark-brown eyes as Pasha. He pulled Dima to him and stroked his cheek. 'They are good children, though perhaps a little wild, eh, you monkeys? I have always encouraged them to be free-thinkers. And I must warn you, in this house we do not believe in discipline for its own sake, and certainly not in the nursery.'

'I am glad to hear it,' I said. 'Being too strict with children is a failure of imagination.'

'Good, good,' he replied vaguely. 'You see, Miss Freely, their poor mother is ill, and I am very often away on business. They have not had an easy childhood.'

'Oh, I'm so sorry.' Miss Clegg had intimated that Mrs Kobelev had some kind of health trouble, but she didn't know the nature of it; all she had heard was that the poor lady hardly left the house. 'Is she . . . is she well enough to meet me?'

Mr Kobelev called to his daughter. 'Sonya! Why not take Miss Freely to meet your mother straight away?'

Sonya frowned. 'If you think it is the right time, Papa . . .'

'It's never the right time. Now will do as well as any.'

So I was shown immediately to Mrs Kobelev's room, the heart of the house, dark and hot and smelling of face powder and eau de cologne and slept-in sheets and violet lozenges. I stopped in the doorway, uncertain how to advance; but after a moment or two my eyes became accustomed enough for me to make out a great deal of furniture, occasional tables and objects, and a chaise longue pushed against the wall, with a figure lying under several rugs.

'Enter.'

'Mama? Here's Miss Freely – the English governess.'

'How do you do, Miss Freely?' Sofia Pavlovna Kobelev turned slowly and I saw a thin, expressionless face.

'Very well, Madame. I am sorry to find you indisposed.'

'Yes . . . please, forgive my English, I do not speak it these days.' She spoke in a monotone, barely moving her lips; and altogether she was so slight and so still, underneath her rugs, that I wondered if she was paralysed. 'Tell me, have you met my little ones, how do you find them?'

'Well, we've hardly met, but I'm sure we will get along very well. I shall bring you a timetable of their lessons . . .'

'My husband will be in charge of all of that.'

'Oh, yes, I see – well, perhaps you would like me to give you a report on their progress each week, or month?'

'Each month, yes, indeed,' Sofia Pavlovna agreed faintly.

'I think that's enough, Miss Freely,' said Sonya. 'Shall we go?'

I followed Sonya out onto the landing, where Pasha was waiting for us.

'So you've met the invalid,' he said sardonically. 'Don't expect her to show any more interest in you.'

'Your poor mother. What is . . . is she . . .' I didn't know quite how to ask.

'My mother has neurasthenia,' Sonya said, pursing her lips. 'She's suffered from it for many years, since Dima was one or two. It's a nervous disease. She has to stay in bed most days, although now and again she manages a meal downstairs. Liza and Dima visit her in the evenings, if she is feeling well enough. We're all quite used to it – but for goodness' sake, don't worry her with the children's progress. If there's anything you need, my father is the one to approach. Now, let me show you to your room.'

Her tone did not invite further discussion, and I discovered that this was the rule of the house. Mrs Kobelev's illness was not mentioned, and we steered the course of our thoughts around her like ships beating against the wind.

Sonya said goodnight at the door of my bedroom, a small, high-ceilinged chamber with grey silk curtains that seemed shamefully luxurious to me. The one tall window was almost entirely obscured by the large fleshy green fans of a horse chestnut tree. I removed my soggy shoes and for a long time after she had left me I leant out of the window, breathing in the leafy sweet air. It was still light, hours after darkness would have fallen in Cornwall; this added to my disorientation. A woodpigeon sang, hidden somewhere inside the tree, and stopped – sang, and stopped – as though listening for an interloper. In the silence that followed, I found myself holding my breath.

*

Governesses are famously long-lived. When I met her in 1914, the Kobelevs' retired governess Mamzelle was in her mid-eighties, timid and furry as a vole and still running errands for the whole family. She had outlasted all her relatives in France. As I write this I am not far from eighty myself. A whole lifetime has passed since I went to Russia. My daughter Sophy has grown-up sons of her own. My husband, Paul, died six months ago, and since then I have the strange sensation that the present, my creaky old body in the little terraced house in Hackney which we bought together, is no longer my home.

For several months Sophy has been trying to persuade me to clear the attic of a lifetime of accumulated papers, and I have been feebly resisting. She is quite right that it must be done, of course; I know that. I am merely taking a moment to gird up my loins before I dredge Slavkin's story up from its decades of silence. Last week Sophy, running out of patience, hauled several boxes down and left them by my chair.

'Have a look through, Mama, and on Saturday I can throw out what you don't want to keep.'

A peculiar smell wafts up to me from the boxes. It brings back my time in Russia even more clearly than its contents – the rank tobacco everyone smoked incessantly, the poor-quality 'wartime' paper, the fumes from the oil lamps. As I sift through I feel bemused by the scraps that have survived, from the utterly banal and pointless (a little printed prayer with a saccharine painting of St Barbara, a half-empty notebook) to things that grip my heart – letters from my parents and copies of my own letters to them, pages of earnest pieces of self-criticism written during the days of our commune, newspaper articles about Slavkin's inventions, and photographs. Overexposed and faded, all that is preserved in the pictures of our young selves is a smudge of shadow for eyes and, on every face, a smile.

All week I rehearse how I am going to open the conversation with Sophy. Paul wanted us to tell her everything years ago, but I persuaded him it would be too confusing, too painful. Now he's gone, it is frankly a worse moment than ever to begin, but I have no choice. 'I'll come back for you if you don't,' he whispered – still managing to joke, even at the end.

I find myself writing an account for her instead, using the papers as my starting point. This way, I think, will be more truthful – more complete – than if I stammer it out incoherently. Immediately I am amazed by how vividly the memories rush to my pen – voices, images, jokes. I remember my brother Edmund at Charing Cross station walking down the platform, waving goodbye to me and pretending to fall off the end. I remember Miss Clegg's sonorous elocution as we crossed Europe, giving me advice on where to buy a winter coat for a good price, and how to avoid the multitude of unsuitable situations that Russia would present. 'The Kobelevs are a respectable old Moscow family,' she kept repeating, all the way across Europe. 'You will encounter nothing untoward with them, I assure you!'

I can feel even now the tiny, rebellious frisson that rose up in me in response. I assure *you*, I thought, I'll do my best to encounter untowardness. 'Untoward!' shall be my motto.

And in so far as such an aim can be judged, I think I was rather successful.

2

My charges – Liza, aged eleven, and Dima, aged nine – were dear, good, funny children, and clever, just as their father had said; Liza was a bookworm with an eye for the unsuitable books in her father's library, and they both spoke three languages – Russian, English and French – with passable fluency. They *were* a little wild, perhaps: they could not sit up at the dinner table without arguing, shouting, and dropping food on the tablecloth. They rarely took exercise, instead romping about indoors, breaking precious objects in Mr Kobelev's collection. At lesson times I soon discovered where they would be hiding: in the kitchen, where the cook Darya fed them strawberry jam by the spoonful and commiserated with them at their bad luck in having to be educated at all.

'Too much jam is bad for them,' I told her in my broken Russian.

'Ah, nothing can harm the innocent!' came the airy reply, translated for me by Liza in a butter-wouldn't-melt voice.

They had had a succession of governesses, and neither their father nor anyone else would say no to them; they were universally pitied, by servants and family alike.

'We're poor, neglected children,' Dima would say with a serene look.

'Yes, tragic children,' Liza chimed in. 'Growing up without a mother's love!'

During my first week I devised a routine: lessons in the morning, a walk in the afternoon and an evening period for reading and learning poetry. The lessons passed off adequately, when I could persuade them to sit down and concentrate, but the real success was the afternoon walk, without which I suspect I would have soon gone the way of their previous governesses. My governess acquaintances at the Anglican church in Moscow, St Andrew's, where I spent my Sundays, were disapproving of the idea.

'I do not advise it, Miss Freely,' Miss Clegg warned me. 'Besides the dirt, it is quite dangerous, you know. The Russian people are an unpredictable lot. Take the children out for a drive, by all means, and a walk in the park, but on foot – no. You're not in Truro now!'

Dirty the streets often were, particularly in spring and autumn, but I had always loved walking, and saw no reason to stop in Moscow. Most Russian children, it seemed to me, were brought up in an absurdly cosseted atmosphere, ignorant of the world outside their immediate household. Talking to the servants was disapproved of, even in liberal households such as the Kobelevs', and even when they had little playmates among the servants' children, they were allowed to lord it over them in an unattractive way. As long as I was their teacher, I was determined that Liza and Dima would have a very different education.

Their nurse, Nyanya, who was against any kind of change, was horrified. 'Oh, she's a cruel one,' she wailed, 'dragging the poor little crumbs out around the city! They'll come home like stones, they will, it's their poor kidneys that will suffer!'

The children themselves rebutted her. 'Oh Nyanya,' they cried impatiently, 'don't fuss! It's warm outside! We *like* going with Miss Gerty.'

It had not always been so. On one early outing both of them lay down on the pavement. Telling them that English children of their age could walk several miles without complaint did not, unfortunately, rouse them to patriotic competition. Several peasants stopped and watched, full of outraged sympathy for the little children so mistreated by the foreign Miss. At last I turned to one of them, a fine figure of a man with dramatic moustaches and beard.

'Please, carry them,' I stammered.

He berated me as he hoisted them up, one on each shoulder, and Liza translated his remarks with relish. 'He's saying you are vicious woman, and you have destroyed our dear little legs with too long walking.'

'Tell him that your dear little legs still seem to work very well when you are playing on the slides.'

'He says all foreigners are same – come to Russia to steal our national treasure.'

'Oh, for goodness' sake.'

We continued on our walk, Liza and Dima waving triumphantly as though they were at the head of a victory procession, and attracting the delighted attention of a crowd of street urchins. When the peasant set them down at Smolensk market, they skipped a good half-mile home without noticing.

Moscow is a city that insinuates itself cunningly into one's affections. At first it fascinated and slightly repelled me, as some vast medieval fair might. I was still ignorant of politics, yet as a Chapel girl I couldn't help but be shocked by the contrast between the golden domes and palaces and the crowds of beggars at their doors. The architecture, with its strange excrescences and decorations, struck me as a wild attempt at grandeur that understood nothing of the true properties of beauty. Yet slowly I came to know its little courtyards, its secret gardens and alleys, its cool green boulevards cast in relief against the bustle and noise. It was impossible not to be charmed by the wooden houses and the bandy streets, the little churches squeezed into every corner. There was a sort of unexpected joyfulness about it all, unlike any other city I have known.

Liza and Dima and I explored together, discovering the river with its busy traffic, the markets – the birds on Trubnoi Square and the flowers on Tsvetnoi Boulevard – and the grand new mansions decorated in the latest styles. Our trips often included a visit to the grocer Eliseyev's to gaze at the displays and drink a glass of flavoured mineral water, which I allowed Dima to order.

'Which syrup do you prefer, sir?' the tremendously solemn, white-coated assistant would ask, using the polite '*Vy*'.

Dima would flush with pleasure. 'Three lemon ones, please . . .' And when the sparkling drink had gushed out of the silver siphon and the syrup was swirling in the glass, he might add, as one man to another, 'I used to like the strawberry but I've grown out of it now.'

17

The streets were always busy; hawkers stood on street corners selling knitted goods and garden produce, brushes and brooms, newspapers – there was an extraordinary array of different publications – hot pies, ice-creams, chestnuts. An increasing number of motor vehicles weaved noisily between the elegant carriages and the trams. In response to Dima's urgent requests, we often passed by one or other of the grand hotels, the Metropol or the National, in the hope of glimpsing a chauffeur, in leather goggles and hat, in the act of cranking up his motor car, swiftly mounting his seat and roaring away, to the accompaniment of several deafening explosions.

Dima was a straightforward little boy, happy as long as he was well exercised and well rested. Liza was more complicated, and I was glad of the opportunity, while walking, to encourage her to talk more openly. Her thoughts often shocked me.

'I hate to eat,' she told me one day. 'I prefer to be hungry.'

'But why, Liza?'

'Look at my sister Sonya. She is fat, all she thinks about is clothes, and her marriage.'

I couldn't help agreeing that Sonya was not the most sympathetic of characters. She was making the arrangements for her marriage to Petya Ostroumov, the son of a prosperous manufacturer from St Petersburg, at the time. The plans seemed to result in tearful scenes with her father every other day, stamped feet, and the imploring figure of Mr Kobelev outside her bedroom door, begging her to be reasonable.

'Well, I don't like to hear such unkind remarks – but, Liza, you don't have to be like your sister. You can study, and work, and you certainly don't have to marry unless you want to. Your father has often said as much.'

'What could *I* do?'

'What would you like to do?'

'I'd like . . . to look after animals.'

'You could train to be a vet.'

'A vet! Me!' She was delighted by the idea, and still more so when, as a result of a conversation I had with her father, she was presented with a puppy. He was named Frank, and joined us on our walks as soon as he was old enough. Liza doted on him.

The shadow of their mother's illness fell over all her children, but Liza was the one, perhaps, who suffered most. She was four when her mother took to her room; no doubt it was hard to understand that her withdrawal was not deliberate. Dima had been too young to realise; he loved Nyanya with all his heart, and still occasionally fell asleep cushioned on her vast, wheezy bosom.

*

We were at the Kobelevs' country estate, Mikhailovka, when the war began. I remember so vividly where we were sitting, looking down to the bend in the stream where the cattle were drinking. Mr Kobelev stepped out onto the veranda, rubbing his forehead.

'Dears, it has happened. Russia has declared war on Germany.'

The prospect of war had been hanging over us, and we felt a sort of ghastly relief when it was finally announced. I thought about but dismissed the idea of going home. I was enjoying myself, and like everyone I was convinced that it would be a short war. Only a handful of governesses in Moscow left at the outset, provoking Miss Clegg's contempt. 'We should support our Russian allies,' she sniffed. Later, with the sinking of HMS *Hampshire* in 1916, travel to Britain was considered too dangerous and I became used to the idea of staying in Russia.

The post arrived fairly regularly and I kept up with news about my brothers and my parents. James was training to be a doctor in Bristol, but Edmund had just left school. He joined up immediately. How could my parents have let him, that gentle, diffident boy? Or had they even encouraged him? He had been accepted to read Mathematics at Oxford; surely he could have been of more use in logistics, or munitions, or anywhere but on the front line, but it was quite possible that my mother wanted a soldier son to boast of . . . I lay awake many nights wondering whether I could have changed his mind if I had been at home.

In the box I find the letter he wrote me from his barracks in Bodmin, scribbled in his unformed, boyish hand:

Dear Gerty,

I hope you are still enjoying yourself with the Rooskis! I have joined the Duke of Cornwall Light Infantry, there are about three hundred of us here, the

most decent chaps you could imagine – Cornishmen
all. This evening we had a sing-song, we almost lifted
the roof off the old shack! So you needn't worry about
me – we'll flatten the Hun at a hundred paces with a
din like that . . .

3

In the second box of papers, inside my copy of Chernychevsky's *What Is To Be Done?*, I find a half-written letter home to my parents, dated December 1914, and never sent. I suspect I abandoned it. Banal and schoolgirlish as it seems now, I knew it would have shocked my parents.

Dear Pappa and Mamma,

I am glad to report that my Russian has improved somewhat and I am now more able to take part in the Kobelevs' evening gatherings, which are very convivial. I am given charge of the Samovar, quite a complicated matter, for the Russians are even more particular about their tea-drinking than the English!

We scarcely ever number fewer than a dozen, and the conversation covers every subject imaginable. Pasha Kobelev is in his first year at Moscow University, and his student friends come to visit very frequently. One of them – Nikita Slavkin is his name – entertains us with all sorts of original suggestions – quite 'avant-garde'! Last night he suggested that Russian children should be taught to walk on stilts, to overcome the huge distances in the countryside!!

He believes, as we all do, that this war is quite unnecessary, a piece of Imperial conceit on a vast scale. I wish I could have convinced Edmund of this. I thought he was planning to study?

*

Nikita Slavkin sat a little apart from Pasha's other friends, arms wrapped around his long, knobbly legs, pale and awkward. He had very short, almost colourless hair that revealed a bumpy scalp, and slightly protuberant pale-blue eyes. He ate a great deal of sandwiches, swallowing them whole, like a snake. When the conversation turned to women's rights Pasha drew him in.

'Nikita here has some ideas, don't you, Nikita? He's an inventor, he's inventing all sorts of contraptions that will change women's lives – and all our lives . . . Come over here, tell us.'

Nikita stood – upright, he was absurdly tall and skinny – and blushed even under his hair. When he spoke, his voice was strangely deep and a little too loud; he looked embarassed by that too. 'Just the outlines.'

But Mr Kobelev was encouraging. 'No, tell us. It sounds fascinating.'

'Well, one of my inventions is a lightweight chastity belt, woven out of steel thread—'

The room erupted into protest. Everyone was disgusted, either on liberal, conservative or squeamish grounds. Mr Kobelev's aunt, Anna Vladimirovna, wanted him thrown out of the house. Pasha laughed so much he fell off the divan. Slavkin stood there, his large hands hanging by his sides, vulnerable. 'Of course, I have not perfected the material yet . . .'

A neighbour of the Kobelevs, Marina Getler, who was studying medicine, looked as though she might punch him. 'Don't you see, modern women need freedom,' she hissed.

His full, pale lips trembled a little. 'I do see, yes,' he muttered. 'That's my aim.'

Slavkin had just moved into the small bedroom next to mine, which Mr Kobelev had offered him in exchange for a few hours' work a week on his catalogue. At twenty-two, the same age as me, he was four years older than Pasha and seemed a decade wiser; I had the impression that he had been born with the grave air of a professor. A scholarship student from Siberia studying physics and engineering at Moscow University, he was already known to many of the artists and poets in the avant-garde for his inventions, which he claimed would 'drive forward the steamer of Modernity'. The poet Mayakovsky dubbed him the 'Futechnologist'. The new, non-objective art that fascinated all of us during those years was not simply a style to Slavkin, but the key to existence in the modern world. To his mind, its geometric shapes and grids, combined with the right technology, would not only define how society would look in the future; they would also shape the thoughts and emotions of its citizens.

Long before the Revolution Slavkin was thinking how

design could improve people's lives. He invented steam-powered domestic appliances to ease the burdens of housework and laundry. He imagined multi-purpose objects for urban life – unbreakable rubber crockery sets that you could fold together and use as a pillow; a port-able shower-bath; a telescopic hat with a telescopic feather that packed away as flat as a piece of paper; a kit for a ceramic stove made of 150 interlocking pieces; spec-tacles with different-coloured, slot-in lenses, depending on how you wished to see the world that day.

He was not, at first, a popular addition to Gagarinsky Lane. Sonya made it clear that she found Slavkin un-couth, while Anna Vladimirovna claimed his 'village voice' gave her headaches. The servants were upset by the way he crammed his room with junk for his in-ventions and insisted on doing his own laundry, which dripped morosely over the nursery bath.

The loyal Pasha, however, wouldn't hear a word said against his friend. He teased Sonya and Anna Vladi-mirovna about their attitude, which he claimed was a medical condition, Snobosis. The two young men were inseparable, arriving at the dinner table in the middle of a conversation, too intent to notice what they were eat-ing; sent on an errand, they would be found halfway up the stairs, hours later, still embroiled in the same debate. It was Pasha who gave Nikita the nickname Camel (legs and eyelashes, he explained), although he also described Nikita as a mythical creature – 'half Moses and half the camel he rode on, with a heart made entirely of *schenki pushistiye* – little fluffy puppies'.

Those evenings, those three long pre-Revolutionary years with the Kobelevs seem almost as distant now, as mysterious and poignant as the jewel-rich illuminations in a Book of Hours – glimpses of a world so far removed from my present existence (the Formica tabletop on which I spread out the contents of my boxes from the attic, the two-bar electric fire at which I warm my old lady's hands, my solitude) it seems quite incredible to me that I ever experienced it.

As I read my letters I strain to catch again a whiff of the stuffy, overheated air of Mr Kobelev's dark-green study, lit by the rosy glow of the large fringed brass lamps and the dark glitter of the wall sconces; his ethnographic collection spread over every surface: shamans' drums, Chuvash jewellery, painted wooden figures, little bronze stags; the pale glimmer of the stove and the step at its base where Liza and Dima perched with the puppy Frank sprawled at their feet; and in the centre of the room, the great vessel of the high-backed red divan, crammed with shining, excitable faces, shouting each other down . . . Slavkin, still just an unknown student, showing us his new inventions, one after the other: the Electric Housemaid, the Automatic Carpet Beater, the flat-pack hats; billows of smoke hovering in the light, shrouding Mr Kobelev's expression, and Mamzelle, the old governess, smiling timidly, on the edge of things; music cranked out of the gramophone, and me at the samovar – dark-haired, pale, with serious grey eyes –

still a little shy, frowning in concentration as I add the hot water ... 'No, no, too weak, girl!' exclaims Anna Vladimirovna, poking me with her lorgnettes, and Mr Kobelev's exasperated response, 'My dear aunt, you'll tan yourself like a saddle.'

Those three years were my university. At home, for all my minor rebellions, I had never dreamt of challenging my parents' articles of faith. Conversation consisted of a paternal monologue, broken occasionally by murmurs of agreement from the rest of the family. Any note of discord roused my father to spittle-laden fury. In Moscow I discovered a household where the most absurd and opposing views could be voiced, disagreed with, argued over or renounced without any tempers lost or touchy Chapel gods invoked.

'Sing,' Mr Kobelev liked to say. 'Every bird has a song.'

Pasha, who reminded me of my brothers, said, 'Yes, Miss Gerty, I'm sure you have the voice of a nightingale.'

'Do stop it, Pasha, or I will sing, and then you'll regret it.'

I listened, read and thought, and began to wonder in particular about the nasty old man by whom my parents set so much store, who trifled with his followers' affections (poor Job, poor Abraham); who set up Adam and Eve to fail and then bequeathed the pain of childbirth on all women in memory of Eve's misdemeanour; who allowed – no, planned – for his own son to be tortured.

Meanwhile Liza and Dima grew up and flourished; I was proud of them. In the autumn of 1915 Liza, and a year later Dima, began to study at secondary school (in Russia called the Gymnasium). Travel to Britain was still out of the question, however, so I stayed on with the Kobelevs, as all their former employees appeared to do. I caught a tram each morning up the Boulevard Ring to a school on Tverskaya Street where I gave English lessons, and walked the children back from school in the afternoon.

The post became erratic, and communication with my parents infrequent. What, after all, had I left behind in Britain? My brothers had moved away, and all that awaited me in Truro was my father, who seemed to dislike me, and my mother, who thought me unnatural. One sunny morning in 1916 I went to the hairdresser's and asked her to cut off my dark plaits; I remember the sensation of release as they fell to the floor. I had grown a little plumper in Russia, a fact that Nyanya was always complimenting me on. 'How pretty you are, Mees Gerty, now you've filled out!' At home, my mother used to bewail, unanswerably, 'What are we to *do* with you?' In Moscow I felt I'd found a reply for her.

Then in November 1916 I received a letter through the diplomatic bag. I have it here – a black-rimmed envelope addressed care of the Foreign Office, King Charles Street, London, in my father's dark, decisive hand.

'Dear Gertrude,' wrote my father.

It is with profound sadness that I write to tell you that your brother Edmund has been killed in action on the

Somme, at Ancre, on the night of the 16th–17th October. His Commanding Officer tells me he fought bravely. Of course we expected nothing less. He is now at peace with the Lord. We will hold a prayer meeting at the Chapel in his memory and I will pray for you then. I trust that you are safe and well, it is only a pity you are so far from your family at a time when your mother needs you.

Yr. affec. Father, S. M. Freely

I suppose it was unfair of me to blame my parents for Edmund's death. Even if they did encourage him to join up, they had done no more than millions of other families. And yet as I re-read that letter now I feel a rush of the rage I harboured against them for years. That nasty little dig: 'It is only a pity . . .' The sanctimonious: 'I will pray for you then.' Those phrases released me from my filial duty. I never wanted to see them again. I ripped up their unread letters. I hid in my room to cry, too angry to accept sympathy. I kept dreaming of my poor dear little Ed, my poor boy, how I'd abandoned him. Fighting sleep, I lay in bed making inventories of every detail about him: his babyish cheeks; how he blinked when he was excited, rapidly, trying to get the words out; his fine, clean, squarish hands with large pale moons on each nail; the way he ducked his head a little under too many direct questions – each day feeling him slipping away from me, solidifying into a few stock images.

'All true Socialists take a defeatist position,' said Pasha that winter – the first time I had heard the term. 'This war was inevitable, a result of Empire. Colonial policies produce an excess of weapons, raw materials and manufactured produce, then they need a war to soak up the glut and keep the prices high. Under this system, war is not only simple – the underclass fights it for them – but essential.'

I was speechless.

He went on casually, 'And the irony is, now it can only be good for the Revolutionary cause – the greater the war the better, because the result can only be chaos and the destabilisation of the regime. It's bringing the Revolution closer every day.'

'Pasha—' I was so angry I shook all over. 'I never thought I would hear you say such a disgraceful, cynical thing. If the Revolution depends on the death of innocent young men, it isn't worth a jot.'

'Oh Gerty, I'm sorry.' He came towards me, but I rushed out of the room.

It was Nikita Slavkin who set things right, knocking on my door late at night. 'Miss Gerty, may I talk to you? I think you misunderstood.'

'Do you?'

'Please, let me explain. We Socialists would abolish war entirely – we agree, the blood of a single human being is more valuable than any notions of patriotism.' He sat down, not looking at me. 'It's primitive behaviour. My mother died just as stupidly, for no reason at all, of a minor infection after childbirth. My father would not take her to the hospital – he sat and prayed over her. If she had been treated she would still be alive . . .'

He said gently, 'At least let your brother's death mean something. Revolution will redeem all these sacrifices.'

Slavkin had grown in authority over the past couple of years; we often found ourselves turning to him for the final word. It struck me that his childhood in an Old Believer community, a type of strict Orthodox sect, had much in common with my own Chapel upbringing. We had both jettisoned a cruel, overweening god, yet against our will we were both left with a sense of loss – in my case intensely so after my brother's death. We rejected the father, but we could not rid ourselves of the beauty of the son's example, or a belief in the unity of all things. I loved hearing Nikita talk, not just for his encyclopaedic knowledge and flights of imagination, but for his almost mystical sense of the patterns of the universe.

Among my papers is this copy in my own hand of an article by Slavkin that impressed me deeply:

'Behold the Lamb of God, that takest away the sins of the world,' said John the Baptist, when he first saw Jesus Christ. For he understood that Jesus was to be a sacrificial lamb in the *pagan* sense: an innocent creature condemned to death. In medieval Christianity the sacrifice of the Lamb of God was explained as redeeming Man's original sin. Yet in John's time, for both Romans and Jews, a sacrifice was a form of sorcery – an offering to the gods, or God – an arbitrary blood-letting that was capable of altering the course of events. A sacrifice may bring about dramatic change; although, as the myths show time and again, it may not be the change we wished for.

In modern times similar brutal sacrifices are still made, if less consciously: injustices occur that are so outrageous, so discordant, that the great kings and governments who carelessly order these vile acts are, to their astonishment and incomprehension, destroyed by them. The Pharisees sacrificed Jesus to shore up their earthly power, and this brutal and cynical act destroyed the Jewish people's political status for thousands of years. In 1905, the Tsar ordered his Cossacks to carry out a massacre in front of the Winter Palace, and all of Russia rose up in protest.

Poor Jesus, the man, understood that only by dying could he bring about a Revolution. 'Except a corn of wheat fall into the ground and die, it abideth alone; but if it die, it bringeth forth much fruit.' Alive, he was merely a Jewish prophet; dead, he was the agent of a change in human experience for centuries to come. In our unified world the smallest action can set off a reaction that reverberates throughout the galaxies. The bacterium kills the great Elephant, and after death the helpless Lamb rises up again as a mighty leader; the weakest becomes the most powerful; the peaceful one, who never retaliates, is the all-conquering King of many nations.

We Socialists, who dream of a great reformation of the human spirit, we are also helpless against the powers of the world. Yet we feel the great swell of hearts behind us – millions all over the world – the weak who shall become all-conquering. We are willing to make any sacrifice for them. We shall be the microscopic action that sets off a vast reaction, that creates the future.

Dear, kind Mr Kobelev, with his conviction that Russia must not let down her Allies and that elections were all that the country needed, now seemed to be speaking from some fast-receding shore. I signed up for a course in political education; my little exercise book of notes on Proudhon and Engels and owning the means of production has, for some reason, survived, complete with doodles in the margin. Yet politics always remained opaque to me, however hard I tried.

Revolution, on the other hand – or at least the revolution that Slavkin envisaged – was clearly visible. It was the longed-for precipice just downhill of us.

4

On 3 March Mr Kobelev arrived back from his club out of breath, his face scarlet, his eyes full of tears, with the news that the Tsar had abdicated. We embraced each other, cried and rushed out onto the streets, swept up on the general tide of euphoria. It all happened more or less just as a revolution should, with dozens of symbolic moments – the burning of Tsarist regalia, huge demonstrations in the streets, exultant groups of citizens drinking the contents of a few looted stores.

Over the years I have often been asked about my memories of the February Days; in fact I gave a talk once on the subject to the Hackney Women's Reading Group, one of a number of Socialist organisations I've belonged to. They were appreciative of my talk, which they preferred to the one I gave on the Great October Revolution, when Lenin and the Bolsheviks seized power in October 1917. My view of Lenin's Revolution was flawed, they told me, too personal, lacking a proper sense of the collective or the heroic. The inconvenient truth was, of course, that October had none of the ingredients of a people's revolution – no processions, and no symbolic removal of the tyrant's flag, because there was no tyrant by then. There was street fighting in Moscow, but, thank goodness, not too close to Gagarinsky Lane.

In late October, I remember, snow threatened but did

not come; the air was oppressive and the sky low and bulging, until one longed for the flakes to start falling. The first we knew of any disturbance was gunfire in the afternoon. Mr Kobelev telephoned friends of his in the City Council and learnt a few details: the Bolsheviks had announced they must act to defend the Congress of Soviets, they had driven out the Provisional Government, it was a coup. We were not overly excited by this information, for there had been rumours of coups several times already that year. We could hear heavy fighting in other parts of the city, however, so we settled in at Gagarinsky Lane and played card games with the children to pass the time.

After five days it finally began to snow and the city fell quiet. Pasha and Nikita were keen to find out news and I volunteered to go with them; I think Mr Kobelev felt that my presence would act as a brake on their spirit of adventure. As far as I was concerned, after so long cooped up inside the house, I was ready for anything.

We turned towards the centre of town; Pasha and Nikita were deep in conversation, and did not include me. The snow was still falling, those large, soft flakes that give one the impression that gravity is not holding things down quite as reliably as it should. It was the middle of the afternoon, but the streets were almost empty. On Mokhovaya Street Pasha said, 'What's that?' and we saw the body of a man in the road. From the way he was lying, awkwardly, his leg bent beneath him, it was clear from a distance of fifty yards that he was dead. Snow had already settled on his face and his clothes. The three of us passed him on the other side of the road. We did not say another word about it, but after a few moments I realised we were on Vozdvizhenka.

'Perhaps—' My voice came out in a croak; I cleared my throat and tried again. 'Perhaps we might drop in to see Miss Clegg and the Beloborodovs?'

'Yes, yes,' agreed Pasha, with relief, and Slavkin, as if noticing that I was with them for the first time, turned to me, smiled and nodded. I felt an absurd, self-congratulatory flush.

Miss Clegg let us in herself. 'I did tell you that your habit of taking walks around Moscow was unwise.'

We entered the Beloborodovs' large, modern apartment, decorated in the art-nouveau style, and Miss Clegg brought us into the drawing room to join the family. Monsieur Beloborodov, who was talking with his brother-in-law Prince Svyatinsky in front of the fireplace, had made a large amount of money by investing in the railways and was destined for great things, according to Miss Clegg (as of course she would say). Madame was quite young, perhaps still in her twenties, although she adopted the gloriously condescending airs of a dowager.

'Little Miss Freely,' she drawled from her chair. 'Do sit down with us. And of course this is Pasha – how is your father, my dear boy?'

We drank weak tea from little porcelain cups and spoke of this and that. The snow pattered against the window panes and the wind – or was it distant gunfire? – boomed in the chimney. Prince Svyatinsky, who was a collector of minerals, spoke of a rare specimen – jeremejevite – that he had found for sale in the market.

'It was being sold by a peasant – goodness knows how he had laid his hands on it. My great-uncle would have given his eye teeth for such a specimen!'

Slavkin perked up. 'I thought only a few examples were known?'

The Prince's little black eyes fell on Slavkin. 'Are you interested in minerals? You must let me show you my collection . . .'

They fell into conversation: Nikita, unwinding his limbs one by one from the gilt chair he had been torturing and beginning to gesture as he warmed up, and the little Prince, charming and portly, with the mannerisms of a grande dame. For all that he looked like an aristocrat in a Bolshevik cartoon, he was a serious scientist, and in later years would become a professor at the Sorbonne.

'Is your friend at the University?' murmured Madame Beloborodov.

'Yes, he is studying Physics and Engineering, but he also attends lectures in the Geology faculty. He seems to know all the professors.'

'Really? Prince Svyatinsky and his wife have had some bad luck. A fire in his house on Myasnitskaya, they think a sniper shot caused it. He and my sister are staying with us here.'

'I am so sorry,' I answered. 'Can anything be saved?'

'His collection, thank heavens, was unharmed. Now they plan to sell it', she lowered her voice still further, as though uttering a rude word, 'and leave for France.'

'I see,' I replied slowly, wondering why I was being

favoured with this confidence. The subject of exile, never far from the thoughts of the Russian gentry in those days, was nonetheless considered in poor taste.

'Perhaps,' she breathed scarcely audibly to me, 'your friend might have connections in the University who would be interested?'

I nodded. 'Yes indeed.'

'They cannot make an open approach, you understand. This needs to be handled with the utmost discretion.'

I reported this conversation on the way home.

'Perhaps they hope to keep the sale a secret from the rest of the family,' commented Pasha.

'Poor Prince. That collection is his great joy.'

'Excuse me,' muttered Slavkin, beginning to walk faster, striding out like a racehorse. 'I must talk to – I think I know who . . .' He disappeared around the corner, still muttering to himself.

A few weeks later he and a student friend of Pasha's, Fyodor, arrived at Gagarinsky Lane in a cart with a package wrapped in straw. It took both of them to lift it across the yard. When it was finally installed in his workshop, the packing came off to reveal a sizeable piece of some dark, silvery mineral.

'I have arranged it all,' said Slavkin, beaming. I'd never seen him so exhilarated. 'The collection will go to the University. Would you be able to give us your help, Miss Gerty? Next week we must pack everything up. The Prince and Princess are delighted – they plan to leave for France a couple of days later. He gave me this as a thank-you.'

The times brought out unexpected qualities in all of us but even so I was impressed, as was Mr Kobelev, who embraced and congratulated him.

'Well done, my boy – you must have managed the negotiations with great tact. Perhaps you will do the same for my collection one day?'

'Yes, yes!' Nikita, shiny with happiness, rushed off to see to his present, which was my first glimpse of the mineral iridium. He didn't offer any more details, and I – always a little shy of him – did not enquire.

We spent several days packing and sorting the pieces at the Prince's house. I was finishing up a last few tasks when the Prince came up to the gallery for the first time. He went straight to his study without greeting us, and Nikita – a little surprised, perhaps, but still beaming, excited by our work – immediately hurried over to speak to him. I could not see the Prince, who was concealed behind the door of his study, or hear their conversation, yet I read its course clearly in the lines of Nikita's body. Before even a word was said, as soon as Nikita saw the Prince's face, I could feel the enthusiasm flowing out of him. His shoulders drooped; I could sense, rather than see, his anxious frown. He plucked nervously at his sleeve, and shuffled from foot to foot, backing away from the fury directed at him. He shook his head.

Now the Prince raised his voice: 'Robbery!' he shouted. 'They never had the slightest intention to pay!'

Nikita, cowering before him, still shook his head, 'That wasn't what we arranged . . . I had no idea . . .'

He flinched as though he had been hit. The study door

slammed shut, and Nikita took a handkerchief from his pocket and wiped the Prince's spittle off his face. He walked slowly back towards me.

'He says – he says they've forced him to sign the collection over to the state. They told me they'd arrange the money side of things, and I believed them. I should have pressed them, but . . .'

'You mean the University aren't paying him at all?'

'A pittance.' Slavkin grimaced.

We set out through the darkening streets towards Gagarinsky Lane and he went over and over the episode. 'What a fool I am, what a fool – I thought they would be honourable, I should have insisted on a contract . . .'

'I suppose now the collection will be at the service of the people,' I said at last, timidly.

He looked at me for a moment as if about to say something, then changed his mind. He stood up a little straighter. Then, quite unexpectedly, he took my arm and tucked it under his, his slow, sweet smile lighting up his face.

'Gerty, I think you must be the most rational, sensible woman I know,' he said.

We walked together through the icy streets and past the Central Post Office, pockmarked with bullet holes. His arm felt very warm against mine.

The Svyatinskys donated their collection to the Soviet State, against their will, and in return were permitted to leave for France. The Svyatinsky Theft, as the episode became known in émigré circles, was much cited as evidence not just of the Bolsheviks' greed, but the naivety or, worse, the corruption of the Russian intelligentsia who did not go into exile. It gave Slavkin a certain notoriety abroad, but in Moscow, where 'Revolutionary Justice' was the slogan of the moment, it brought him the approval of the Bolshevik leadership and a position at the newly established Centre for Revolutionary Research, where he began his work on iridium alloys – the first step towards the Socialisation Capsule. It is a thought that I still find disturbing. Surely Slavkin's future was already fixed in his genes, in his genius. Yet if I'd never suggested that visit to the Beloborodovs, might he have remained an anonymous scientist all his life?

*

'Boots to beard, I'm a Muscovite – where else in the world will I live?'

Mr Kobelev refused to be concerned by the increasingly menacing tone against the middle classes in the winter of 1917. 'There is much that is good about the new regime, even if I disagree with it in many ways; it's my duty to stay.'

Russia withdrew from the war and despite the catastrophe of the German invasion across a vast area in the south and west of Russia, he was still optimistic that the various Socialist parties would solve their differences and a democratic system would develop with time. He summoned the servants and told them that they were free to leave his employ, if they wished, and one by one they melted away, all except the yardman Yasha,

41

the cook Darya, and one of the maids, Shura. We unpicked the fur collars from the children's coats and took care not to look or behave in a 'bourgeois' manner on the street. My English classes were in demand; I took private clients as well as continuing to work at the school on Tverskaya. The children's schooling, as well as Pasha's university degree, limped on through endless strikes and political meetings. Sonya visited us often, exhausted and sad. Her husband, Petya, had been left severely disabled by injuries incurred on the Austrian front, and poor Sonya struggled to care for him. In this way we lived more or less uninterrupted at Gagarinsky Lane until the following spring.

One May evening in 1918 I couldn't sleep. I leaned out of the open window, gazing into the dark spring night. A car, its headlights extinguished, cruised quietly down Gagarinsky Lane. Underneath my window it stopped and several men jumped out. They ran up to the gate and banged loudly. This was not the first time that the house had been searched, but the other occasions had been in daylight, and we'd had some warning to hide incriminating possessions. I darted along to Mr Kobelev's study. His gun, a Mauser, was lying quite openly on the sideboard. People were shot for less. I thrust it into my bodice, then ran to Mrs Kobelev's room.

'Wake up, Sofia Pavlovna, dear, the militia are here,' I said, shaking her. 'Give me your jewels, quickly.'

'What? Oh . . .' She sat up and fumbled in the chest of drawers by her bed, pulling out several velvet bags.

I could hear voices in the hall downstairs shouting for Comrade Kobelev.

'He's at work,' Pasha told them.

'Look at all this stuff, it belongs to the people. Thieves!'

I peeped over the banisters. There were perhaps four or five of them, swaggering and nervous. One of them casually swept the large china letter-dish off the hall table. It chimed like a bell as it smashed.

'Who are you?' said Pasha. 'Show me your identification.'

'Comrade Kobelev, I'm the Deputy Head of the Smolensk District Soviet.' A man pushed forward to talk to Pasha; I saw it was Prigorian, who had been the Kobelevs' chauffeur until the car was requisitioned. He had always been the image of deference. Now he stood with his legs apart and rested his hand on the gun holster at his belt. 'The people are concerned that your father has been carrying off the treasures he expropriated from the nation.'

'You mean his collection?' I was impressed by Pasha's calm tones. 'You know perfectly well, Prig, nothing has been carried off. My father has preserved large numbers of works of art for the Russian people.'

'Search the house,' Prig told the others without looking around.

They moved towards the stairs and I ran to my bedroom and shoved the jewels and gun under my mattress. My heart was thrashing about in my chest. Voices were raised, there was the crash of a table being overturned.

'Open up or we'll arrest you all,' I could hear them saying outside Mrs Kobelev's room.

I waited in my room.

'Open up, open up at once!' They thumped on my door.

'Certainly not,' I said in my most haughty tones. 'I am a British citizen. You have no right to search my room.' I opened the door a sliver and showed them my passport.

In silence they examined it, one after the other. Prig was called.

'It's true, she's an *Anglichanka*,' he said, looking at me distastefully.

To my amazement, they moved on.

Half an hour later they were gone. When Mr Kobelev returned home, I went to see him in his study. For the first time since I had lived in the house, Mrs Kobelev was sitting with him. I gave them back their belongings.

'Good Lord, Miss Gerty, how can we thank you?' muttered Mr Kobelev.

'No, no, don't thank me – but, sir, is it safe for you all here in Moscow?'

'I've always said the moral course is to remain—' Kobelev began, then checked himself, looking at his wife. 'I don't know.'

Mrs Kobelev, very pale, but upright, suddenly spoke. 'I think we should go south for the summer. Will you accompany us, Miss Gerty?'

'No, Sofia Pavlovna, I must stay in Moscow,' I told her gently. The Embassy had advised British citizens to remain in the capital in case of evacuation. 'But perhaps you'd like me to protect the house, as far as possible?'

'Oh Miss Gerty.' Sofia Pavlovna turned away, unsteady on her feet. 'What you do, of course, is your affair.'

I slept fitfully that night, and woke to hear someone crying. I went to check, but the children were quiet; in the early hours of the morning I heard it again. It was their mother.

We spent the next three days packing away Mr Kobelev's ethnographic collection. We filled crates with straw for the peasant ceramics, then with the contents of the shelves in his study, fragments of embroidery and costumes wrapped in old cloths. All the woodcuts came down from the walls; all the Buryat weapons and animal skins. We labelled every box and Yasha nailed them shut. Then we hired a cart and transported them to the Alexander III Museum, which had agreed to store the collection. It took us four journeys, back and forth.

'I always intended to donate it to the State when I died,' Mr Kobelev remarked. 'This way is better – sooner.'

Travel into German-held areas was not at all reliable, and although Mr Kobelev had procured tickets for them to Yalta, we had no real idea whether they would be allowed to cross into the Ukraine. Sonya's husband Petya had returned to Petrograd; Sonya herself decided to accompany her parents south. Shura, the maid, would go with them to help with Dima and Liza. But the old ladies refused to move; Mr Kobelev was in despair.

'We can't leave you behind, my dears! Come with us, for our sake, if not for yours!'

'No,' said Anna Vladimirovna, definite as ever. 'Much too hot! Not at all good for the health. Sonya, my girl, you will ruin your complexion.'

'But my dears,' said Sonya, kneeling beside her chair, 'it might be dangerous for you here, and very hard – who will look after you?'

'We'll look after ourselves, won't we, Mamzelle? We'll manage very well.'

No argument would change their minds, and as I promised to care for them as best I could, Mr Kobelev finally agreed they should remain. In any case, as he admitted, it was quite possible that the journey itself would be just as dangerous for them. The trains were uncomfortable places these days, so it was said. Even more deadly than the borders and the militia were the typhus lice, hopping through the packed carriages. He insisted on leaving me the Mauser, which I took with some trepidation, having no idea how to load or fire it.

'We'll be back soon,' said Mr Kobelev, his kind face creased by anxiety. 'We'll be back in the autumn. All of this will have blown over by then. A Government of National Emergency is what's needed—'

'Don't be a fool,' murmured Sofia Pavlovna, almost inaudibly. 'It would be better if we forgot this life completely.'

It was another lilac-scented day in May when the old carriage was loaded up and a horse was hired to take them to the station. The children were dressed in their travelling clothes, heavy with the coins and jewellery that Sonya and I had sewn into the hems. They complained bitterly. 'We can't wear these clothes! We're not puppets, you know!'

The children's excitement gave the last moments an unexpectedly cheerful tone.

'I'll sit next to Mama,' Liza kept saying. 'I'll take care of Mama.'

'Yes,' said Dima casually, 'that's your job, and mine is to deal with any bandits we come across.'

We couldn't help laughing at the bloodthirsty look on his face.

'Where is Nikita?' wondered Mr Kobelev. 'Miss Gerty, you must embrace him for us. I am sorry not to say goodbye to him.'

'Goodbye, Miss Gerty,' said Pasha, doffing his cap and grinning at me. 'Now I'll never be able to convince you how much I love you!'

I laughed. 'Pasha, you are ridiculous —' I stopped; he had already turned away and was talking to Yasha, telling him to drive on.

'Oh, do take care,' I said after them. 'Take great care . . .'

In the end the Kobelev family left the house on Gagarinsky Lane almost without noticing, talking and arguing among themselves.

5

I found the two old ladies standing forlornly in the hall and led them back to their room overlooking the court-yard.

'We are all tired, I think,' sighed Anna Vladimirovna, adding unexpectedly, 'Perhaps you would sit with us for a cup of tea, Miss Freely?'

She was frightened, I saw, and no wonder. But I suddenly felt that if I sat down I would start crying and not know how to stop.

'No, thank you. I must see to a few things, and then perhaps we will spend the evening together?'

Two heads nodded, eager to please.

'We will have a little soup, a *soupchik*.'

They agreed again, more happily; there's no Russian alive that is not soothed by a little *soupchik*.

I wandered into the study, now furnished with ab-sences: squares of dust on the walls, pale patches on the parquet. With all the packing I had not slept more than five hours for the last couple of nights and everything had the dreary, gritty texture of sleeplessness. The empty shelves were scattered with dead woodlice. Prig's people had smashed the pretty gilt sconces on each side of the fireplace, perhaps imagining them to be made of real gold.

Why was I here? There was a part of me that felt

miserable for remaining. Should I have accompanied the Kobelevs? I loved them more than I did my own family, and yet I'd let them go alone, into danger.

Perhaps there was more of my father in me than I imagined. An image of him sprang to mind, red-cheeked and sandy-browed with great quivering lobsterish whisps, snapping at me, 'Make up your mind, girl!'

Well, I had.

A cold draught suddenly hit the back of my knees. Slavkin was standing in the hall, gazing around him with a look of desolation.

'Have they gone? Have I missed them?'

'Yes, they left half an hour ago – they asked me to say goodbye to you for them; they were sad not to see you.'

'I was at work.' His chin trembled. 'How bare it all looks . . .'

'Mr Kobelev said he'd always planned to give it all to the people.'

'It's for the best. It was much too dangerous to keep the collection here.' Slavkin's voice betrayed him with an alarming squeak. He turned his back on me and clumped up to his room.

For several days, Slavkin and I barely saw each other. In the evenings I heard him stomping to and fro in his room; occasionally I fancied that he was listening to my movements, as I tended to the old ladies. The house felt strange, like a ship adrift on a silent sea, a huge empty ship with an echoing hold. The weather had suddenly turned cold and windy; in the evenings the chestnut branches flexed and slapped against the shutters like ropes. The rafters creaked and moaned and occasionally fell quiet; then I felt the presence of Slavkin most strongly. I didn't seek him out; I was too shy of him. His brilliance rendered me absurdly prosaic and tongue-tied, blushing, a caricature of an English governess.

And yet sometimes, across the noisy evening gatherings, I had caught him looking at me as though we understood each other. We were outsiders in that house; we were not liberals, we didn't understand doubters. We had little to lose.

'What *can* he be doing all the time?' wondered Anna Vladimirovna. In the empty house, even Slavkin's 'village voice' was apparently better than nothing. 'Doesn't he want to come and sit with us? Can he be quite *well?*'

'He's probably busy with his contraptions, Anna Vladimirovna,' said Mamzelle soothingly. 'Scientists are not quite normal.'

I was working longer hours than ever at the English school on Tverskaya, lessons that were now paid mainly in kind – half a loaf of black bread and a smoked fish for the present continuous. One pupil, a Georgian, presented me with a bag of good black tea. Oh, the old ladies were happy.

'*Vous êtes trop gentille*,' said Mamzelle tearfully.

'Take some, do, to that strange boy,' said Anna Vladimirovna.

At my knock, Slavkin opened his door – even a little too quickly, as though he were waiting for me – and made me jump, and some of the precious tea was spilt. And then he hurried to relieve me of the tray, and I recoiled, trying to protect the cup, and there were apologies and counter-apologies, and I was blushing so hard, and my heart was racing, that I couldn't help laughing, and he looked at me in embarrassment, drawing back.

I had never seen the inside of his room. The walls were covered in notes and equations, pieces of newspaper, scribbles and rather beautiful sketches. There was a series of X-rays that seemed to show a skeleton walking with a stick and sitting on a bench. Posters covered one wall. In one corner was a camera on a tripod, and in another, a heap of rubbish – quite literally, without any exaggeration, rubbish. Broken wooden crates, bits of old planking, dirty bottles, rags, stones . . .

'Goodness,' I said, 'this is your work?' I was conscious of a note of incredulity, and added, 'I know you are very busy, Nikita Gavrilovich, as always—'

'I am.'

'Perhaps one day you will explain it to me.' I turned to leave, embarrassed.

'Wait.' He took a step towards me. 'Why are you here? Why didn't you go south?'

'What do you mean?' I stammered. 'You know why. British citizens have been told to stay in Moscow—'

'I don't think you remained here just for reasons of safety,' he said quietly.

I was speechless. At last I said, 'I don't know, I felt there'd be something for me to do here—'

'For the Revolution?'

'Well, yes . . . For the people, for my pupils, you know . . .'

He gazed at me, and I had an extraordinary sensation – as though it were the first time in my life that anyone had really looked at me.

'You're an unusual person,' he said. 'Aren't you afraid?'

'No, for some reason, I'm not. I feel . . . light. I feel that I'm changing, day by day.' I laughed. 'I know that must sound foolish.'

'Miss Gerty,' he said, 'you could never do a foolish thing. It makes me happy to hear you. We are in the first stage, you know, and everything is rough and crude and even cruel, but we have a chance—'

'A chance to reform society, you mean?'

'Oh, not just society – ourselves! Transform our own souls, even our bodies – we can be different.' He paused and then looked at me intently. 'I'd like to—' he said and immediately looked away, confused.

'What?'

'I'd like to visit you.'

I did not look away. Afterwards, thinking about it, I was amazed that I held his gaze so coolly, although my heart was rattling in my chest. 'Of course,' I said. 'Please do. '

*

My sitting-room floor in Hackney is littered with balls of paper. If this account is to be worthwhile at all, it seems to me, it must be as honest as I can manage. A dozen times I have found myself veering off into comfortable euphemism, torn out the page from my typewriter, and started afresh. The truth, my husband used to say, however shameful, however inconvenient, is the great healer. Isn't that time? I'd ask. Yes, but the truth is the surgeon. It sets the bones. Otherwise time will heal them crooked . . . His voice so close, in my head. I rip out yet another spoiled page. How could he leave me to tell it on my own? Out of nowhere I begin to cry, noisily, into the silence.

After a while I quieten down. I wipe my face on my sleeve. I thread a clean sheet of paper into the typewriter and begin again. The truth is the surgeon.

*

Later that night, after I'd cooked for the old ladies and listened to yet more of Anna Vladmirovna's endless supply of family stories, which could all really be boiled down to the simple maxim 'breeding is what matters', I lay in bed and listened to the wind – an unsettling tune with no comfort in it. Various conversations I'd had with Slavkin repeated and fragmented in my mind. 'Revolution . . . once in a millennium . . . transform ourselves, reform ourselves, unform . . .' Russian prefixes scuffled about drearily like the chestnut leaves on the window. I sat up in bed. There was someone at the door.

'Who is it?'

Slavkin – a tall, awkward figure silhouetted in the doorway 'It's me, comrade. You weren't sleeping, were you?' His voice gave way a little.

'No.'

He approached my bed. I did not move; my mouth was dry. He crouched beside me, avoiding my eyes, and spoke in a ponderous monotone.

'Comrade Freely, I have long thought you a very rational, intelligent woman. I have known your positive attitude to the Revolution and to women's rights for some time, but when you told me your reasons for staying in Moscow, it struck me that you would see my situation clearly, without sentiment. I hope I deduced this correctly . . .'

He gulped audibly, and in the half-light I saw his Adam's apple leaping up and down in his throat.

'In order for me to work productively certain physical comforts are occasionally necessary. For some time now I have been wanting urgently to visit you with the proposal that we might . . . we might become intimate, so to speak. That in the light of the new world we are building, we might ourselves enjoy free, mutually satisfactory, er, beneficial . . .'

He hesitated.

For a moment my mind whirled. Then I noticed that he was trembling, the hand clutching his knees white-knuckled.

I reached across and touched him.

'Oh, comrade—'

Suddenly we were together, and he was kissing my face, and pushing up my nightdress, and we were both shaking with urgency, and I was only astonished that I had never felt his hands on my waist before, or touching my breasts, and he was hurrying, hurrying, and pressed himself upon me, cried out, and a moment later fell still. I was aware of a wet patch on my thigh. The whole had taken perhaps five minutes.

My heart was galloping, I could not quite understand what we had done. After a while Nikita raised himself from me, stood up and straightened his clothes.

'I greatly value and respect your honesty and your generosity,' he said, serious as ever.

I sat up, flooded with shame. I covered myself with the sheet. 'Oh . . . I see.'

He was avoiding my eyes again. 'You will assist me on my great task, I hope, comrade. We will work together, shall we?'

'Yes indeed,' I answered.

'Well, good night then I'm tired,' he said, retreating. 'A peaceful night . . .'

Was that a 'dear one' that I heard at the end of his sentence? Perhaps it was. When he was gone I got out of bed, took off my nightdress and washed, staring at myself in the mirror. My shame evaporated and I was filled with joy. What had happened? It was very puzzling. I had only the vaguest knowledge of such matters, only my mother's hissed and encoded warnings. For some reason, however, I was certain I would not fall pregnant or catch anything nasty. Shame? No, no, here in Soviet Russia there was no place for shame – here men and women were equal, we were honest with each other and we had no time for sentiment. And yet for some time he had been wanting urgently to visit me! I could hear my mother's poisonous tones: 'I'm afraid you're not the type men like, dear.' Every cell in my body rejoiced that night: she was wrong, wrong, wrong.

*

For several long days afterwards, I saw nothing of Slavkin. I began to dig the children's vegetable plot in the courtyard, tripling its size, thinking of the winter ahead. In the afternoons I brought the old ladies outside and settled them in the shade of the lilac trees in the corner, where they watched and chatted.

'I can't think why we troubled to go all the way to Mikhailovka all those years,' Anna Vladimirovna said. 'Why, it's just as pleasant here, without that terrible travelling!'

'It was only an hour on the train,' I reminded her.

'No, no, much longer, and quite dreadful.' In some way Anna Vladimirovna seemed invigorated by the strange new situation in the house, less tetchy, more energetic. 'Where is the boy? Is he avoiding us?'

Oh dear God, did she somehow know how desperately I was asking the same question? My every nerve was alive to his presence in the house, and listening involuntarily to his movements in his bedroom, his arrivals and exits at strange hours, exacerbated my insomnia terribly.

As time passed it seemed to me that he had shown disrespect, if not for me then for the principle of self-transformation that he had spoken about so warmly. Taking my courage in both hands, I decided to approach him myself. In the new world men and women must be honest and direct with each other; it was no good hanging back like a blushing damsel.

I knocked on the door of his room that evening, my hands sweating uncomfortably.

'Enter!'

'Comrade Slavkin,' I began, 'I'm afraid I am disturbing you in the midst of important work, but it is essential that we discuss the matter of living space. We are here in possession of almost two hundred square metres of living space, enough by government standards to house at least another twenty-five people. Don't you think we should report this anomaly?'

As honest as I intended to be, this was the subject that I lit upon in the awkwardness of the moment.

'Oh, yes indeed, comrade,' he said. 'The fact is I have been thinking about exactly this problem . . .'

I could see, now, that he was blushing. Yes, blushing! A deep pink all down his neck and under his hair. He looked up at me almost beseechingly, like a boy gazing up at his teacher. A chill passed through me at that moment; if I had only heeded it, how much pain I would have saved myself. But I suppose it was already too late. I steadied myself, and spoke to him as gently as I could.

'Please, you have no need to feel awkward with me.'

'What? No, no—' he stammered.

'Really, it's not necessary. We are adults, we are responsible for our own actions.' I smiled, to show I meant it. 'Now start again. Tell me what you have been thinking.'

He gazed at me doubtfully for a moment. Then a

smile began, and spread and spread. 'Dear Miss Gerty, comrade, what a wonderful person you are! A true Revolutionary! I am convinced that if you will help me, we will succeed. Will you help me? Will you?'

He was almost on his knees before me, beaming, looking so young, and I couldn't help laughing and agreeing. 'Of course I'll help you, Nikita, but with what?'

'With my institute – my scientific institute for the purposes of creating the true communard! You, Miss Gerty, you are the perfect woman to lead our Russian *dyevushki*, you have already the spirit of English egalitarianism in your veins . . .'

We talked long that night, Nikita was inspired and eloquent. In the early hours of the morning, without any awkwardness, we suddenly found ourselves making love on his rusty-springed bed. The feel of his skin against mine was intoxicating.

Immediately afterwards, as we lay in each other's arms, we agreed that the physical side of our friendship was no more than that, part of a friendship. Romance, we both said, was a product of an outdated social order, a trap for women that turned them into second-class citizens. 'I have the greatest respect for you, Gerty,' Nikita said to me earnestly. 'In fact I'm very fond of you – but I am not and I never will be "in love" with you. I reject that state of exaggerated ego in which each partner wilfully creates an ideal beloved of the other.'

I agreed with him and added, quite casually, that sexual desire is natural in both men and women – even if the words caused a foolish hot flush to creep up my cheeks.

We both concluded that the important thing was to be rational about such things, and not to let emotion mislead one.

June passed in this way, and July. In what spare time I could grasp from the round of English classes, looking after the old ladies, tending the vegetable patch and trailing from shop to shop to find food, I packed away the Kobelevs' things, determined to keep them safe if I could. 'Loot the looters!' Lenin had announced, and all over Moscow people were taking his words to heart. The Civil War brought news of more horrors every day. In July, they reported that the Romanovs were killed – the poor girls, the little boy. I didn't tell the old ladies. By force of will, I shut my mind to all of it and concentrated on the house. Nikita worked with me, room by room. He was good at cleaning; as a child, he told me, he had helped his mother who always had a new baby to nurse.

Together we scrubbed and polished the floors and stored all but a few essential pieces of furniture and household equipment in the stables. We took down the heavy, swagged, fringed curtains and packed them in cloth dotted with camphor. Day by day, more sunlight poured into the house – even into poor Mrs Kobelev's room. We flung open the doors and windows and the lush summer seemed to rush indoors. Like an old beast led out after the winter, the house pulled itself upright and pricked up its ears. The years dropped away from it. The lack of the Kobelevs themselves was like a stitch in my side, a constant, anxious ache – but at the same time exhilaration bubbled in me, just below the surface.

I hardly slept, I worked like a dog, I didn't recognise the wild-eyed, exultant girl I saw in the mirror, biting her lip to stop herself from laughing out loud.

I spent my evenings playing canasta with the old ladies, my ears pricked for the sound of the front door closing behind Slavkin. Then I excused myself and went to bed, waiting, shivering with excitement, under the covers for the door to open quietly and Nikita's long silhouette to approach. Every evening I was sure he wouldn't come, sure that I didn't deserve so much happiness. Every evening he appeared, and silently, passionately, we embraced. Sometimes he was too hasty – I remember crying out – although later he was always tender, stroking my cheek. Afterwards we would lie in my bed and drink Armenian brandy. Nikita would talk, his long face animated and glowing like an El Greco, imagining a new way of living. Together we planned a commune – a place where a group of us could live together, and be moulded and changed by communal living, its problems and its rewards, into real Revolutionaries, people capable of building Communism.

'But the Kobelevs, what would they think?'

'Well, the alternative is Prig and his louts – they will be back any day now to give these rooms away to whomever they choose.'

'You're right.'

'We'll invite Marina and Vera, and others – this way we can choose suitable participants rather than have to take Prig's people.'

Nikita was not the only one to have this idea – ideological communes were springing up all over Moscow. They were a rational response to the life we found ourselves living, with such scarce resources and such high hopes.

So we invited Fyodor Kuzmin, a student friend of Pasha's, to join us, and Volodya, the yardman's son, when he returned from the army. Marina and Vera Getler, neighbours and old family friends, agreed as well. Together we wrote a Manifesto. We renamed various rooms: Mr Kobelev's study became our communal meeting room; the hall became a 'Red Corner' with political reading material. For the first time in my life, I felt that I was engaged in a mighty, vitally important task. I had never been so happy. Fyodor took some photos of us on the steps of the house – Nikita and I, standing close together, beaming straight at the camera.

I often find myself staring at those photos now. It's hard to make sense of what became of those two smooth-skinned children the girl now a bent, wrinkly old woman, while across the Soviet world, from hoardings and murals, book covers and film posters, the boy smiles on unchanged.

*

One evening towards the end of August Nikita and I heard a muted knocking and voices at the front door. We leant out of the window into the warm summer night. Two figures were waiting in the street; we could hardly make them out in the twilight.

'Who's there?' Nikita called quietly.

'Good Lord, can that really be you, Nikita?' came a familiar voice. 'Get down here at once, you dog, open the door to us.'

Pasha and Sonya Kobelev had returned to Moscow.

'Friends! My dear friends!' shouted Nikita, galloping downstairs and flinging open the door. I hurried behind.

'My goodness, Miss Gerty! You look beautiful! Have you been waiting for me?' Pasha stepped indoors. 'Don't touch me, Nikita, for goodness' sake; we must fumigate these clothes, there are infections everywhere. Just get us some water to wash with, there's a good girl, Gerty—'

'Oh – yes, of course.' I brought a basin and as they washed they told how they had travelled south – their week-long journey, unable to leave their seats for fear of not being able to force their way back into the train, poor Mrs Kobelev delirious with fever, begging for laudanum. Outside Yalta they had found a small villa to rent and had installed themselves safely. The area was now under White control, from whom the Kobelevs had little to fear, even if they disagreed with their politics. 'My father plans to stay the winter there, at any rate, and then decide what's best.' Pasha said quietly. He looked tanned, if thin and tired. 'They're quite happy – the children swim and sunbathe all day long. Even my mother seems rather better. But Sonya and I couldn't allow ourselves to swan around like that for ever. Once they were settled in we decided to come back. To do our bit for the Revolution and all that. You can't imagine what all those Whites are like – they really are clankingly awful. Their politics are

62

one thing, but do you know they talk about nothing but duck shooting? And their moustaches . . .'

I smiled. 'Well, if they have substandard moustaches, of course. What did your parents say when you told them?'

'My mother wasn't happy,' Pasha shrugged. 'My father understood. He was anxious about us, of course, but I think he was proud.' He blinked. 'And of course he plans to come back.'

'Once things have settled down,' I said – Mr Kobelev's mantra. 'By spring, once things are a bit calmer—'

Slavkin, who had been pacing about the room during this conversation, suddenly interrupted.

'Yes, yes, but Gerty, perhaps you'd empty the water for us, would you?' He pushed the basin into my hands, slopping it over my dress. 'My word, I have been missing you both!' he burst out before I'd left the room. 'I've an idea, a plan. I had no one to discuss it with . . .'

I couldn't help stopping and looking at him in astonishment.

'Of course Gerty and I have talked it all over,' he stammered, embarrassed. 'She's been a wonder, but—'

'Gerty is a wonder,' said Pasha. 'We all know that.'

'But I need other progressive minds to discuss my plans with, you understand.'

My face was burning. I emptied the basin in the laundry and sat there for a long while, until I calmed down.

The following day, Nikita drew me aside and said, without looking me in the eye, 'We've always been friends, comrade. I hope you will do me the honour of remaining my friend even if certain aspects – which were always quite separate from our friendship – are no longer appropriate to our relationship.'

Part of me had guessed immediately what he was about to say, but nonetheless I was silenced for a moment. I stared at him and stammered, 'What aspects?' And when he took a deep breath and was about to tell me, I interrupted, 'No, no – but why are they no longer app—' the word he had used failed me, 'no longer app— app—'

Slavkin looked at me. He seemed puzzled. 'Are you all right, Gerty? Perhaps you should sit down?'

I sat on the stairs.

'The fact is, that now Pasha and Sonya are here, and all our members are about to move in, the time has come to devote ourselves to the commune, do you see? We must all make sacrifices and our – our physical intimacy is one of them. We cannot have couples, with secrets and so on, forming divisions within the group. We must be a collective.'

I said nothing, determined not to cry. To my horror, he crouched down in front of me and put his hands on my shoulders. 'I must tell you, Gerty, how grateful I am for your friendship. I've never known anyone like you. You have taught me so much about the human spirit, what generosity it is capable of . . . With you in the commune, I think we have a chance of making it work.' He gave me a little squeeze and left. Was it my imagination, or was he almost jaunty as he stepped out of the front door?

I lay hunched over on the stairs for a long time, feeling

the sharp edges of the mahogany panelling pressing into the skin of my forehead. Tears dripped onto the stair carpet, soaked in, and disappeared. Then I heard someone coming and struggled upright, straightening my clothes. Neither Slavkin nor I mentioned our liaison to the others – why would we? And I was grateful, on the whole, that none of the members of the commune noticed anything amiss – my low spirits, or the way Slavkin seemed to avoid me, or a thousand other pinpricks that pierced me each day.

So at the end of August 1918, the Kobelevs' house on Gagarinsky Lane became the Institute of Revolutionary Transformation, and we – its raw materials, aching to be transformed.

6

The Institute of Revolutionary Transformation
MANIFESTO

WE, the Comrades of the Institute of Revolutionary Transformation – declare war on:

The Private – from now on there shall be no I, only We.

The Old – in this new world we shall build everything anew – Society, Family, Art, Science, Language, Nature, ourselves.

The Ego – the enemy within ourselves that sabotages all attempts at true Communism. It shall be dragged out and crushed.

We hereby renounce, joyfully and wholeheartedly, certain frills that society prizes: sexual activity, romance, wealth, power, marriage, family, success, luxury, leisure.

Comrades shall be expected to comport themselves with the iron discipline of Revolutionaries – chaste, frugal and dedicated to the cause.

All property shall be held in common, and all decisions shall be made by the commune as a whole. There shall be complete equality between comrades.

The non-objective aesthetic of the avant-garde will transform our commune and our city. The New World will look, feel and think in the language of Modernity.

We celebrate comradeship, cooperative effort, and every form of creativity.

And so, we aim to transform *our own selves* into true communards, capable of inhabiting the Communist State.

All Hail the Revolution!

Signed: Nikita Slavkin, Pavel Kobelev, Sofia Kobelev, Dr Marina Getler, Vera Getler, Gertrude Freely, Fyodor Kuzmin, Vladimir Yakov.

Institute of Revolutionary Transformation,
Gagarinsky Lane, Moscow.
20 August 1918

*

The day began in the IRT with the clanging of Mr Kobelev's huge copper gong – one of the few possessions of his that still remained in the house – at six each morning. How delicious those summer dawns were, the morning sun through the poplar trees dancing on the ceiling of my bedroom. I dressed rapidly; everything was quicker now – no dreary lacing of stays, no elaborate hair arrangements. All the female members of the commune – Sonya Kobelev, the sisters Marina and Vera Getler and I – wore our hair short and had exchanged our corsets and underpinnings for loose cotton dresses, and all of us were amazed at the difference it made. Whereas before we were hardly aware of our bodies and gave them no thought, except to feel uncomfortable, now suddenly I noticed the muscles sliding under the skin of my arms, I felt the air on my legs and the sweat trickling down my torso on hot days. And if I was careful, and worked hard, and concentrated on such matters as the muscles in my legs, the fresh morning air, and so on, then I found I could keep my mind off dark thoughts for whole hours at a time.

At six-thirty we sat down to eat breakfast in the airy, high-ceilinged dining room with its large windows giving onto the garden and listened while one of the members read something suitable – Gorky, perhaps – a relief, as the food was best not dwelt on. It was usually *kasha*, buckwheat porridge, or perhaps *blondinka*, as we called millet porridge, with salt fish. Even in the summer, when supplies were relatively plentiful, there was already the sensation of dread before you had started your bowl . . . the last spoonful was drawing near. You took smaller and smaller bites and you savoured the feeling of food on your tongue, in your mouth; you never swallowed too quickly. You found different ways to eat your portion; a slice of bread could make a whole plateful of tiny balls of dough. I remembered little Liza's words, years before –

'I don't like to eat, I prefer to be hungry' – and I understood her better now. The only way to overcome hunger was to welcome it in.

At the time we were brisk with ourselves. Communists are too tough to whine about hunger, we said. We joked about the Moscow Slimming Diet and then we changed the subject. But all these years later, I still have what my little grandsons call 'the tins' – the hoard of tinned and dry foods that I keep piled up to the ceiling under the stairs. My daughter Sophy tells me I am absurd, but I can't help it. If you've once been hungry like that, you never quite feel safe again.

After we had scraped our bowls clean, if it was not a working day, we sat in the garden and debated how to run the commune. We set it up as if we were establishing a small independent state. We had a Customs House, run by two Customs Officials to whom all members handed over any food they came by. A Finance Ministry controlled most of the money the members might earn, apart from a small amount to be kept by individuals. A Triumvirate of Food Commissars was in charge of buying and bartering the supplies for the month. Small articles such as soap, paper, pencils, hairpins, and so on were in theory available from the Shop Without a Clerk, which was in a cupboard in the meeting room; a small red book was provided for members to note down what they had taken, and we relied – in this as in all our arrangements – on the communards' good faith. All these positions were rotated weekly, and those who were not assigned any that week were expected to show solidarity with their labouring comrades. For example, while the Ironing Brigade was at work, volunteers might entertain them with songs or funny anecdotes.

Almost despite myself, I loved it all . . . so many jokes, so many passionate debates. We pinned up reproductions of non-objective pictures we admired. We painted slogans on the walls: 'Come on, Live Communally!' in yellow letters on the red wallpaper in the hall, and in the study a quote from Gerrard Winstanley: 'Live together, Eate together, Show it all abroade'. In Slavkin's workshop, which he set up in the empty drawing room, we nailed a banner along one wall: 'We have nothing to lose but our chains.' ('And that hammer . . . I'm sure I left it here somewhere,' added Pasha, of course.) The men's dormitory was Mr Kobelev's bedroom, while at first the female members of the commune had the small, separate bedrooms at the back of the house. Then Dr Marina (as we called her, although she was still in training) disagreed with this arrangement.

'Why do women need privacy? Only to hoard some kind of private property, some frippery; or to indulge in private fantasies instead of working; or perhaps to facilitate sexual relations, which would be the most offensive reason of all . . . We women, more than any men, need to rid ourselves of the insidious reactionary voice in our head – look pretty, be charming, please everyone! A collective life will help us to be free of it. We assert our right to a communal women's dormitory. They are only partition walls between the bedrooms; I propose we demolish them.'

Tall and thin with short dark hair, constantly smoking and grave as a Spanish hidalgo, Dr Marina was the most militant of all of us. She had already spent three years struggling against the casual chauvinism of her male colleagues, and no battle was too small to fight.

'Well said!' approved Slavkin. 'Everyone, share your thoughts on this suggestion.'

'Let's hope the house shows a proper Revolutionary spirit and doesn't collapse on us all,' ventured Pasha.

'They're such nice little bedrooms,' Vera said wistfully.

She could barely have chosen a more outrageous description, in our terms.

'Nice!'

'Perhaps you mean *cosy*!'

'Verochka, you should be ashamed of yourself! Explain to your sister that we're in the middle of a Revolution, Doctor—'

'Let's vote on it – who's for the women's dormitory?'

The motion was carried unanimously, even the blushing Vera putting up her hand, and the following week the three back bedrooms were knocked into one. Sonya, Dr Marina, Vera and I moved in together, and it did mean that there was little time for vanity – and even less for introspection. At night, when I couldn't sleep, I still felt desolate – although what right did I have when Nikita had been so honest with me from the beginning? But at least, day by day, my ego was being eroded – 'dragged out and crushed', as our Manifesto said. I was changing, little by little, and the pain it caused me was only natural. It was a sacrifice worth making for our cause.

'The children seem to be turning everything upside down, Miss Gerty!' Anna Vladimirovna kept saying querulously. 'In my day, Father would have sent them to bed with no supper.'

'Well, that's more or less what happens these days too.'

'*Nichevo strashnovo*,' Vera soothed them. 'Nothing to worry about.' Vera, who wasn't remotely interested in politics, was probably the most generous and selfless communard of all of us. Kind and plump, with shiny dark hair and huge blue eyes, she often helped me with the old ladies, who adored her. 'Let's listen to the gramophone, shall we?'

'If you say so, my dear . . .'

Dr Marina and Vera had brought the gramophone with them; in the evenings we played 'Sensation Rag' and Marion Harris singing 'I ain't got nobody', and danced on the lawn. Pasha asked his aunt to dance, and Nikita led out a shy and delighted Mamzelle. I hung back as each song ended, hating myself for minding that he never asked me. Later, under the warm night sky, we lay on the grass, told stories and read poems. The one I remember best was the Futurist poet Khlebnikov's 'Incantation by Laughter', which, read aloud, always reduced us to helpless snorting heaps:

> O laugh it out, you laughsters!
> O laugh it up, you laughers!
> So they laugh with laughters, so they
>   laugherise delaughly.

O laugh it up belaughably!
O the laughingstock of the laughed-upon –
    the laugh of belaughed laughsters!
O laugh it out roundlaughingly, the laugh of
    laughed-at laughians!
Laugherino, laugherino,
Laughify, laughicate, laugholets, laugholets,
Laughikins, laughikins,
O laugh it out, you laughsters!
O laugh it up, you laughters!

*

'Miss Freely,' said Miss Clegg, striding into the hallway one hot August day. 'I made a promise to your poor parents. I cannot abuse their trust. I simply will not allow you to remain in this house a moment longer.'

It was some months since I had last seen Miss Clegg. Her appearance, however – solid and weathered, still topped by her small crocheted cap – had scarcely changed. I admired her for that. There were not many who had stayed so unbowed by the hardships of the Revolution.

'Miss Clegg, how kind of you to think of my parents, and me. But there is no reason to feel concerned, I assure you. I make a reasonable living by giving English lessons, and I'm among friends. I've lived here for over four years now – I feel at home.'

Her eyes flickered over our 'Red Corner' with its slogan and portraits of Marx and Engels.

'Miss Freely, you know I am not one to mince my words. You are living in a house of ill repute. Your name is connected with the most depraved behaviour. There are those at St Andrew's who would refuse you entrance to the hostel, but I have used what little influence I have to persuade the Reverend Brown that we must offer you this charity.'

'Please thank the Reverend for me and tell him that I'm in no need of assistance.' I smiled at her and attempted to be firm. 'Now, if you will excuse me, I have a meeting to attend.'

'Miss Freely! I will not be sent away like this—'

'Well – then perhaps you'd like to stay for our evening meeting? You will see that there is nothing remotely depraved about it.'

It was perhaps unfortunate that she attended the session at which we set up the Commissariat for Clothing.

'Comrades!' began Slavkin, once we had all gathered. 'Good, all here, and we have with us also an acquaintance of Comrade Freely's. Welcome, Comrade Clegg.' He nodded towards Miss Clegg, who was perched on a chair in the corner, her expression a wonderful mixture of excitement and disgust. 'Now we must discuss the matter of the collectivisation of our clothing. We have already decided to pool all our possessions for the common good. We have handed over our income and our valuables. How can we, therefore, allow one member to walk about in an astrakhan coat, while another shivers in a cotton jacket?' As he talked, he loped about on his long, knobbly, Bactrian legs.

'Quite right,' said Dr Marina. 'Clothes only provide fuel for vanity. We cannot have them creating inequality between us.'

'I don't see anyone in an astrakhan,' commented Pasha.

'Pasha, you're a . . . a Galliffet,' Sonya said, frowning at her brother (the latest term of abuse, it was a reference to the French general who suppressed the Paris Commune). 'A wool coat, then. You know what he means.'

'I am not! I just don't think this idea is radical enough. Why do we need clothes at all? It's warm at the moment, clothes only get dirty and need washing, as well as promoting inequality. I mean, even collectivised clothes – give one man a smock, and he'll look like a wastrel; give the same smock to another and he'll wear it like a hero,' he ran on. 'Everyone knows that. Only the naked body can be truly equal.'

'I'll second that,' Volodya, the ex-soldier drawled, speaking past the soggy cigarette stub that lived in the corner of his mouth. 'Clothes off, everyone!' He stood up and took off his jacket with a flourish.

Miss Clegg made a noise in her throat, something like 'Oglf.'

'Well, in that sense nudity wouldn't be equal either, would it? Some people are better made than others, there's no escaping that,' snapped Fyodor. 'We need clothes for protection and warmth. Enough of this oafishness.'

Even then, of course, fault lines existed within the commune. Volodya, just back from the trenches and

75

highly suspicious of anything that smelt of refinement or intellectual snobbishness, did not blend happily with Fyodor's rather prissy emphasis on 'Revolutionary culture' (that is, neatness, politeness and meticulous self-discipline), and Fyodor disapproved of Pasha's jokes.

'Don't be so hasty!' Pasha retorted. 'Haven't you heard of the nudist movement these days? They dance with only a loin cloth, or a fig leaf, or something. I'm sorry to say I haven't seen it yet. Anyway, I think some of the other members agree with me. Didn't I hear Comrade Clegg expressing an interest?'

Miss Clegg, chins quivering, stood up. 'I didn't come here to be insulted. This is the last time I offer the hand of friendship to you, Gertrude Freely.'

'Oh Miss Clegg, please don't be offended. It was a joke, that's all. Pasha, come and apologise, won't you? She didn't understand . . .'

But she had gone, rushing out of the house, clutching her bag to her chest. I went back into the meeting, where we decided on the finer details of laundry and mending, and established the Commissariat, to start work with immediate effect, the first Underwear Commissar being Pasha himself, who promised to work hard and absolve himself of the crime of ruining my reputation for once and for all at St Andrew's Hostel for Governesses.

'I couldn't let that nasty woman take you away, could I, Gerty?' said Pasha, not particularly repentant.

*

However much I resisted her attempts to interfere, I was still full of gratitude to Miss Clegg for bringing me to Gagarinsky Lane, for unwittingly allowing me the chance to participate in the task of auto-transformation. Mankind, we believed at the IRT, was only a half-designed product that had taken shape by accident rather than through conscious choices. In many ways we were not so different from the millions who seek self-improvement today – the spiritual questers, and those in therapy, and the readers of self-help literature; like them, we were hopeful that with self-awareness human beings are capable of living together in harmony.

'It may sound an insurmountable task,' Slavkin said, 'but the whole history of man is really a long, slow war against our base instincts. A couple of centuries ago it was acceptable to burn witches and to hang pigs for heresy. In this context you see a large part of the road has already been travelled . . .'

Pasha, who was fascinated by Freud, argued for a psychological approach, and from the beginning all of us were expected to write accounts of our Revolutionary Development (a few of which I still have in my dusty cardboard boxes) – the steps that had led us towards the commune, that we read aloud to the other members. He also suggested episodes of 'group criticism', at which people were encouraged to express any emotional difficulties they might be experiencing as a result of our communal life. We attempted to solve disagreements in this way.

Fyodor saw simple discipline as the key. The

Revolution, as he perceived it, was chiefly a matter of efficient organisation and training. He and Nikita clashed over this view.

'I can't help it, Fedya,' said Nikita. 'Your picture of the future fills me with dread.'

'You're too emotional about it,' snapped Fyodor. He was rather cherubic, with very red, full lips. 'Behind all your talk of technology is a sentimentalist.'

Nikita, in fact, was an unusual mixture of the pragmatic and the idealist. He understood better than any of us that from now on, in human history, man would be formed by machines as much as the other way around. Man *would* have extraordinary powers – the power to fly like a bird or swim in the deepest oceans, the power to throw up mountains, even blast out of the shell of the Earth's atmosphere – thanks to the advance of technology. His focus, therefore, was on designing the machines that would reshape man's psychology.

Towards the end of 1917, he had begun work on his first psychotechnological device, the Propaganda Machine. This 'audio-visual sensory chamber that aimed to convert an individual's mindset from bourgeois to Revolutionary in a single, twenty-minute session', as the *Encyclopaedia Britannica* later described it, was no more than a rusty upside-down grain hopper from the back stables bolted onto the Kobelevs' open carriage. Nikita insulated the hopper with thick cotton wadding and covered it with canvas, all but the funnel, which peeked out at the top. We coated it in what should have been Revolutionary red paint, but dried a sickly salmon pink, so from the outside the whole thing resembled nothing so much as a colossal, plumply upholstered bosom on wheels.

To enter, one mounted the steps of the carriage and squeezed through a door cut in the side of the hopper. The benches had been removed and instead there was a single large chair, heavily padded, with a footstool, while the curving wall in front was entirely covered by a white screen. The patient seated himself in the chair and was strapped in around the waist, legs and arms. A sizeable helmet was lowered to restrict his viewing solely to the screen. Then the door was closed and the anti-bourgeois vaccination began: a series of short films and flashing images, accompanied by a soundtrack played on a gramophone lodged at the top of the funnel. The images were very large and close; the sound was slightly distorted by the acoustics within the hopper, and rather loud. Meanwhile canisters of different, powerful smells were discharged into the hopper; the temperature was raised by means of several gas lamps and, at certain moments in the session, the whole construction could be violently and unexpectedly pushed and joggled from the outside. We hoped the combination of these effects would produce an indelible impression on the brain. Night after night, we pooled our ideas and experimented with the Propaganda Machine settings – the right images, the snatches of speech, the timing – searching for the irresistible *coup de foudre*, the touchpaper to light people's hearts.

What will people think of our efforts now? As I

write this, in 1974, the dreary banner of realpolitik with its stench of atom bombs and oil fumes seems almost to have smothered any talk of a better world. Of course there are my friends in the Women's Reading Groups and the anti-racist organisations; there are the demos and the strikers. But outside a few places like our little radical republic of Hackney – after Vietnam and Watergate, Hungary and Prague, hasn't idealism been universally dismissed as a shorthand for naivety and self-indulgence? Graham Greene expressed it succinctly in *The Quiet American*: 'God save us always from the innocent and the good.' This cold-war generation will probably say that we were impractical and unrealistic – 'not living in the real world', as the patronising phrase goes.

And yet the truth is that the realities of our life in 1918 ground us between their hard edges in a way that most people today would find unbearable: we were constantly hungry, we were cold, the country was in chaos. Despite it all, we set out on the hard, hard path of change. We were not daunted, we were tenacious. The real cause for astonishment, to my mind, does not lie in our failures – of which of course there were many – but in the incredible extent of our success.

7

'The city of the future looks more like a village every day,' remarked Pasha in the summer of 1918. It was true: harebells and cow parsley now flourished in the strangely empty, hot thoroughfares. Shopfronts were boarded up, most of the markets were closed down, and the onion domes were stripped of gold; day by day evidence of the city's flamboyant pre-Revolutionary life faded from the streets. Muscovites left in their thousands, and even when Moscow was declared the capital city in March, the government ministries did not plug the gaps.

As though reclaiming their territory, the rats came out into the daylight – too many even to be kept down by the packs of stray dogs and cats, abandoned pets that had, so it was said, developed a taste for human flesh. The birds seemed to have lost their fear of humans. Once a flock of rooks attacked me as I walked home – perhaps I passed too close to their nests. I flung up my arms to shield myself and they stabbed my hands and the back of my neck with their beaks.

After our measly breakfast, we joined the crowds of people trudging to work in the middle of the road. Occasionally a lone tram, faces crammed against its windows, would divide them; silently, the crowd closed up again in its wake. Gone were the costumes of Imperial Russia –

the vivid blues and reds of the dress uniforms, the merchants in fur coats and their wives in sarafans and pearls, the priests. Everyone now dressed in a jumble of drab khaki, old suits and plain dresses – partly due to the lack of clothes on sale, and partly from expedience. An epaulette, a smart collar or even a pair of spectacles was enough to single one out as 'bourgeois', and the city was full of characters who looked forward to an opportunity to mete out punishment to the bourgeoisie.

Occasionally I came across friends of the Kobelevs who had not gone into exile. They were classed as 'former people', prevented from working in any but the most menial jobs. I was overwhelmed by the stoicism with which they adapted. An old general, a cousin of Sonya's in-laws, now worked as a lift operator at the Metropol Hotel, while his wife sold clothes she sewed out of old curtains. 'It's not so frightful,' he told me. His skin hung in pouches around his face and he had the sallow glaze of malnutrition; the plump ones seemed to suffer the most. 'I'm sorry to say that in the old days we didn't do all we could to prevent this.'

One heard this sentiment again and again. 'We have brought this on ourselves,' Prince Lvov commented when he heard about the October Revolution. In August the Committee for the Mobilisation of the Bourgeoisie began to organise 'former people' – even the elderly – into labour brigades to sweep the streets and the yards; others, one heard, were forced out of their beds to feed the electricity stations in the middle of the night, and, in winter, to clear snow from the railways. It was a horrible sight. Occasionally they were beaten up, but even if they were not physically attacked they were taunted and abused by passers-by. I was so grateful that the Kobelevs did not have to endure it.

Our little republic at No. 7 Gagarinsky Lane kept to its own rhythm; behind our gates we were building a very different revolution from the one we saw on the streets. Yet we couldn't help but be aware that this new-born Bolshevik world – 'Sovdepia', the land of Soviet deputies – was encircled and isolated, battling for its life. There was war at every compass point, and several in between – against the Germans in the Ukraine, the British in the north, the Czechs on the Volga, the Whites on the Don, and the Japanese in the Far East. In the summer Trotsky introduced martial law, and conscription sucked up many of the pupils at my school – either into the ranks or as far from them as possible. Every day we saw peasants marching through the streets to join their new regiments. A more pitiful fighting force would be hard to imagine. Many of the peasants seemed to be visiting the city for the first time and were terrified of the traffic, sparse though it was. They would break formation and huddle by the side of the road, peering anxiously to left and right; then get their timing completely wrong and scuttle out just as a lone vehicle approached them. They seemed constantly to be asking the way, usually to a church, which they called by their own names: 'Girl, if you please, can you tell me how to find "St Michael no-hair" or "Mother of God with the oak tree"?'

We had no accurate news about what was going on

outside Moscow – or, rather, we had no way of gauging its accuracy. Our information came either from the propaganda posters and slogans that papered the capital or rumour. No one paid much attention to the endless articles in *Pravda* about the Red Army crushing the Whites under the boot of the proletariat.

'What, he has boots?' as some old fellow was said to have remarked. 'This Mr Proletariat sounds like a rich man!'

We thought the whispers in the market were more plausible, those that told of the White leader Denikin's army of forty – a hundred – five hundred thousand, armed by the Germans. The papers reported the cruelties they inflicted on any Red soldiers they captured, which, on the whole, we believed: we already had years of experience of Cossack behaviour against unarmed demonstrators, let alone on the battlefield.

'Our skinny Revolution, in birch-bark shoes, clutches on to its little victory by a whisker,' Nikita put it.

And so we understood why Trotsky ordered Tsarist army officers to join up and fight for the Red Army, and also why he took their families hostage to keep them loyal. The army was starving and short of every type of equipment; so we accepted the need to send the brigades into the villages to collect food, and even to break up the factory committees. We understood – although it was also true that we preferred not to dwell on such matters.

*

I continued to teach English more or less without pause through all the upheavals. It was as though the overthrow of Tsarism had released a surge of energy among the working classes – a huge impulse towards learning and self-betterment of every kind. After the Bolsheviks took power many of my younger, middle-class pupils left to go abroad or to the country, but their places were taken by double the number of adult students, who seized their first opportunity to study. English seemed a more or less random choice; they could just as easily have decided on book-keeping, chemistry or statistics. They were endearing students, eager and demanding. Many of them were barely literate in their own language, let alone in a second. I remember one jowly young man, always quick to criticise my teaching from a Marxist perspective, asking, 'And how do you pronounce this letter, with the eye at the bottom?'

'Which letter?' I was confused.

'Why, this one! It's a Russian letter too, but I don't know ' He stopped suddenly, blushing. He was pointing at an exclamation mark. I murmured to him that we'd discuss it after class. These new students had a good deal of pride; it did not do to embarrass them.

America was their passion: the construction of the Brooklyn Bridge, and Detective Pinkerton, and Charlie Chaplin, and the new 'jazz' music, the tango and the foxtrot (considered decadent, of course, by the authorities, but exciting nonetheless). 'Americanizatsia' and 'Fordizm' were the words on everybody's lips. I taught from a copy of the *Illustrated London News*, by good fortune kept since 1916, which showed recent technical innovations in the USA and Europe. My pupils learnt useful terms such as 'cable traction', 'gasoline engine' and the 'dynamo-electric machine'. Sometimes I taught for ten hours, and then went on to see my private pupils. If I worked hard enough, I might be spared another wakeful night.

One hot Friday in late August I walked from the school to the Hotel National at the bottom of Tverskaya. The streets were dusty and quiet. A young guard, barely seventeen, slouched at the main door of the National, drawing pictures in the dust with the end of his bayonet. I fumbled in my pocket for a permit and held it up to show him.

'I've come for a meeting with Comrade Pelyagin.'

'Huh,' grunted the guard, jabbing his bayonet in my direction, making me jump. He laughed, pleased with himself, and gestured towards the ruff of other permits at the bottom of the blade. 'Stick it on with the others. Don't cut your little white hands, will you?'

'Nothing white about my hands,' I retorted sharply, sliding on the scrap of paper.

The hotel lobby smelled of *makhorka* – cheap tobacco – and stale alcohol; the fleshy, heroic marble figures holding up the ceiling and the remnants of the marble floor contrasted bizarrely with its new role. I climbed the grand art-nouveau stairs to the office of Emil Pelyagin, a Party official who, so the director at the language school had told me, wanted private English lessons. He was part of the Department of Industry that continued to operate from the National after other departments moved over to the Kremlin.

'Enter!'

Pelyagin did not look up as he said this and my first sight of him was of a round, startlingly white bald patch surrounded by black brilliantined hair. He was peering closely at a file in the centre of his desk, while on either side of him stood a tower of other books and papers. A poster hung on the wall behind him: 'Exterminate the idler and the filcher!', with a worker smiling unpleasantly as he stamped on a runtish wrong-doer.

'Ah, Comrade Freely, very good. If you wouldn't just mind waiting while I finish a small piece of business off?'

I sat in the corner of his office while he called in his secretary. 'Bring me those papers, comrade, and don't muddle them up as you did yesterday.'

His secretary, a tall, serious girl who looked somehow familiar, did as she was told. I waited for almost half an hour while Pelyagin worked through these papers, speaking petulantly to the girl now and again. I may have been wrong, but I got the impression that this behaviour was partly for my benefit.

At last he waved the secretary out of the room and stood up. He was barely any taller on his feet than sitting down and as slight as a twelve-year-old, in a dark suit with a celluloid collar. I stood, and sat down again quickly, embarrassed by my extra foot of height 'So, you are the English teacher,' he said, very dignified. 'Are you trained?'

'Yes, comrade.'

'How quickly can you teach me, then?'

'Well, it depends how much you know already, how fast you pick it up . . .'

Self-importantly, he began to declaim: 'Daisy, Daisy, give me your answer do—' He managed to give it the flavour of a report on production levels. 'Brazil, where the nuts come from.'

'Very good! Where did you learn your English, as a matter of interest?'

He blushed. 'An acquaintance of mine had a gramophone record which we enjoyed listening to, as children . . . Now, comrade, get started. We must not waste time!'

Apart from his snatches of music-hall songs, it turned out that he knew little more than the alphabet. I learnt later that he had taken up English in response to a directive issued by the head of his department, one of a flurry of orders that were only fleetingly complied with by most government officials. Only Pelyagin, with his dogged determination to finish any job once started, plodded on with his lessons.

On that first day, the room filled with a rich smell of beef stew, a waft from the Party members' evening meal bubbling in the canteen, which must have been quite near Pelyagin's office. It came upon me suddenly, as I was going over the present tense, and caused me to lose the thread of what I was saying.

'Yes, where was I? You are, we are . . .'

Pelyagin had the decency to look embarrassed, and at the end of the lesson, as he paid me in large sheets of uncut Kerenkas (the old currency that had officially been banned), he said rather tentatively, 'Lenin himself has stated that it is essential for key Party workers to receive fuller rations, in order that they may carry out their Revolutionary duties effectively.'

'Yes, indeed,' I murmured, not catching his eye. A sliver of humanity, just the smallest glimpse, is enough, after all, to prove that it is present.

'I think you are a Party member yourself?' Pelyagin went on.

'No, not a member, but I consider myself a loyal supporter of the Revolution.'

'Yes — I've heard about your Institution, and Slavkin, is that his name?' He stood up to dismiss me. 'Perhaps you will tell me about it in our next lesson.'

I hurried straight from the National to meet Pasha at the Commissariat of Enlightenment, where he was working in the Department of Museums, thanks, really, to his father's reputation as a collector. Pasha and I had been appointed to the commune's 'shopping triumvirate'; we'd arranged to visit Smolensk market together that evening.

All day I had been aware of this task ahead of me, a knot of apprehension in my stomach. The markets were periodically closed down by the Soviet, in an attempt to control all the food distribution in the capital — and ultimately to abolish money altogether — but as most of Moscow's citizens received either a ration that would have killed them off within a couple of months, or nothing at all, we were forced onto the black market.

The traders swirled and eddied, vanishing from Kuznetsky Bridge only to pop up in the Sukharevka market, regrouping in the suburbs and then creeping, street by street, back to the centre. Each time the Red Guards knocked them back more viciously, confiscating their goods, beating and arresting them. It was a frequent sight; the rumour flitted around the stalls – 'They're coming! The dogs are coming!' In moments the goods would disappear, people would scatter, and the one woman who did not pack away her bread rolls fast enough would be knocked to the ground and her goods gobbled by the guardsmen ... The pavements around were often stained with blood, but even that didn't stop the traders.

That day there was an old woman selling bowls of steaming *shchi* – cabbage soup – outside the entrance. A few men were spooning it in hurriedly, bowl only inches from mouth, and I found myself staring at them, my mouth watering. They must have had tongues of leather to eat it so hot.

'Come on, Gerty,' Pasha urged me. 'We don't want to hang around.'

'Hey, that's my spoon, you thieving yid!' yelled the trader at one of her customers, who was moving a little too far from her patch.

Pasha and I bought dried fish and rusks, millet and barley, and from a tall, well-built woman, even a couple of pounds of butter – half melted, so I bargained her down a little.

'Take it, and good health to you,' said the woman

cheerfully. 'The devil of a life this is anyway. I'll leave for home now, and you better hurry too; I've got a feeling those Red bastards will be along soon.'

'Why's that?' I asked.

She lowered her voice. 'Old crooked legs over there is packing up and leaving, and he's . . .' She knocked her fist quietly on the palm of her other hand. I understood her – he was a *stukach*, an informer, who knock-knock-knocked on the police door.

'I'm one of the sort who can see that kind of thing,' the woman murmured. 'Always have been able to. If you like I'll tell your fortune, and I won't charge too much either.'

'That's all superstition,' said Pasha. 'You must forget such nonsense now.'

'Nonsense? And me only offering you a favour, *bozhe moi*.'

I felt it then – a ruffle, like a wind, from the other end of the market. Shouting. 'Comrades, beware!'

'Pasha, they're here, the guards are here—'

I saw them – one shoving the butt of his rifle in a trader's face, bright red blood, several more pushing further into the market, glints of their rifles, ripples of people panicking, crashing into each other, a child's screams . . . We squeezed past the butter lady's stall and ran across the bare expanse of the square. I heard my breath loud in my ears. Shouts behind me. Then bang! A rifle shot, my knees buckled. For a moment I thought I had been hit. 'Let's go, let's go,' hissed Pasha in my ear. He hauled me up by the arm. 'It's just the shock, you're all right', and we reached the side streets and dived into

91

a courtyard, slid down the wall. Pasha was still holding me by the arm.

'Oh, Gerty,' he whispered after a moment, giving me a lopsided grin, 'you are my one true love, even though you do fall over in the most inconvenient places.'

'Just – stop, Pasha,' I spat back at him, furious. I was shaking, I could hardly get my words out. 'Why do you still have to talk like that? In the old days, it was a joke that we all understood, but—'

'What?'

'Well, we're all trying to be honest now. Sincere.'

'I suppose I must mean it, then,' he whispered, still smiling. 'I love you, Miss Gerty. Especially when you're telling me off.'

'It's so easy to mock the governess, isn't it?' Tears of rage pricked my eyes. 'All your Revolutionary ideas, and at heart you are just a snob, like your aunt.'

At home I avoided the others, who were returning from their work in dribs and drabs, and took our purchases to the kitchen. I went into the cool back larder and leaned against the wall until my breathing settled down and my heart stopped pounding.

None of us said much about the fear that we felt on the streets. All around us were those whose suffering was much worse – the soldiers fighting the civil war, the civilians in the paths of warring armies, the pathetic, half-starved 'former people'. The Kobelevs – I wondered, as I did several times a day, how they were managing in the south. At the IRT, after all, we were in the vanguard of history; we were Revolutionaries, who had nothing to fear from the future. In those fluid days it felt as if fear itself was a cause for guilt or a failure of faith. It was quite common for me to return home and find my fingers white-knuckled and clamped to the stick I carried. I would slip quietly into the back rooms and wait until I was able to enter the communal sitting room with a smile.

I was never going to be much use to the commune in terms of scientific or philosophical understanding, and no doubt I was such a dullard that people like Pasha would always use me for the butt of their jokes, but I did have a role – a useful one – and Nikita always showed how much he appreciated it.

'Ah,' he used to say when I appeared, 'here's Gerty, cheerful as always! English phlegm . . . that is what this commune needs.'

8

On Friday evenings, as long as we had enough fuel, the IRT bolstered its Revolutionary spirit by taking a communal steam bath. No other form of washing could ever be so good for morale. While it heated up, filling the air with the tang of woodsmoke, we ate outside on the terrace under a sky filled with violent, flaming cobs of cloud – caused, so people said, by the huge quantity of munitions dust and gas in the atmosphere. Then we made our way quietly across the yard; we'd voted for no talking in the *banya*.

I slipped out of my clothes in the women's section and entered, shutting the door quickly behind me. One by one we took our places and settled down. I breathed in the sweet, resiny steam and leaned back, feeling the painful tensions of the week begin to relax, the clamp of anxiety loosen. There was only the creak of wooden benches and the occasional sigh; and from the men's side of the partition, the slap and shuffle of bare feet. Around me the women lolled, eyes closed, rosy and sweating, at ease. Dr Marina ladled water onto the stove. Thick, blinding steam billowed out into the room and then there was nothing, nothing at all, but the heat, and my breath in little gasps, and the prickle of sweat on my skin.

The habit of modesty had been fiercely bred in me, and at first, I confess, I found the *banya* uncomfortable.

It had seemed wrong – animal – to walk about naked, and I didn't enjoy seeing these women reduced (as I saw it) to cows in a barn, with their undignified female shapes. Then Dr Marina noticed my awkwardness and forced me to look through her medical dictionary. 'For goodness' sake, Gerty, look at elephantiasis,' she said. 'No, wait! Look at psoriasis . . . Well, you feel squeamish about these poor sufferers, I quite understand. But why shy away from normal, healthy, strong bodies? That I can't comprehend.'

Dr Marina was not the subtlest of teachers, but in this case her incredulity made us both laugh. 'I mean, look, this poor man with the strawberry nose – it's drink that's done that – you'd have to be a stone not to feel for him! But what could be wrong with your body, or mine for that matter?'

So now if I felt shy, I took a deep breath and observed quite dispassionately how my mother's remarks bobbed up in my mind, unsinkable:

'Whatever shall we do about her nose?'

'It's a pity she didn't inherit my chest . . .'

'Oh dear, how she does overheat, it isn't attractive!'

And just: 'Oh dear. Oh dear, oh dear.'

I observed how I constantly compared myself with the other women around me. Then I sliced those thoughts out, surgically, using Dr Marina's words as the knife: 'A normal, healthy body – a thing of beauty.'

Not for the first time, I noticed the wave of pleasure it gave me to identify a splinter of the old me – of the old, pre-Revolutionary world – and to destroy it.

For the last couple of weeks, however, there had been a new preoccupation to distract me during the steam bath. Since the IRT's decision to collectivise our clothes, clean laundry was issued each Friday evening from the general store. We were meant not to sift through the clothes rail, but simply to take the outfit closest to us; but in practice the last members to be kitted out had an eccentric time of it that week.

As I lay with my eyes closed, outwardly calm, I observed that my ears were straining to hear who had already left the *banya*, and that my muscles were actually tensed, ready to jump up and push in front of them, even though there was at least another half an hour of the steam bath left. The collectivisation of our clothes had clearly not yet succeeded in eliminating vanity from my soul. I did my best to be firm with myself, although I did notice (still without opening my eyes) that the others were cutting short their *banya* as well.

After another fifteen minutes I went into the wash-room, took a bucket of water and scrubbed myself, briskly but thoroughly, for ten. Only then did I approach the laundry dispensary in the changing room, taking note of the distinct quickening of my heart when I saw how few clothes were left on the rail. Almost all the other women had already taken their pick. Dr Marina was still dressing; she had the rather nice jacket I'd used a couple of weeks ago. I saw a cotton skirt – good; a shirt with no collar and a flannel waistcoat, rather large, but all right. But underwear . . . oh, underwear! I couldn't help a lurch of disgust at the tattered, greyish bloomers that lay at the top of the underwear basket. But here, yes, another pair, really quite acceptable. I hesitated. It simply would not do, my conscience told me, to mind so much about bloomers. It was over just such matters as these that we had to be strict with ourselves in the Institute. Quailing a little, but determined, I took up the tattered pair, noticing that they had some truly repulsive yellowish marks.

'Have you everything you need, comrade?' Vera bustled over, her kind, plump face strained with anxiety over this important moment in the Laundry Commissar's week. 'Here, let me help you, Gerty – there's some better ones here, wouldn't you prefer—'

'The most important thing, Verochka, is not to care.'

'Oh, well, of course, but really I wouldn't have thought it matters – look, there's a nasty stain on those—'

'Shall I sign here?'

The delicious, unravelled feeling of the bath suddenly reasserted itself; I beamed at Vera as I interrupted her and, surprised, she smiled back. All this pettiness, these belittling preoccupations were falling away; the process of conquering the ego could only become more joyful. I dressed quickly and hurried to join the other members in the drawing room. It was time for our evening meeting.

*

In the early days of the IRT, many of our evenings were spent listening to and discussing each member's piece on their Revolutionary Development. They were varied.

Fyodor, smacking his rosy lips, gave us a curt few lines on his father's incompetent management of their family estates and his own determination to learn a profession – engineering – and to devote his life to the technological advances that would make Communism possible. 'The tasks of our commune', he said, 'are discipline and efficiency.' They were his two favourite words. 'We must mould men and women as punctual and regular as machines.' If mild depression assailed us at these words, we tried not to let it show.

Marina wrote about her life as a trainee doctor, Vera as a nurse and Volodya described the trenches; all of them, in their different ways, driven by a sense of the injustice of the autocracy.

That evening after the steam bath, as we drank the hot water flavoured with a little grated carrot that we called tea and smoked our 'goat's leg' cigarettes rolled out of newspaper, Sonya read us her account. We breathed the cool, scented air and listened to her little well-brought-up voice floating out of the darkness, describing the failure of her marriage. In 1915 she had married Petya, the son of a manufacturer of dandruff shampoo – we had all witnessed her tantrums over the guest list, the invitations, the wrong kind of quails' eggs – only to wave him off to war just a few months later. In 1916 he was badly wounded and lost a leg to septicaemia. Throughout 1917, while he was ill, she devoted herself completely to him; I remember how impressed I was by this new side to her character. But as he recovered, all her attempts to be a good wife were met by increasing hostility on his part and frustration on hers. They had married young and in haste – Sonya, I suspect, had been longing to escape the shadow of her mother's illness – and the foundations of their relationship had been shattered by war. What common ground was there to sustain them in this new situation? When he and his mother moved back to Petrograd, Sonya came back to Gagarinsky Lane, and soon afterwards left Moscow with the family for the south. I thought the marriage would probably have foundered even without the injury, but of course that didn't stop Sonya from feeling that she had failed him at his most vulnerable.

'*Ptichka*,' said Pasha gently, 'Little bird, you know that it was his decision as much as yours, even though he didn't admit it. He went back to Petrograd and he didn't even ask you to come, did he?'

Sonya's voice caught. 'Well, perhaps he just assumed I would. But he used to look at me with such hatred – he used to rail at me, abuse me, as if he blamed me.' She cleared her throat. 'And then, of course, I saw him again in Yalta . . . It was while my father still thought there might be a chance for them to leave immediately for Turkey, before he decided to rent the villa. I bumped into my mother-in-law who told me where she and Petya were staying; they fled Petrograd just about the same time we left Moscow. "Don't imagine he's longing to see you," she said grimly – there was never a great deal of warmth between Evgenia Maksimovna and me.

'He was in bed when I came, and made no attempt to sit up. It was only a couple of months since I'd last seen him but he seemed to have swelled up – I don't know, perhaps it was some health problem – and his face was quite different, eyes and mouth tiny in big, pallid cheeks. I was shocked, and perhaps it showed on my face, because he was immediately angry, accused me of all sorts of vile behaviour—' She hesitated, and laughed. 'Well, it's ridiculous, but he accused me of having an affair with you, Nikita. "That student, I've seen how he looks at you." His mind was filled with every sort of warped nonsense. Then just as I was thinking I would have to leave, he burst into tears, and told me I was well out of it. "I couldn't look after you now, could I? It's better this way. You must live your life, and I'll try to do something with mine, God knows what—" I cried too, and for a moment we sat together quietly, without speaking, and I thought we understood each other. And then he suddenly sat up and hissed into my ear, "The least you can do is get me some money! Ten thousand roubles – come on, I know you can lend it to me!" He pushed me away as hard as he could. Hating him, I went and sold some jewellery, and returned with a wallet. And then I made up my mind. I couldn't go abroad with my parents. The only choice left to me, from the moment I left my husband, was to try to do something towards the Revolution.'

Sonya stopped. She was blushing. 'After that we returned, and you know it all from then on.'

Anna Vladimirovna spoke into the pause that followed, 'My dear,' she drawled in her grandest voice, 'it's really not suitable to repeat all that in public. I tell you this in your parents' absence.'

'Oh, Aunt, but—'

'Don't interrupt. But I must say that boy was extremely badly brought up. You did the only thing you could, dear.' She sank back in her chair, then suddenly added with a mad glint in her eye, 'If I'd been there I would have horsewhipped him myself.'

She laughed with all of us, still nodding fiercely. 'I would have. Bring the whip! Swish, swish!'

'You did well,' Nikita said.

Sonya looked up at him and I saw that she was crying. 'No,' she retorted. 'I did not. That's what I mean – *now* I must work hard and do well. All my life I've wasted time, squandered my privileges, but now—'

'Now,' murmured Nikita, 'you have changed.'

He was looking at her and I couldn't help breaking in: 'Well, yes,' I blurted out. 'Yes, but we've all changed, haven't we?'

Nikita turned toward me, frowning slightly, and I hurried on, 'I mean, we've all changed, but obviously we've still got a long way to go, or I have, in any case . . .'

He leant back in his chair. Even in the height of August he was still pale, and in the dark garden, in his white shirt, he looked almost ghostly. When he spoke we all fell quiet.

'This week I suggest each of us devotes some thought to identifying what we have to do to become more measured, rounded characters. This will stand us in good stead in communal living. Each of you has thought hard about what made you a Revolutionary. Now you must try to identify the task that your story sets you. And how should each of us know what that is? Well, it's quite simple. It is the thing that is hardest for you to do, the thing that terrifies you, that makes you feel least comfortable. Not something that is hard for your neighbour, which might be perfectly simple for you. But the one area that you think impossible for yourself.

'Fyodor, for example – your task will be to exercise your imagination. You are a scientist, hard-working, logical, methodical – a list of your good qualities could go on for hours, we all agree. A free-flowing imagination, however, would probably not be on that list, don't you think? This week I suggest you engage in some form of abstract self-expression – dance, art, music.

'Marina, your task is to be spontaneous, irresponsible – to allow yourself to be silly.

'Vera, yours is to identify what you really want – not just what others want of you.

'Sonya? Yours is to forgive yourself. Set down your burden of guilt. You acted as best you could, in the circumstances. There are no Christ figures now to set ourselves up against and fail. You are flawed, as we all are, but you were honest, you showed courage. There's an arrogance in guilt – it suggests you think you could, or should, be infallible. Let go of it.

'And Gerty?' He turned to where I was lurking in the corner, hoping to be forgotten, and I felt almost panicky at what he might say. He looked at me for a moment. 'Yours is to believe that you are a full citizen of the world, as important as anyone else, as clever and as lovable. Be proud, be boastful this week, Gerty.'

*

A letter arrived from Mr Kobelev.

'Dear children,' Pasha read aloud,

'I write to you like some Eastern potentate, sitting under the shade of a pomegranate tree. Liza and Dima are supposed to be doing their lessons at the table with me, although at this moment Liza is whistling to a lizard while Dima attempts to trap it under a box. They have a great desire to keep one as a pet, but so far the local lizard population, wily Tatars that they are, have had no difficulty evading them. Your mother is resting, but this morning she was gathering peaches in the garden. After a difficult first couple of weeks, her health is much improved by this move – we should have decamped years ago. We eat fruit from the trees, we sun ourselves, and apart from my sallies into Yalta to find out news, we see no one. In short, all is well with us. And how is it with you, my dearests? This letter is being carried to Moscow by an acquaintance of ours. Please telegraph c/o Yalta Central Poste Restante. I am afraid that your mother is worrying about you. My regards to Miss Gerty; tell her that her pupils are missing her.

'With fondest love, your father A.A.K.'

'You see?' said Pasha to his sister. 'You are feeling guilty for abandoning people, and all the time they are sunbathing and stuffing themselves with peaches and pomegranates.'

103

'What wonderful news—' I gulped down the lump in my throat. 'You must have been so anxious about them.'

Sonya laughed and unexpectedly hugged me. 'Dear Gerty, I know how much you have been worrying about them yourself. My mother, gathering peaches! And the little ones are having a real Crimean summer.'

I extracted myself a little awkwardly. We were picking raspberries together in the thicket at the back of the laundry house. Cool morning shadows lay across the yard and the birds were chattering and splashing in the water trough, but the sky was already its brazen, flat, August blue. As Pasha came out with the letter I had just been calculating that we might make two dozen pots of raspberry jam from this harvest, and another two dozen of blueberry, and later there would be blackberries, if only we could get hold of enough sugar – that would provide our vitamins for the winter.

'We may not end up measured characters, but we'll certainly be rounded, if you have anything to do with it,' remarked Pasha. 'I hope you're feeling proud and boast-ful, Gerty.'

I laughed. 'Yes – proud, boastful and rounded, that's how I'm feeling.'

It was typical of Pasha to have noticed Slavkin's words; I wondered if he had also noted their effect on me. Ever since that evening I had been feeling – what, exactly? Expectant, a little flustered, excited – I thought I knew what he wanted of me. I wondered when would be a good moment to approach him, whether I dared disturb him while he was working. Now, propelled by the good news from the Kobelevs, I decided to take the plunge.

'My basket's full. I think I'll take these indoors and prepare everything for jam-making,' I said casually. 'Do you mind finishing off?'

I left the raspberries on the kitchen table and slipped quietly across the yard to the stable where Nikita was working on the Propaganda Machine. Whatever the commune thought of privacy, that day I wanted some time alone with him. I leant against the wall and watched him as he concentrated. He performed a little dance around the PropMash; bending down, twisting, fixing, standing back, contemplating, diving in again to drive in another nail. He was grinning to himself, occasionally laughing under his breath, muttering. I found myself smiling too. My stomach was fluttering.

It was not until he almost tripped over my feet that he noticed me.

'Oh! Devils. What time is it? Is it dinner?'

'No, no, I just wanted a talk with you, please, Nikita—'

'Oh.' Reluctant, he straightened up, keeping one hand on the metalwork as if still feeling the PropMash's pulse.

'Yes, I wanted to ask you to explain a little more about what you said. The task you gave me at the evening meeting on Friday, you know, about being . . . about being as important as anyone else.'

'Of course.' He frowned. 'I thought it was clear – you were to remind yourself that you are a full citizen of the world I meant you have a tendency towards servility.'

My heart sank, but I was determined to finish what I

had come to say. That was the point, after all, wasn't it? I should stick to my guns. 'You also said I was as – as lovable as anyone else.'

He picked up a box of nuts and bolts and began sorting them intently. 'Yes.'

'Nikita, probably it sounds absurd, but I must tell you how deeply I still feel for you. I'm devoted to you ...' I was babbling. I took a breath and started again. 'I can't help hoping that perhaps, one day, when the commune has achieved its purpose, we might be again ... you might feel—'

He interrupted, clearing his throat. 'Comrade ... is this necessary? We are all friends within the commune. There's no need for this exaggerated type of ... this emotional excess. We have made a promise to each other not only to be chaste, but to give up this type of romanticism. Let's not mention this conversation again.' He put out his hand for me to shake, but he avoided my eye. 'All our energy must be for our work.'

I swallowed, not trusting myself to speak, hanging on to his hand.

He looked at me at last, and surely there was a little shred of feeling in his glance? 'I do understand, Gerty. But you must see that that was a moment which passed. You're making such progress, you know – don't give up.'

*

It was far too hot to make jam, but I had no choice; the fruit would not last more than a day. I left Nikita and returned to the kitchen. Like an automaton I plodded through my tasks while Sonya and Pasha joked and chattered, still in high spirits. Inside I shrivelled. I couldn't believe my presumption, my *idiotic* stupidity. How could I have misunderstood Slavkin's instruction to me so completely? I had taken even fewer steps down the road of transformation than I thought. I would have to be much, much harder on myself from now on. How difficult it must be for Nikita to deal with someone so stubborn – with such a servile personality. He had been perfectly clear, hadn't he?

In the evening Fyodor helped us seal the jars.

'So how is your artistic development progressing, Fedya? Are we going to be treated to an art exhibition? Or a ballet?' teased Pasha.

Fyodor reddened a little, but did not speak.

'A mime?'

Suddenly I couldn't bear it. 'Oh, for God's sake, leave him alone!'

Pasha gazed at me for a moment, and then turned towards Fyodor. 'Please don't mind me, Fedya. I'm sorry if I upset you. I haven't been given my task yet, but I can tell you already what it will be: to stop my idiotic joking and be serious. So forgive me for fitting in a few last bits of nonsense. I don't mean to offend . . .'

'No, no, I don't take offence,' Fyodor answered quietly. 'I know you all think me pompous. It's just that I'm no good at this sort of banter, you know – I never have been. As a child I was brought up alone, and my parents were always rather melancholy . . . I don't see the point of taking up painting or sculpture; frankly, that would just be a waste of materials. But I do have one very meagre gift, which I've been working on a little this week' – he looked embarrassed – 'although you must forgive me if I am not terribly skilled . . .' Fyodor glanced around at us, hesitating, and began to sing: 'Alone I go out on to the road; the flinty path is sparkling with mist . . .'

We stopped, electrified by his fine, sweet tenor voice. He sang all five verses of Lermontov's poem, standing up straight like a little boy in the choir. Simple and un-adorned, they seemed to express the essence of human isolation.

When he finished, he just stood there, motionless. I turned away to hide my face; I was so moved.

'Well,' said Slavkin at last, beaming, delighted. 'Now we see the whole Fedya. Wonderful! This is genuine pro-gress.'

'Fyodor, that's beautiful,' exclaimed Pasha.

Fyodor was embarrassed and puffed his chest out in a particularly irritating way he had. 'Yes, Nikita, you see I will do anything you ask of me, as best as I can. I don't mind making myself look foolish for the sake of the com-mune. But . . .'

'But what?'

'Don't you think you're getting distracted from the real work? Frankly, these "self-improving" ideas are all very well, Slavkin, but singing isn't going to make the factory wheels turn.'

None of us was at all convinced by these remarks. Fyodor laughed in a pleased way when we begged him to sing something else. Later on, Nikita commented that we shouldn't forget that our goal was to be transformed, that is to change form, not content – to change how we are, not who we are. 'It's very clear to me, if not to you, that all of you already possess the qualities of true communards. It's just that some of them may have been obscured by the different priorities of the Old World.'

I received these words of encouragement as if they were spoken only to me, drips of balm to my soul.

9

Autumn painted Moscow every shade of red, as though for a vast performance. 'The streets are our brushes, the squares our palate,' announced the poet Mayakovsky, who planned to revolutionise nature permanently by giving the trees in the Aleksandrovsky Gardens a coat of scarlet paint. Each day more avant-garde decorations appeared, plastered awkwardly over Moscow's crumbling set. There was neither money nor materials for the radical changes the artists longed for, but here and there Constructivist monuments to Revolutionary heroes, hastily cast in concrete, went up. To educate the public, abstract art was hung out on the street, causing consternation: 'They'll be telling us to worship the devil next!' wailed one old babushka at the sight of a Malevich. The vast head of Alexander III was toppled from his statue outside the Cathedral of Christ the Saviour and little children amused themselves by sliding down his nose.

Everywhere, fluttering from every fence post, were slogans and tattered decrees:

'Go to sleep quickly – your comrade needs your pillow!'

'24 August. Nationalisation of Clothing – any person in possession of more than one overcoat to come and hand it in to their district Soviet, on pain of imprisonment.'

'All ropes on church bells to be cut.'

'Tax: On Hats – 30 roubles per item. On Pianos – 50 roubles. On Armchairs – 40 roubles.'

'We must crush the Hydra of Counter-Revolution with Red Terror!'

'Smash the Imperialist Bourgeoisie!'

'Push the Bourgeoisie out of their nests!'

Scribbled all over these official announcements were appeals for missing people: Valentina Yurievna Yukova, aged sixty-four; Oleg Borisov, aged six; Georgy Alexandrov, aged four.

*

Pasha's account of his Revolutionary Development was really the story of his love affair with the avant-garde. He began with the lectures on Cézanne where he and Nikita had first met, then broke off and recited the poetry of Mayakovsky to us, leaping about with excitement. I couldn't quite believe in Pasha's commitment to the Revolution – his dandyism seemed to undermine it, his moustache that he couldn't resist trimming and curling even when it could have got him beaten up on the street, his (to my mind) ridiculously affected Scottish accent when he spoke English; above all his constant, ironic commentary on life. Yet he was entirely serious about art and the theatre. He insisted on dragging us to the theatre several times a week, to dramatic groups in factories and hospitals, barracks and converted churches, to performances that never had props and often lacked scripts or plots.

111

'Don't you understand, Gerty, you Galliffet, here you can see the new world as it's summoned into being, one performance at a time.'

I often just wished I could have stayed at home in Gagarinsky Lane, rather than in these large, draughty halls full of rowdy workers, who heckled and occasionally stormed the stage if they felt the villains weren't getting their comeuppance quickly enough.

Slavkin's talks were more enjoyable, even though the Futurist revues in which he participated always ended in commotion. I remember one evening at the Café Pittoresk on Kuznetsky Bridge, decorated with abstract reliefs that jutted out from the walls and threatened to poke you in the eye. Slavkin's lecture on the PropMash was followed by an act in which all the performers wore machine costumes made out of cardboard, eight or nine foot tall. They looked imposing but their voices were inaudible. After a while, tired of listening to muffled and incomprehensible fragments of poetry, the audience began to shout and throw things at the tiny stage.

'Call yourselves men of the Future?' yelled someone. 'You're not Futurists, you're packets of biscuits!'

He leapt up on the stage and took a swing at the tallest robot. The Futurists threw off their cardboard tubes and a brawl ensued.

'You pineapple-munchers! You donkeys! You . . . you . . . talcum powder!' the poets shouted, enjoying themselves.

Through the crowd I suddenly caught sight of Emil Pelyagin, my student from the Hotel National. He looked out of place and panicky. I pushed my way through to him.

'Comrade Pelyagin! What brings you here?'

We had talked about the event, I remembered. Pelyagin was having three hours of lessons a week, spread over two days, during which we discussed all sorts of subjects – politics and history as well as our childhoods (both spent in small towns), the IRT and Slavkin's inventions. I had become quite fond of him.

He turned, and smiled – an awkward little closed-mouthed grimace – and immediately solemnised his face. 'Comrade Freely,' he said, with a bow. 'Well, as a government official I try to keep myself abreast of developments in culture.'

I felt myself blushing, ridiculously. 'Well, it's ... it's very kind of you to come. Would you like to meet Slavkin, now you're here?'

'Certainly.'

I forced my way over to Slavkin, but Pelyagin was stuck behind a group of boys who were rather the worse for alcohol.

'Oh, Nikita, my pupil wants to meet you – go and rescue him, won't you?' I gasped.

Slavkin, a foot taller than anyone else, passed through the crowd with ease, occasionally lifting tussling boys out of his way. With an amiable smile he arrived at Pelyagin's side. Slavkin spoke civilly to him. The episode, framed by the flailing arms, yells and yodels of the crowd, played out like a scene in a silent film. 'No, no, I'm quite all right,' I saw Pelyagin answer, pulling himself upright, craning his neck back to meet Slavkin's eye. Slavkin put a hand on his shoulder to guide him through the mêlée. Pelyagin shook his hand off, a mulish look on his face. Slavkin tried again. Pelyagin shrugged him aside, quite violently this time.

I tried to signal to Slavkin to leave him, but neither of them looked across at me. They were glaring at each other and I watched, with a sinking heart, as Slavkin took Pelyagin forcibly by the shoulders and propelled him across the room to me. I'm not sure his legs weren't lifted off the ground.

Before I could say anything Slavkin bundled Pelyagin out through the fire escape. I squeezed after them.

Out on Tverskaya Street Pelyagin shook Slavkin off and brushed down his jacket.

'Please forgive me, comrade, if I was mistaken,' said Slavkin gravely. 'Gerty asked me to come and help you. These days the kids do sometimes get carried away.'

Pelyagin cleared his throat. 'There was no need to manhandle me.'

Slavkin shrugged.

'Well, I'll be on my way, Comrade Freely,' said Pelyagin. He didn't meet my eye.

'Oh, won't you wait a moment—'

'Come on,' Slavkin turned away brusquely. 'Time for us to leave, Gerty.'

Pelyagin spun on his heel and departed. At our next lesson, I apologised, tentatively, for the unfortunate misunderstanding and Pelyagin brushed it off. 'Don't give it a thought.'

In the years since I have probably wasted not just hours, but whole days wondering about this episode, and even so I still can't work out if it had any bearing on the course of events.

*

The commune gained two new members that month: Ivan Matryossin and his wife Nina, dancers who had recently arrived in Moscow from Kiev. Pasha discovered them sleeping in a corridor at his office and brought them back to live with us, claiming they couldn't be closer to the IRT philosophy. What this turned out to mean was that they couldn't have been closer to *his* philosophy, both avant-gardists through and through. Ivan and Nina showed no interest in communal living, missing our evening meetings due to their performances, refusing to collectivise their clothes, and living the life of a perfectly ordinary married couple in the night nursery, where – worst of all crimes – they hoarded food. Fyodor agitated to expel them, but it became quickly apparent to the rest of us that Ivan and Nina had something extraordinary to offer the commune. This was the Model T.

In Kiev they had spent a year working on a new type of eurhythmics, which they called the Model T system (for *telo*, body). It had two aims: firstly, healthy physical exertion, which they claimed exercised not only the muscles but the internal organs, the immune and nervous systems; and secondly, psychological training in 'the rational and optimistic rhythms of the future'. With the efficiency of a Ford production line, we would be trained up physically and psychologically for Communism. The movements, many of which were quite beyond me, had names such as 'Tearing out the Bourgeois Liver', 'The Power of the Turtle', 'The Gulls of the Soul'. They were accompanied by sounds, from a growl that came from the Turtle to the abundant flatulence that Nina produced when performing the movement to cleanse the bowels. She assured us that it would not take long, if we practised regularly, before we too would learn the same skilful control of the body.

To my surprise the Model T was an instant success, for Nina's confident direction somehow released us all, even me, from inhibition. We spent those warm September evenings in the Summer Gardens twisting and stretching our bodies in time with her, mooing and whinnying with abandon. Groups of children might run to watch us, shouting, 'Here come the grunters!', but an hour of Model T left me strangely dizzy with happiness, loose-limbed as a drunkard. Afterwards we would stroll through the park, kicking the drifts of leaves, full of hilarity and nonsense. It worked better, even, than the *banya*. Bad temper, resentment, unhappiness – not to mention hunger and weariness – floated from us. That night I would sleep quite still, without waking or turning about, and wake with a smile on my face. The giggling children were nothing compared with the blissful calm of that sleep.

This was all the more useful for, as the first thrill of the commune faded, tense moments seemed to arise between us more and more frequently. These were never, needless to say, about politics, or morals, but usually over some idiotic detail. One evening Fyodor accused Sonya of having eaten a hundred grammes of her bread ration on the way home, driving her to tears, at which Pasha swore at Fyodor so inventively that Fyodor threatened to move out. Another time Vera and I fell out over how long she took to do the ironing. These were nothing, however, compared to the incident between Dr Marina and Volodya.

There had never been much love between the two of them; he thought her stuck up, while she detested his swearing, spitting and general air of undiluted *muzhik*. There was already a tension in the air when she raised the subject of the Shop Without a Clerk, from which stock had been disappearing without being noted down.

'And I can't help wondering why four bars of soap would have been necessary to anyone; I checked all the washbasins in the house, and each of them has soap.'

There was a pause. Nikita looked around. 'Now is the time for anyone to speak up. We are living in trust; if someone had a reason to take more soap, tell us, and we'll try to understand.'

'Well—' Volodya started.

'I thought so,' snapped Dr Marina instantly. 'You traded it for cigarettes, yes? For tobacco?'

Volodya glared at her. 'Oh, so you'd made up your mind about me already? What, I was stealing soap from all of us to keep myself in fags? Well done, Doctor, very trusting.'

Nikita held up a hand silently.

'I'm sorry,' Dr Marina muttered.

'You'll never change, will you?' Volodya paid no attention. 'Looking down at me, Marina Getler, that's all you've ever done, you bloody bourgeoise . . .'

Slavkin just said, 'Volodya.'

Volodya took a breath and visibly tried to control himself. 'All right, I'll tell you what I did with the soap.'

Dr Marina took a sharp intake of breath –

'I'll tell you: I took it to barter for a barrel of sunflower oil, best quality. Someone offered it to me down at the railway station, he'd heard I had soap.'

– and let out a shriek. 'You took it to barter, without consulting the rest of us! Haven't you understood anything about how we are trying to run the IRT? You stupid, ignorant—'

'Enough,' interposed Slavkin, but they were beyond reining themselves in now, both on their feet, shouting at each other.

'It was for the commune, you nagging old cow, don't you see? A whole barrel! I didn't have time to consult with your ladyship—'

'You brute, you take us for fools – you'd take advantage of all of us given the chance, just to satisfy your disgusting libidinous self-indulgence, wouldn't you?'

'You stupid bitch, what are you talking about now?' yelled Volodya.

'You're using the Revolution as an excuse to exploit a gentle soul—'

'Stop.' Slavkin was on his feet between the two of them. 'Quiet – don't speak.'

Volodya, leaning towards him like a bull ready to

charge, was breathing heavily. He could have snapped Nikita in two; I marvelled at Nikita's calmness, his strength.

'Now – let us try to understand. What are you saying, Doctor? Please be careful not to express groundless prejudice.'

'I'm asking, can it be right for one comrade to take advantage of another's gentleness of character?' Dr Marina's voice was shaking.

A long pause.

'Are you talking about any comrades in particular?' asked Fyodor. 'Because if so I think we should know.'

'Marina, darling, please don't,' said Vera. She was blushing hard and her eyes were a little watery.

Dr Marina's face was flushed, her eyes glittering. 'Yes, I am, as a matter of fact,' she said. 'I'm—'

'She's talking about me, of course,' Volodya interrupted, clearing his throat. His voice was calm but he smiled a tight, angry smile. He went over to Vera and took her hand. 'Verochka and I, we are very happy to announce to you all that we are occasionally sleeping together. Or rather not sleeping, having sexual intercourse. Seeing as you all seem to think it's your business.'

'Oh!' Vera started to cough and the tears trickled out of her eyes.

Aghast, I glanced towards Slavkin. 'But we've all promised Nikita to be celibate,' I burst out. 'You . . . you mustn't, you know . . .'

Beside me, Fyodor's face was turning scarlet. 'You

119

decadent! How dare you twist Revolutionary language for your own ends! You have betrayed a trust! You have debauched an innocent girl!'

'Say that again,' growled Volodya. 'Repeat that, if you dare, you toad.'

Pasha stood up as well. 'Wait, Fedya, can't you see their point of view, too?' he asked Fyodor. 'They've decided to love each other openly – to have a "socially affirmed sexual life", haven't you heard Kollontai's expression?'

'*Milaya* Vera, sweet Vera, I never made you do anything you didn't want to do, did I? It was your choice too, wasn't it?'

Vera was shrinking into the corner of the divan. 'Yes, Vova, it was my choice,' she whispered.

Volodya sat next to her and put his arm round her. 'You are treating us like children.' He turned to Dr Marina, menace in his voice. 'Every individual is free to make his or her own decisions now, even if you disapprove of them. What do you want, a priest to come along and marry us?'

'She's not free to make that decision!' snapped Marina. 'She'll fall in love with you, you brute, and you're just amusing yourself.'

Nikita sat back in his chair as though all the energy had flowed out of him. 'Vova,' he said quietly, 'no one is denying that you are perfectly within your rights. But, my dear friend, aren't we devoting all our strength, every minute of precious time, to achieving other goals?' We are in the very first stages of the commune. If you have affairs, not only will you spread disharmony among your fellow commune members, you will be distracted from your Revolutionary work. And what about children? This is no time to bring children into the world. With children, you have a family unit, the basis of all bourgeois life—'

'There are methods, you know, for not having children.'

'Slavkin is right,' snapped Fyodor. 'We must make sacrifices, Volodya. Those methods are not reliable in any case. Only if we learn self-control can we become true Revolutionaries.'

I didn't trust myself to speak; I couldn't look at Slavkin.

'Oh, you are a herd of nanny goats,' interrupted Nina, who was lying voluptuously on the sofa. 'What are you all making such a fuss about? It's normal. Look around you, everyone's doing it!'

There was a pause.

'Camel, we don't want to let you down,' said Volodya at last, almost pleading. 'Tell us what you want us to do.'

Nikita stirred. He looked painfully disappointed, with dark shadows under his eyes. 'Pasha is right, you can make your own choices. But we are attempting to put the needs of the collective before our own, do you understand? We must not have the commune splintering into sub-groups. In our Manifesto, we wrote that we'd abolish the private and the domestic. How will you avoid that?'

'We're not married,' said Vera timidly. 'I mean, it's not as if we're in love or anything,' she added, blushing.

Slowly, with purpose, Nikita spoke. 'I want you to promise that you will cease these sexual relations.'

Volodya made an exasperated gesture. 'Really, Camel?'

'Yes. Or you must leave the IRT.'

'For fuck's sake . . .'

Nikita stood up. 'I think you should talk privately and come to a decision. Will you stay and abide by the rules of the commune, or go? Why don't you let us know tomorrow?'

We were silent as he left the room. Vera was crying quietly.

'Verochka, darling,' said Marina, throwing herself down beside her sister, 'we promised Mother we'd stay together and look after each other. I beg you not to go with him—'

'Oh, leave her alone,' spat Volodya. 'Stop bossing her, Marina, for once.'

I slipped out of the room and went to check on the old ladies in their bedroom. Mamzelle was not well – she had a chest infection – and as I settled her for the night I was aware of Anna Vladimirovna watching me. No detail ever passed her by.

'You're shaking, Miss Gerty,' she said. 'Are you feeling well?'

'No, no, I'm a bit tired, that's all. I shall go straight to bed now.'

As I left the room, I heard her say in a loud, hoarse whisper. 'I've always said it doesn't do to let peasants have too much of a say. Now he's ruling over them all like a tsar.'

The following evening Volodya and Vera announced to the meeting that they wanted to stay in the commune.

'She wants to stay, and I don't want to go on my own,' said Volodya, with bad grace.

Fyodor raised his eyebrows. 'You can hardly participate with that attitude.'

'No, no, you know how much I think of the Camel. I said already, didn't I? He's got a brain, he has, and I want to give him a chance to make things fairer.' Volodya stood up straight and looked Nikita in the eye. 'You have my word, Camel – I'll give it my best shot. That's all I can promise.'

Nikita smiled at him, his sweet, whole-faced beam. 'I'm so glad, Vova. We'll vote on it straight away. Shall we give them a chance? Any member can be expelled if the commune feels they are poisoning the atmosphere. Put your hands up those who want them to stay.'

Dr Marina, Pasha and Sonya put up their hands straight away; Nina and Ivan casually signalled yes. Slavkin joined them, and I did too. Only Fyodor remained firmly against.

'Well, you are on trial, Vova, Verochka. Be aware that we will all be watching you to see if you are keeping your word. All right?'

'All right,' they said. Poor Vera bowed her head. 'Thank you, everyone, for believing in us,' she said.

'And you, Fyodor, you need to drop your resistance now and assure us that you are cleansed of negative feeling.'

'I think this is a mistake, you know. They broke a rule once, they are sure to break it again.'

'The commune has voted. You must back down now, don't be proud. Remember, pride is only the ego, not your essential being. I think you had better do an hour of the Model T.'

'Really? Oh, no, I'm worn out, Nikita, please—'

'One hour tonight, Fyodor, and remember to think cleansing thoughts as you do it.'

'But—'

'No pettiness.' Slavkin was almost shouting. 'We will get swamped in this pettiness!'

10

By the end of September Slavkin's Propaganda Machine was finished, and we were spending several evenings a week administering anti-bourgeois vaccinations at a rate of twelve an hour. A couple of photographs have survived. In one, Volodya has his arms draped around Nikita and Pasha, three young men smiling into the evening sun. Behind them is just a glimpse of the Machine, obscured by the gaggle of children that have crowded in to stare at the camera. At the side you can just see Fyodor admonishing them, sun glinting off his spectacles. He looks so young too, with – I can hardly believe it – what looks like a stiff collar. In the other – the clearest image of the PropMash that we have – Nikita and Sonya stand together in front of the steps. Sonya is speaking, gesticulating with one hand and pushing her hair back with the other. Nikita is gazing at her, smiling a little. I feel I can remember this exact moment, that exact look.

Some evenings we managed to hire a horse to draw the PropMash to its location of the day; occasionally we all dragged it together – it wasn't too heavy with eight or so of us pulling. Immediately a crowd of noisy, excited children would gather. We didn't plan a venue, just stopped in whichever yard or park that Slavkin chose, but the lack of publicity made no difference. The street kids did that work for us, shouting into every house we passed, 'The PropMash is coming!' The queues soon stretched down the street.

'Our medicine has an advantage over bacterial inoculation,' Slavkin would announce benevolently to the crowd. He wore a doctor's coat with a pair of pliers in the pocket and some nasty brownish stains here and there. 'Ours is highly infectious. Each inoculation achieved here today should spread to a further forty or fifty. At this rate we'll cover the entire Russian population in a hundred and seven and a half working days!'

We stacked up the gramophone records and filled the olfactory pumps with scents, loaded the films and rigged up a curtained cubicle around the Machine. We charged a rouble per vaccination, although we waived the fee for almost everyone except prosperous-looking people (and there were few enough of those).

'Be aware,' boomed Slavkin, drawing himself up to several inches above his full height by means of an inconspicuous cardboard box. 'Once initiated, the process of vaccination cannot be interrupted under any circumstances. We cannot let you out, you must simply endure until the end. Otherwise it may have serious consequences. Do not attempt this if you have weak nerves or any other debilitating condition.'

The people in the queue shivered in pleasurable anticipation at these remarks and settled contentedly down to wait. They had no view of the Machine and could hear only muffled sound effects, including, occasionally, the screams and yells of the patient undergoing vaccination. These, too, seemed to increase their eagerness for their turn.

Each patient climbed up into the landau and squeezed in through the door. Once he or she was in the seat we fastened the straps and lowered the heavy metal helmet. Then the inoculation began. The temperature was slowly raised to that of a steam bath. The film began – a crude attempt at the technique Eisenstein would later develop – images inside a factory were cut with some unpleasant scenes at a slaughterhouse, and some of us dressed as high capitalists forcing our servants to grovel under the table. Volodya, as one of the servants, rather spoilt this part by grinning at the camera. More scenes from the factory, fainting workmen, emaciated children, cut with close-ups of babies crying, priests performing a burial and a piece of meat being fought over by stray dogs, and suddenly – the crisis of High Capitalism, a scene of hell given added shock value by us drumming the outside of the Machine and shouting down the ventilation tube. Then the olfactory pumps would switch from charred rubber, rotten meat, petrol and so on to the soothing scent of bread and grass, and a gentle breeze would dissipate the boiling heat of the factory that they had been trapped in. Abstract images of great beauty, simplicity and power were interspersed with images that dwelt on construction, brotherhood and harmony. The words of Lenin and Gorky could be heard at first in the distance, so one strained to catch what they were saying, then they slowly came closer, speaking in low, conversational tones; explaining simply and kindly what

Socialism meant for all of us, for the individual. 'Henceforth, no one need feel in the wrong' is a phrase that stuck with me. 'Guilt is not a Socialist emotion.'

The patients, reeling and dazed as they emerged from the Machine, were led to a small roped-off seating area known as No Man's Land for at least ten minutes' recovery time. Suitable reading materials were handed out. They were usually eager to talk the experience over with others, and 'PropMash Friendships' became a well-known after-effect. There were even some 'PropMash Marriages', apparently. Dozens had to be stopped from just walking straight back around to the end of the queue. 'But I love it,' I remember one wailing. 'I want it!'

The most ardent supporters of the Machine were Slavkin's friends in the avant-garde. Early on the artist Tatlin was inoculated, and raved about it to his friends, bringing a crowd the next day that included Popova, Stepanova and others. They dragged Slavkin out into the crowd and gave him three cheers. Nikita, typically, blushed and didn't know what to say, especially when the poet Bryusov launched into criticism of the exterior of the Machine: 'Where are the clean lines, where is the modern approach here, my dear friend? If it must be mammary, at least you might aim for a firm young bosom rather than this squashy old teat!'

Nikita, who hadn't given much thought to the exterior of the Machine, muttered, 'I suppose it's a mother.'

Tatlin laughed, delighted. 'Yes – a monument to the Mother who feeds us all! PropMasha, perhaps.'

Mayakovsky, who was filming in Petrograd at the

time, came later and charmed everyone in the queue. He scribbled a *chastushka*, a little two-line rhyme:

> Slavkin has found out what's best –
> To the future in a breast!

Thanks to all of this, Slavkin became quite well known, and at the IRT the trickle of curious visitors and fans grew to a stream. For a time we got no peace. Then Volodya fixed a lock on the gate and found an orphan, Kolenka, from the gaggle around the Machine one night. Kolenka's job was to answer the doorbell and ask for a password before letting anyone in. If a guest did not know the password, he announced very fiercely, 'The IRT are labouring in the red-hot forge of Revolution!' and did not open. He turned away not only fans, but also inconvenient visitors like Prig, who returned several times with resettlement plans. Every now and again Kolenka wandered off to play somewhere and then we had to climb through the rotten plank at the end of the garden, but apart from that it worked well. He became a member of the commune, ate with us in the evenings and slept in the men's dormitory, and seemed to grow several inches a month.

In short, the Propaganda Machine was a triumph – in all ways but one. Slavkin's great wish was to win government support for it. He envisaged a future in which it was put into mass production and distributed across the country. But the Party leadership itself – unsurprisingly – was otherwise engaged. Each member of the Ispolkom was sent a personal invitation to the PropMash, which they ignored. Finally, at the behest of his artist friends, Anatoly Lunacharsky, Pasha's boss at the Commissariat of Enlightenment, consented to a vaccination. He talked briefly with Slavkin; Nikita was nervous and distracted; he kept rubbing his hands together, blinking and laughing oddly. I could see that Lunacharsky thought him strange. There was a long, awkward pause and then he said, 'Well, is it time?'

'Yes, yes . . .' Slavkin leapt forward to help him up, banging his head on the landau. Lunacharsky – who was quite tall – compressed himself into the space and we began the inoculation. When he finally emerged he was smiling in a restrained way. He put on his hat and shook Slavkin's hand. 'Let me congratulate you on a very fine piece of circus,' he said. 'Such things are still important.'

'Circus? Not just . . . not only . . .' stammered Nikita. 'Really?'

'We are administering a vaccination! A permanent immunity to bourgeois attitudes!'

'I do congratulate you,' murmured Lunacharsky, 'and admire what you have done.' He said it with the smiling charm for which he was famous, but the dismissal, nonetheless, was firm. 'And I hear that your work on iridium alloys is remarkable,' he added.

We packed up and trundled the Machine home with none of our usual exhilaration. Nikita was gloomy and irritable, and for the first time in over a week, we did not take the Propaganda Machine out the following evening.

*

I sit here surrounded by my papers in my neat little modernist armchair, produced for the masses and sold inexpensively. On my walls are prints of paintings produced by the Russian avant-garde, now celebrated and sold for vast sums. If I look along my bookshelves, the lettering on every cover, every magazine – if it does not intend to look deliberately old-fashioned and folksy – is the plain sans serif of avant-garde pamphlets. From the new concrete towerblocks soaring up all over Hackney to my teacups, knives and forks, the stuff of our lives now echoes the drawings of students who worked at the Moscow design studios Vkhutemas in the cold, dark winters of the Civil War.

And I wonder about the Propaganda Machine and many of the designs of the Russian avant-garde. They were playful – the whims and self-dramatising jokes of clever children. They were also deadly serious, made in conditions of real suffering. They seemed insignificant among the clanging chaos of the Revolution, but they were levers to change lives, alter thoughts, create new ways of living; this we knew, straightforwardly, just as we knew that a teaspoonful of air resistance could make us fly, a wisp of steam could drive a locomotive. On their own merits they have survived: now, decades later, our houses, clothes, china, patterns, magazines, objects look and feel as they do at least partly because of the Soviet artists and poets who imagined them.

Yet, extraordinary as this achievement is in itself, it would not have satisfied their creators. The modern aesthetic was always a means to a far greater goal – a just society. And I can't help thinking as I look around at my comfortable house and our well-designed modern city, how did we become so childishly easy to please, so unambitious? Why did we settle for so little?

*

Among the papers from the Institute that have survived is a scribbled account in my own hand entitled 'The First Journey to the Future – 25 October 1918'. As I reread it, I suddenly feel the most extraordinary sensation, a sort of muffled, tingling wave of emotion, part agitation, part excitement. I laugh out loud, and the sound rackets alarmingly about my house.

Slavkin was despondent for several weeks after Lunacharsky's snub. Once the whiff of entertainment had tainted the PropMash, he lost all interest in it. It was true, also, that as time went on we became more aware of the arbitrary effect it had on people. Many felt benevolent and peaceful and reported greater faith in the future of the Revolution, but some made cynical remarks, such as, 'Socialism don't smell so good in real life, though, do it?' And there were also cases when patients behaved erratically: several became amorous and forced themselves on to passers-by; one elderly man ran around making chicken noises. In another, very unfortunate case, a woman experienced some sort of mental crisis and emerged convinced that she was the Tsarina, a delusion that I believe persisted for some weeks. She caused chaos by insisting on inspecting the queue as if they were troops on parade and growing tearful when she saw the state of their buttons.

'How can I have wasted my time on such nonsense?' Slavkin groaned. 'Superficial, pointless. I'm a fool. We need something that works at the level of atoms – of particles.'

He was already turning to the latest ideas on particle physics and to Einstein's revelations.

On the evening of 25 October, Slavkin was exuberant. He sat on the floor in front of the lit stove and read from a pamphlet by the light of a couple of smoky, stinking *nyedyshalki* – no-breathers, wicks stuck in pots of oil.

'Listen to this,' he said. 'Time is our medium now. It's by Khlebnikov. "Until now, the brain of the people has been hobbling about on three legs (the three axes of place). We, by cultivating the brain of mankind like farmers, will attach the fourth leg to this puppy, namely – *the axis of time*. Lame puppy! No longer will your miserable yelping grate on our ears!

'"People of the past are no wiser when they assume that the sails of the State can be hoisted only on the axes of space. We, draped in our cloak of nothing but victories, build our young union by raising a sail on the axis of time, and warn you that our scale is greater than Cheops, and our task is bold, magnificent and stern . . . *Black sails of time, now sound!*"

'You see?' he went on triumphantly. 'He's talking about Einstein's Theory of Relativity. How many centuries will it take to build Communism at this rate? Our real task is to find an application for Einstein's theory, to accelerate our passage to the future. We can't dawdle around on the edges as we are now – taking a step forward, then running backwards, squabbling, concerning ourselves with superficialities . . .

'We have put in place the basics of the commune. Now it is time for the real work to begin. We need to have a real understanding of Communism, what it will *feel* like in our bodies and our souls.

'I have prepared a dose of a narcotic that is used by the Siberian animists. I recognised the mushrooms in the market – they used to grow near my village. There are mild physical symptoms such as contraction of the pupils, perspiration and increased heart rate, which will cause you no ill effects. The psychological effects are more extreme. You should experience a miraculous heightening of reality, lasting for some hours. They will lead you into another world – a world of joy, clarity and sensual delight. And this is where we use the Propaganda Machine. I have prepared new stimuli, all is fresh and ready. Each of you will undergo a vaccination. It will have an unimaginably powerful effect on a brain under the effect of the narcotic. I shall take some readings from your brains – the frequencies at which the particles vibrate – this will not take long. Then you will need to rest until the narcotic wears off.'

'What on earth gave you this idea?' asked Fyodor, frowning.

'The shamans use the mushrooms to discover their totems and to form a bond between the tribe. They claim it as their magic, when of course we know it is merely the physiological effect of the drug on the brain. It allows the individual to escape his own consciousness, even if only for a few hours, and to experience a sense of union with all existence. Shamans and witch-doctors of all religions see this as oneness with God. We understand it in simpler terms – it is the sensation of Communism.'

'Might it not damage the brain?'

'Oh no, the physical effect wears off within twenty-four hours. I have discussed it with Marina. But the psychological effect can be life-changing. This, after all, is what we are hoping for.'

There was a pause, doubt in the air.

'I didn't know you were planning something like this,' murmured Fyodor, always cautious.

'Count me in,' said the dancer, Ivan. 'Nina?'

'Darling, you know me, I'm ready for anything.'

'Me too,' drawled Volodya from the corner.

'How about you, Gerty?' asked Sonya.

I took a deep breath and glanced at Nikita. 'Yes. I'll do it.'

'Bravo, Gerty!' Pasha smiled at me. 'If Gerty can overcome her fears, then you all can.'

One by one, they agreed, even Fyodor. We ate the dried mushrooms then and there, before anyone could change their mind: all of us except Slavkin and Marina, who were to look after us. While the drug took hold, on Nikita's instructions, we prepared ourselves by loosening our clothing and removing our shoes and stockings; washing our hands, face and feet; carrying out a few of the Model T exercises and drinking a glass of water.

Nikita attached three rubber pads to our foreheads, and two behind each ear, to monitor our neurological energy patterns. Then we waited to take our turn in the PropMash. As I wrote in my account some time afterwards:

My mind feels beautifully relaxed and I stare at the halo of light around the lamp when my name is called. My limbs are heavy and I am glad of Nikita's guiding arm as he helps me into the Propaganda Machine. The helmet presses down on my head as though the whole weight of the atmosphere were concentrated on me and I am suddenly very afraid, but Nikita's eyes are fastened on mine, infinitely reassuring, and I find myself saying, 'I love you so much.' And he gazes back at me without saying anything but in his eyes is written clearly that he loves me too, more profoundly than I have ever been loved. And I relax into the seat and relinquish myself to the pain and horror of the Machine, because I know it is an expression of his love, and even the screams that I hear coming from my mouth, and the sweat, and shudders of terror that rend my whole being, are enfolded and cushioned in the vast sensation of warmth and tenderness that I feel from him. And therefore when the Crisis is over, and my tears are drying on my cheeks in the soft breeze of Socialism, my heart almost bursts with joy.

And when we had waited while Nikita took further readings of neurological energy patterns, he and Marina led us gently across the courtyard to the *banya*, the steam bath, which they had fired up, using some joists from the stable roof, and we gasped at the delicious sensation of heat. We shuffled off our clothes, and splashed water onto the stove. Nakedness, under the influence of the drug, felt like perfection, like innocence. We were in the Garden of Eden again. After a few moments of blindness a leg emerged, a breast, a dangling arm, with bony joints sliding under the skin or smooth and massive. We were quiet and utterly at peace.

Later Slavkin spoke. 'Each time we – just we few – allow ourselves to imagine a harmonious world, we bring it closer. We are creating the future here, in our minds. The neurological patterns you are now experiencing will be its foundations. Just share your thoughts with us. You know the answer, if only you can discover it within yourself. Inside your imagination lies the blueprint for the future. How, why, what you will into being – this is the choice that confronts you, and all of us.'

This journey was followed by several more. They played a remarkable part in bonding our small community together, at least in the short term. No one reported any ill-effects from the narcotic. Volodya and Vera acquiesced to the will of the commune. Fyodor accepted Slavkin's leadership. Ivan and Nina co-operated more fully. I felt happier, less suspicious of Sonya. We worked together harmoniously, and when Slavkin began to talk to us about his plans for the Socialisation Capsule, they did not seem far-fetched in the slightest.

11

Slavkin now made an extraordinary leap from his work on iridium alloys into quantum mechanics. His notes on the Socialisation Capsule have been much reproduced in the decades since his disappearance and the scholarly literature on them is extensive. Nonetheless I reproduce below the text of the final lecture he ever gave, in January 1919. This was what Slavkin was working on in his workshop during those cruel winter months – his last, astonishing achievement before what many consider the greatest feat of all, his disappearance.

Particle physics was in its infancy, yet in this text Slavkin intuited truths about the quantum world that mathematicians and scientists would begin to understand only decades later. Indeed, there is a school of thought in the Soviet Union that suggests the real proof of Slavkin's success with the Socialisation Capsule lies right here, in this lecture – in these ideas that are so flagrantly anachronistic they can have only one possible explanation. He must have achieved his aim and returned to write the lecture later. They also point to his apparent foreknowledge of Eisenstein's theory of montage in the Propaganda Machine, and the amazing farsightedness of many of his other inventions. However, as one who saw a number of the early ideas in development, this seems to me to be stretching things too far.

Still, how did he do it, on our miserable diet of millet porridge, in a collapsing city, among our endless arguments? How did he even have time, after his long days at the Centre for Revolutionary Research and our meetings stretching far into the night? I know he hardly slept, waking at three or four in the morning and padding down to his workshop in his dressing-gown. I know he also made frequent use of the Siberian mushrooms. By the time he woke the commune he had already completed four or five hours' work. Fizzing with energy, robe flying, eyes glittering in his pale face, laughing and jumping about on his bare feet with their long toes, he smashed the gong like a djinn, or an Orthodox saint.

A Short Introduction to the Socialisation Capsule
Lecture delivered by Nikita Slavkin at the Polytechnic Institute on 12 January 1919

The radical problem of Communism is in fact the problem of time. The key to constructing Communism lies therefore in a solution to this problem – a means of distorting or evading time.

Darwin's discoveries did not, as it first seemed, paint a picture of a world solely based on 'survival of the fittest'. Quite the contrary, evolution has given humans (and all living things) a dual strategy for survival – on the one hand, a ferocious survival instinct where it is a question of kill or be killed; and on the other hand, the instinct to work within a community for the benefit of the group as a whole, when that group provides a safeguard for the individual. This last instinct, which is present in the huge majority of living things – from plants to insects to communities of fish or mammals and to humans as well, of course – is the dynamic force behind Socialism.

In general, the history of mankind is the story of the suppression of the 'kill or be killed' instinct and the cultivation of the communal instinct – millennia of slow progress towards humanism, away from barbarism. In this sense the battle between the two impulses is already won; only the march of time stands between us and the ultimate victory of Socialism.

It may be that this Revolution is too early, as Marxists suggest; that the proletariat has not yet reached the right level of development for Socialism to exist. If this is the case, it, too, is unimportant; progress will wash backwards and forwards, and short-sighted people will no doubt announce that Communism is defeated, not noticing that beneath the superficial events of history a huge tide is carrying humankind imperceptibly away from the instinct to slaughter meaninglessly, to force their fellow men and women into economic or domestic slavery, to deny the union of all mankind on grounds of nation, race or religion – and towards unity.

In this generation, however, we long for a discovery that will speed up the process and give hope to the millions of innocents who are suffering now, whose parents and grandparents have suffered, and whose children can look forward only to more of the same.

This is where new discoveries in physics lead us to hope for new approaches.

Recent developments have resulted in not one, but two undeniable Revolutions in our understanding of the world, both of which we owe in large part to the talents of Herr Einstein. One is his Theory of Relativity, which, with one grand gesture, sweeps away all that we thought we knew about the solidity of the world, of matter and time. Herr Einstein has shown us that we inhabit a universe in which nothing is constant and all depends on the state of the other. It is a universe in which the future, the present and the past are curled up together like puppies on a mat.

The second, astonishing revelation concerns the life of the smallest fragments of matter that make up the universe. Planck, Rutherford, Einstein and others, in their studies of particles, have shown us that even the most minute pieces of matter live in relation to all other pieces of matter; that their state is intimately bound up with our own, and not only each physical movement of ours but even, perhaps, each uncommunicated thought has an effect on the behaviour of the physical world around us.

This is the reality of our universe – a state of Atomic Communism, in which we are all inextricably enmeshed in the lives of not only our fellow men, but of the entire world of living and non-living beings. It is a world that needs no biblical God to fill us with a sense of unutterable wonder, nor any priest to convince us of our duty towards it. It is also a world that holds out to us, in its benevolence, the possibility of harmony – not in the far future, but now, in the present. And this harmony is based on the laws of quantum physics, on the inalienable truths of our universe.

In my own laboratory I have made a series of studies of the electromagnetic radiation that is associated with a state of psychological harmony, and those associated with disharmony. My experiments have taken place under proper laboratory conditions without the prior knowledge of the subjects. While they were in the psychological state that I have termed 'Chaos' – i.e. exhibiting signs of distress, pain and fear – I tested the quantum energy states within their brain cells; and equally in the psychological state I have termed 'Order' – i.e. calmness, happiness, comfort.

The frequencies of 'Chaos' showed a marked dissimilarity across the group, as you will see from my results; while, to my astonishment, the frequencies associated with 'Order' oscillated within a range of 0.0007 h (where h is the Planck constant).

When Tolstoy remarked, 'All happy families are alike; each unhappy family is unhappy in its own way', he little realised that his insight was correct even at the level of quantum neurology.

My findings have led me to a further course of study on which I am now engaged. If, as seems to be the case, we have identified the frequency associated with 'Order' at the subatomic level in the human brain, then our next step is to ascertain a method of stabilising the oscillation of the brain particles within this range of frequencies. I am currently engaged in building a Social- isation Capsule, a brain-stimulation chamber of radical accuracy that will create in the brain a steady state de- noting 'Order'. Under this stimulus the brain particles will not only achieve a stable, sustainable mode but will remain oscillating at this frequency for some time, prob- ably months or years, thereafter.

There are various outcomes that may result from this experiment:

In the most conservative, subjects exhibiting the state of Order will be able to work in varied and creative ways towards the establishment of an external state of Order. The experiment will continue on a larger and larger scale, following the mass production of the Social- isation Capsules, and the influence of the Socialised (as they may be known) will spread throughout human so- ciety.

A second possible result involves the natural spread of the state of Order at a subatomic level; within the vast, united web of particles that is our world, a reaction takes place, the 'Socialist' frequency is inevitably communic- ated from particle to particle at the speed of light and alters our planet utterly and instantaneously.

A third possible result concerns the complex nature of light particles, which, it is increasingly suspected, may also apply to electrons and even all particles – the wave-particle duality – which inserts a new level of uncertainty into our knowledge of the Universe. Before being measured, energy, it is suggested, may occupy a type of unknowable, unmeasurable stage between wave and particle. Bizarre though this may sound, it may be that they are impossible to track because they are in fact not a part of our universe at these moments. There are other versions of reality, other dimensions, with which we perhaps share matter; our matter, far from existing solidly in our world, flickers between an infinite number of worlds that all co-exist within this universe. And in this multitude of other realities, all the possibilities thrown up by our reality are played out; every unchosen path is taken, every unsaid word is spoken.

Among these dimensions there is, undoubtedly, a Communist reality; a world where man has lived in harmony with his fellow man since the beginning of history. It is quite possible, therefore, that the Socialisation Capsule will do more than just create a beneficial mindset in patients. If our particles, under the influence of the Capsule, begin to oscillate at the correct frequency for Communism, it follows that we, particle-entities, will immediately be transported to the reality of which this frequency is the dominant feature. We will cease to exist in the reality that is dominated by 'Chaos'. We will exist, instead, in the reality of 'Order'.

Our Time Travel will carry us instantly not to another Age, nor another Place, but another Now.

12

In the first frosty days of November 1918, Slavkin came to one of our evening meetings with a request.

'My dear ones,' he said diffidently, 'you understand that what I am asking you now is quite outside the daily demands made on you as members of this commune. If any of you don't want to take part in this enterprise, I understand. It is for you to choose.'

He produced a piece of paper and began to read from it: 'Tin sheeting, iron bars, copper wire, acid – these are some of the materials that I will need for my new project. If you could help me to assemble them, I assure you you'll be performing a great service for the Revolution.'

We gazed at him without a word. I expect our mouths dropped open. Was it possible that he had not noticed the state of the city outside the house on Gagarinsky Lane? Moscow was returning to the Neolithic age, people were eating rat, and he was talking about bringing home iron bars? Railings all over the city had already been sawn off and carted away, first for one war and then the next. It was a capital offence to steal firewood, let alone the things Slavkin was after.

'I already have a basic engine, which will need modifying, of course, and I have a good part of the metal necessary. What I list here is perhaps 25 per cent of the total,' he went on, looking hopefully at us.

'Is this for the Socialisation Capsule?' asked Sonya.

'Yes. It's about the size of a bathtub. Rather a long one, with a lid - you lie down in it,' replied Slavkin. 'There is one more thing, too, that I need. Something that I know we can get hold of quite simply.'

'What's that – Lenin's balls?' Volodya said, laughing. 'Camel, you're quite something, you are. Even if by some miracle you get hold of this stuff, we'll all be shot on the spot for harbouring it at home!'

'Oh, no, that's something I've taken care of,' he said. 'I have a licence here for my workshop from Lunacharsky. You remember he complimented me on my work at the Centre? I went to him and asked for support. Any work I do here will be listed on the jobs list of the Narkompros. He's including it, in fact, in the anniversary celebrations for the October Revolution – as a way to allow us to requisition scarce materials. He was very accommodating.'

'But what is the other thing you want us to pilfer for you?' asked Fyodor.

'Well, it's nothing we haven't managed to obtain before – just a little iridium.'

Iridium had an almost mystical significance for him, a fascination that had begun in childhood. The success of the Socialisation Capsule seemed to depend entirely on its properties – its extreme density, its resistance to any kind of manipulation, heat or corrosion. He would often talk of it as 'noble', in the alchemical sense: 'Most true and noble metal, essence of metal, ideal element,' he wrote. 'With a shield of iridium, my Capsule will withstand any pressure. It will be invincible.'

Increasingly fantastic accounts of Slavkin's childhood have appeared in the years since he became the Vanishing Futurist. It's been claimed that he was a child prodigy who made his first inventions as a toddler; that he was the son of Bolshevik exiles in Siberia – even the son of Stalin. He never talked a great deal about it to us – just the occasional remark – but he did write his 'Revolutionary Development', that I suppose must now be a rather valuable document. Here, in his own words, he briefly describes his early years. Far from being acclaimed as a prodigy, he was formed by hardship, loneliness – and iridium.

Revolutionary Development
Nikita Slavkin

In the village. Dirt, darkness, old bearded fellows, bitter women, fights breaking out on holidays. Poor, tired mother – babies hanging off her like leeches. Black-faced father, beard like a goat.

Age six I wander into the taiga for the day. Wide open skies, Siberian beauty and wildness all around. Happily eat raspberries, fall asleep by a brook. At home my father is waiting with a whip. My mother screaming at him not to kill me. I lie in bed for a week. At school my teacher – Alexei Yurievich Samarin – a political exile, intelligent fellow, teaches me to fish. I hide at his house many times. Gain the idea that education + intelligence = escape from Father.

Every Sunday to church. My family are Popovtsy, Old Believers. Endless droning choir, deathly boredom. I gaze out of window, dream of fishing. They beat me for not paying attention. Next week I fix my eyes on iconostasis – ugly, gloomy. Only one thing I like in that church – a strange cup, dark silvery metal. Priests carry it to and fro, I don't know why. It gleams in an odd way. Cannot stop staring at it. Later am rewarded by Mother for good behaviour – a candied plum.

Week after week gaze at this cup (despite no more plums). At last can't stop myself – I have to touch it, know how it feels. At end of service, sneak through forbidden door in iconostasis, reach up to take cup from altar . . Shrieking, hollering begins. I run for my life through village to Alexei Yurievich's house, hide there for four days. Great scandal of village, neighbourhood, whole world, apparently. Boy profanes Holy Grail!

Alexei Yurievich and I go to my father to apologise. He slams the door in our face. 'He's no son of mine.' I live with Samarins for two years until begin Gymnasium (secondary school) in Yekaterinburg.

Until I go away to school, my mother meets me secretly each week. I plan to take her away with me when I am grown up. I am thirteen when I receive a letter from my aunt: 'Your mother's dead . . .' Something about the Lord's Will.

In the town museum of Yekaterinburg I see the silvery metal again: 'Iridium. The second-most-dense metal on earth, and the most resistant to corrosion, common in meteorites but very rare on our planet – because, being so heavy, it sank into the molten core of the earth during its early stages of development. Iridium can withstand temperatures of up to 2,000 °C, is nearly unmalleable and very hard.'

I meet Socialists in Yekaterinburg, good people, like Samarins. Science and the Revolution fuse in my mind. I train myself to study eighteen hours a day and eat only once. No warmth in my life until I arrive in Moscow. The great city, traffic, shops – for some months my mouth permanently open. I discover stale rusks, half a kopeck a bag. I meet Mayakovsky, Burliuk – stop myself from pinching them to check they are not statues.

At last, Pasha Kobelev swims at me out of the crowd. 'How about an ice-cream?' At the ice-cream stall, advertisements – 'Duchess *papyrosy* – as smooth as satin', 'Negro coffee – the exotic taste' – we laugh like idiots. I never saw the need of a friend before – limited, perhaps, but efficient. I move in with the Kobelevs. Life begins.

*

The first anniversary of the October Revolution was to be celebrated with all the scale and pomp that the actual event had lacked. The Commissariat of Enlightenment planned a blaze of red flags, great crowds of singing schoolchildren, increased rations and free meals for the people, the hammer and sickle everywhere, and the face of Lenin against snowy roofs and buildings.

Pasha reported on the preparations to us in the evenings – the frenzy at Narkompros as entertainments were commissioned, rejected and re-commissioned by competing organising committees; and artists appeared flourishing designs for the huge sets and floats in the Constructivist style; and performers demanded props, fur coats and bottles of cognac without which their acts would 'simply breathe their last gasp'. An astonishing amount of money had been made available – several million roubles for Moscow alone – and, what's more, the organisers had been given the right to requisition scarce materials, as Slavkin had already discovered.

On the day itself, the IRT and the Propaganda Machine took part in the Smolensk district procession. Slavkin repositioned the gramophone to blare Scriabin out into the street, and each of us, dressed as a capitalist, a general, an aristocrat, etc., minced up to the back of the machine. One by one, we were pushed inside by Dr Marina, dressed as Revolution with a flaming cardboard torch and a sword. Once inside the idea was that we would wriggle out of our costumes and emerge jubilant in simple workers' clothes with cloth caps.

I have never been much of a performer, and my mood was not improved by the fact that the crowds lining the route watched stolidly, only showing excitement when an aeroplane flew overhead scattering propaganda leaflets. 'Cigarette papers, lads!' I heard them shouting. I had spent over four hours that morning standing in line to receive the commune's extra two pounds of bread and fish and half-pound of butter and sugar per person, and I could feel the beginnings of a chest cold.

They were beginning to light the bonfires – there was a huge one on the Lobnoe Mesto, the execution place on Red Square, with a figure of a kulak on top – and fireworks were promised. As the light faded the crowds became more lively; drunken Red Guards shoved and jostled the people as they passed. At last we arrived at the old Governor General's mansion for the free meal provided for participants – a bowl of thin borscht and some kind of meat rissole, we didn't enquire too closely what kind of meat. I looked up and down the long tables, at the people ruminating over their miserable food – just like the soup kitchens in Tsarist times. It all felt a long way from any genuine progress.

'Come,' said Slavkin, jumping up suddenly. 'There's something I want to show you.'

'Oh, Nikita, we're too tired,' cried Sonya.

With relief I joined in. 'Yes, let's go home . . .'

But he glowered at us, almost shoving us in front of him. 'It won't take long. Really, you must trust me.'

We followed him down a side street to a tiny church. The gold had been stripped off its domes, no light shone in the windows, but Slavkin led us to a side door and knocked three times – paused – and knocked three times more. The door opened and Slavkin motioned us inside. The door swung shut behind us, leaving us in darkness.

I breathed in incense and wax, smoke, old cloth; at last, I made out some shapes around me.

I put my hand out and felt Nikita's sleeve; he took my arm and tucked it tightly under his, and we shuffled forwards until we were obviously in front of the altar. I looked around quickly; Sonya was somewhere behind, standing alone. A figure – a priest one assumed – was moving about; the swish of his skirts and the occasional clink of one vessel against another suggested that he was performing the offices of the Mass. A shiver passed through me. By a faint glimmer of light from the window behind him we watched him move about behind the altar, mouthing the words. He raised the Host and after a moment signalled for us to kneel. Without a word we did as we were told, one by one. Nikita and I sipped the watery wine, the first time I had taken communion for years; like me, he seemed to shudder with emotion as he swallowed. It burnt my throat and spread out through my body as though it were neat alcohol. My miserable mood evaporated and I was wildly happy. I squeezed Nikita's hand as we stood and retreated from the altar.

'*Batiushka.*' Beside me, his voice echoed out suddenly. 'Light a match, would you, Pasha? Father, we mean you no harm, but we must ask you to give us something.'

'I know you, don't I?' The priest approached, peering into Slavkin's face. 'You're the boy from Alekseevo ...' His voice quavered. 'Yes, the son of ... I don't remember. I knew your father, didn't I?'

As quickly as it had come, the happiness left me, and I felt queasy.

'Yes, I've come to see you again, with my friends this time,' said Slavkin. 'We need something that you have. Give it to us, and we'll not disturb you again.'

'What can I give you? I have nothing left—'

'I want the cup. Not that one, the other.'

The priest let out a feeble cry. 'But this is the Host! I cannot give it to you – a mortal sin!'

'Then we shall take it, and spare you the sin,' said Slavkin calmly. He stepped forward and removed the cup from the altar. 'Come, everyone, let's go.'

The cup, as Slavkin knew, was another of those made of iridium. It had probably come from the same region of Siberia. On the way back he was jubilant, hopping from foot to foot. 'Now we can build the Future, don't you see?'

When we arrived home he disappeared immediately into his workshop. I lay awake in my bed through all the jagged night, listening as the wind stripped the last leaves off the trees. Even now the old priest's sobs in the darkness sometimes come back to me.

*

'Don't give up,' Slavkin used to say. If you were feeling discouraged, before you'd even uttered a word – just at a look or a sigh, he'd come close to you, take your face in his hands and say it very gently but with tremendous force. It felt loving but absolute. I find myself repeating it now, as I try to marshal my thoughts: don't give up in the face of the mass of detail, the thunder of voices all competing to tell the story of Slavkin's life. Don't give up, despite the horrors. I promised that I'd tell Sophy everything.

In November 1918, just as Slavkin was starting work on the last great scientific achievement of his life, our world was almost drowned by a flood of distractions. Nikita, Pasha and I came home one evening to find our little gatekeeper, Kolenka, sobbing in the street.

'*Sovdepy* – Soviet deputies – they broke down the gate!'

Prig stood at the front door, hands on his hips.

'Good evening, comrades,' he said smoothly. 'As you know, due to the compression of living space throughout the capital, this house is due for resettlement.'

'Prig!' exclaimed Pasha. 'This household is not just any old house—'

'Comrade,' snapped Prig, 'I would remind you that such forms of address are not suitable nowadays. I assure you, there's nothing special about this house.'

There was a pause.

'Please let me explain, Comrade Prigorian,' Slavkin started. 'We are running an experiment in communal living here that, if successful, will be a model to replicate all over the country. If on the other hand we are now swamped by people who do not understand our aims, the whole project will be destroyed. What's more, we have a scientific workshop on the premises that comes under the control of the Narkompros – I will show you the order from Commissar Lunacharsky—'

'I already know about the workshop. Finished, boys?' Prig called to his men. 'Come on—'

'I myself also have special status as a key worker for the Revolution that permits extra living space, and—'

'I know about your status too. However, we have inspected the premises and ascertained that there is at least 500 square metres of unused space.' Prig and his boys clattered across the yard. As they rounded the corner he said, 'I would have thought you would welcome the genuine *narod*, the people, into your experiment.'

I saw Pelyagin the next day for his lesson and told him of our troubles. We had long ago smoothed over the incident at the Café Pittoresk. He had a tendency to see things in black and white, but there was something touching about him, the way his feet barely touched the floor when he sat in his chair, the little, faintly pleading look he gave me as he peeped over the *Illustrated London News* – I couldn't help liking him.

'I will see what I can do,' he promised, nodding seriously at me. He seemed flattered to be asked, which rather reduced my faith in his ability to help.

*

Within days a total of forty-two people had arrived at the doors of Gagarinsky Lane dragging cartloads of belongings and pouncing on every inch of space. Our little Kolenka pounced with them, securing for himself the official papers to a small storeroom off the kitchen. Volodya, Vera and I stayed at home for the whole day in order to fight our corner, but nonetheless we ended up with only three rooms between the thirteen of us – the study, Slavkin's workshop and the old ladies' bedroom. This caused some friction, as Nikita was adamant that his workshop must not be used for any purpose other than the Socialisation Capsule, while the rest of us resisted the idea that we should make do with just two rooms for all the other activities of the commune.

'Nikita,' Marina snapped, 'where are we to do the Model T, now it is almost winter? Where are we to eat communally? Have you gone mad? We are abolishing the private, and you are trying to keep to your ivory tower? I simply don't understand.'

'I know this work of yours is important,' said Fyodor, 'but surely even you can agree that the commune needs more than two rooms.'

'The advance of Science must take precedence,' Slavkin dismissed us.

A metalworker and his family moved into the dining room, seven of them. They told terrifying stories of life in the Volga region under the boots of one, then another army occupation, while they lay in a dugout with the trapdoor closed over their heads and ate beechnuts. At last the Whites were driven out and the local Bolshevik commander gave him a travel pass to Moscow as a worker with a skill useful to the Revolution. His children looked like five tiny old people, eyes shrunken in their yellow faces. Without consulting the others, Vera and I gave them dried apples and pickles from our stores.

Upstairs seven families of factory workers moved in. Servile and monosyllabic to our faces, they were aggressive filchers of any morsel of firewood, any utensil, any scrap of clothing behind our backs. The sign saying 'Institute for Revolutionary Transformation' was taken down by the cadres, and our decorations in the hall – 'Come On, Live Communally!', and the portraits of Marx and Engels in red paint – were covered over with decrees from the Soviet. We fixed locks and chains to our doors, but that didn't stop someone from forcing open the window and stealing our cooking pots and soap. Volodya, Fyodor and I marched into the bedrooms and took back everything of ours that we could identify, although one woman – a dark, mustachioed termagant with arms like Christmas hams – had the gall to cling on to one of our mixing bowls, howling so loudly that she was being robbed, that we left her to it.

The main bedrooms at the front of the house were taken over by a group of ex-soldiers who made all our lives a misery with their constant drinking, fighting and ripping up pieces of the house to burn in their fireplace.

'These people may look like the proletariat, but they were born in Russian villages; you know that really means they are of the Paleolithic era,' said Fyodor. He looked surprised when Pasha and I laughed. 'I'm making a serious point!'

Of course he was; I don't think Fyodor ever knowingly joked in his life. He forgave us then, although not for much longer.

The 'compression', as it turned out, had its advantages. In November the first snows fell and the reality of War Communism under General Winter began to bite. During the winter of 1917–18, we had bartered for firewood and burnt old fences. In 1918–19 wooden bath-houses, sheds, duckboards and shop fronts were burnt as well as whole wooden houses – their inhabitants given twenty-four hours to clear out with their belongings. Moscow's parks were decimated and the Boulevard Ring lost half its avenues. We congregated in the study for our evening meetings and soon to sleep as well, all the mattresses arranged in a star shape around a small metal stove, or *burzhui* (bourgeois person; for its fat stomach, I assume). The stovepipe shot vertically upright and out through the old chimney breast, smoke leaking out of every joint. The old ladies, against their will, came to sleep around the stove too.

'What will my cousin say when he sees how you have treated us?' complained Anna Vladimirovna bitterly to me. 'It's a disgrace! Don't you know I am a Dolgoruky on my mother's side?'

In vain I tried to explain to her that this was the best we could do. Poor things, they suffered from the cold more than any of us.

One evening Sonya produced a telegram from Constantinople.

'All aboard the Eloise sailing Marseilles stop Mama's health not good lack medicines and treatments here stop details on arrival stop 4 x Kobelevs.'

I closed my eyes partly against the fumes of the *nyedy-shalka*, and partly against the tears that welled up against my lids. Since peace had been declared in Europe we had heard that hordes of refugees were leaving Russia for Turkey, France or New York. I hated to imagine their journey with an ill Mrs Kobelev. Dima would now be thirteen, Liza fifteen; old enough to help. Old enough to worry.

'I would like to have the Commune's agreement,' broke out Sonya unexpectedly. 'I want to leave my job. It's such a waste of time! I didn't leave my parents and my brother and sister on their own to fritter away my days in that office.'

I agreed with her. She was working in a government department – the Committee for Sovietisation of the Caucasian Nationalities. As the Caucasus was still over-run by civil war the business of Sovietisation was being carried out by the Red Army, who were fighting in the mountains, killing and being killed in great numbers. Meanwhile Sonya's colleagues consisted of a few officials who saw it as a reasonable way to pass their days, thanks to the office's ceramic stove which they kept alight with Tsarist reports on Caucasian questions. The promise of a ration, however erratic, and the protection of a government position, however sketchy, was enough to keep them at their desks at least for part of each day.

'What would you do instead?' asked Fyodor.

Slavkin spoke up. 'I need a co-worker on the Capsule. I'm making progress, but it will go faster—'

'But we need your ration, Sonya,' objected Fyodor. 'We can't feed ourselves as it is.'

'Yes, I know,' she said. 'I thought I could make a trip to Mikhailovka. Some of the peasants are still well disposed towards our family, you know. I think they would help us.'

'Don't be a fool!' Pasha exclaimed. 'It's much too dangerous. Please, no, Sonya.'

'From each according to his ability,' Fyodor chipped in, raising his voice. 'Each of us must contribute to the commune. We can't carry any dead weights.'

'I will do whatever the commune thinks best,' Sonya spoke up again. 'But as I say, I didn't come back from the south to waste my time. I can hardly bear to see their greasy faces in the department – what clever fellows we are, they seem to say, keeping ourselves warm, our feet under the table, while those fools out there starve—'

'If I succeed in the task I am now setting myself,' said Slavkin calmly, 'the Revolution will, I promise you, make a huge leap forward. This, after all, is our chief aim, is it not? We must keep our eyes on our goal.'

'But – but is Sonya really the best person to help you?' I put in. 'She has little or no scientific education, and—'

'She will do very well,' Slavkin said definitively.

'Wouldn't I be more suitable?' I persisted. 'I could rearrange my English lessons. I at least have an elementary knowledge of physics.'

Slavkin turned his back on me, saying casually, 'No, no, you must continue with your teaching. I will explain to Sonya what she needs to know.'

Sonya began work with Slavkin a day or so later, and with her, he spent longer hours than ever closeted in his workshop.

After making a careful inventory of our stores we decided that in order to survive the winter we would have to go bagging. The whole Russian nation would have starved without bagging under War Communism, despite the fact that it was illegal. It meant setting out into the countryside with a bag slung over your shoulder and bartering with any peasants you might come across – a few pounds of grain in return for the family silver. Talk in the food queues was full of terrible fates that had befallen ordinary folk, fathers of families, young boys, *babushki*, who had gone bagging and been caught by the flying brigades – Red Guards who searched the trains and not only confiscated any goods people might have collected, but quite often shot the bagmen too. But as the alternative was starvation, the tide of hopefuls with bags did not abate.

Pasha and Volodya volunteered to be the bagmen.

'I'll be able to deal with the brigades,' Volodya said. 'I know how to speak to the lads.'

'And I'll hide behind him,' said Pasha. I laughed.

'You're the child of fortune,' I told him. 'Nothing could penetrate your halo of good luck, undeserved though it is.'

Vera and I stitched several pouches into their clothes to carry their goods for barter – a gold necklace of Anna Vladimirovna's, six silver teaspoons, some lengths of cloth, some Kerenkas and other bits and bobs. We also sewed good strong double-lined sacks, in hope.

Later the same week we accompanied them to the railway station, marching in formation and singing Revolutionary songs; Nikita thought this part of the IRT's duty of enlightenment, now we were becoming so well known. Our commune, in Slavkin's words, was to shine as a beacon among the darkness of contemporary society; it should mould not only ourselves, but should attract others, through our example, to the communal life.

It may have been my lack of charity, but I was not convinced that our marching and singing inspired passers-by with anything other than amusement. Grunters in the park, PropMash Doctors, and now a rather out-of-tune marching band – it was no wonder that one article about the IRT described us as avant-garde *chudaki* – cranks. Never mind: in this way we saw our boys off on the train. Verochka bathed Volodya's face with tears and made a surreptitious little sign of the cross over him. Pasha kissed his sister, and made me a funny little bow, and we sent them on their way with renditions of 'Boldly, comrades, in step', and 'Break the fetters, set me free, I'll teach you to love freedom'.

Each day, on my return from work, the quietness of the house was noticeable, the dampening of all our spirits. Sonya and Slavkin worked long hours, and although their behaviour was entirely proper in our evening meetings, I was tortured by their casual reminders to each other, the tag-ends of their working conversations. One week passed, and two, and three, without word from our bagmen.

13

'This commune', Fyodor shouted suddenly one evening, 'is deteriorating into some kind of *synod*.'

We all stopped talking; Fyodor did not usually raise his voice like this, or shake with agitation. 'We are not here to chatter!'

'Calmly,' murmured Slavkin.

Fyodor paced up and down. He didn't meet Slavkin's eye. 'Your approach, Nikita, is – is subjective. It's all wrong. I mean, I don't want to offend you, but I think you're going about things completely stupidly.' He frowned. 'The psychological approach, the self-criticisms – it just leads to talk and more talk. Your work is your affair, but the narcotics, well, to my mind that's just some kind of mysticism.'

Slavkin seemed taken aback. 'Well,' he said at last. 'It is easy for anyone to paint the room black. What do you suggest? Let's see how you'd go about it!'

'We need discipline and efficiency, above all. Self-control. This is the most important transformation. We are getting waylaid by every sort of nonsense. "Don't be distracted" – that's what you say, isn't it, Nikita? The Taylorisation of our daily lives is what we need.'

F. W. Taylor, the father of the 'scientific management' of work, was Fyodor's great hero.

'Oh, Lord!' sighed Slavkin impatiently. 'All that is the work of *clerks*! We're searching for revelations! Haven't I already explained to you many times that in order to penetrate the mysteries of the human soul one must move obliquely, subtly – it's no good approaching it as if it were a steam engine.'

Sonya nodded, and they smiled at each other.

But Dr Marina interrupted, 'No, Nikita. You've had your own way for too long. It's becoming an auto-cracy. Fyodor, you should write out a programme for us. Propose it at our meeting tomorrow, and we'll vote on it.'

'Thank you, Doctor. I will,' replied Fyodor, surprised at this unexpected support.

I glanced at Dr Marina; she was frowning, her face set.

As it was already midnight, we prepared to sleep: washing our faces in a pail of tepid water that had been sitting on the stove and spitting out our toothpowder into a slop basin. In the morning it would have frozen into beautiful spirals. We stepped around the figure of Nikita who sat, sulky and unmoving, in his position to the right of the stove. I suspect the others felt as I did, embarrassed and irritated that he should take this minor challenge to his authority so hard. After some time he turned abruptly to Sonya and murmured something to her. They stood up and, without saying a word to the rest of us, dressed in their outdoor clothes and left the room. We heard the outer door open and close with a thump.

I lay on my mattress very still, very still. A burning sensation inside me caused my chest to pump up and down and my face to contort with pain. A couple of hours passed before Nikita and Sonya returned. They had allowed themselves to get chilled, and spent a long time trying to warm up by rubbing their hands and feet until Marina asked them very sharply to be quiet.

During my long walk to and from work that day I decided that I would vote for Fyodor. It was not an easy decision. But Nikita's petulant expression of the night before came back to me, and the childish way he had refused to speak and then led Sonya out of the room.

Having already made up my mind, I was surprised and impressed when Fyodor stood up and made his suggestions for the Taylorisation of the commune. He was articulate and passionate, and went into extraordinary detail. I put my hand up immediately we were called upon to vote. Ivan and Nina were performing that whole week, otherwise I suppose it might have gone differently. When I saw Dr Marina's arm go up, and Volodya's, followed by Vera's, I glanced involuntarily at Nikita. The look he gave me, of utter misery and disbelief, was like a slap.

'Congratulations, comrade,' he said hoarsely, bowing his head. 'I look forward to starting on your course of work. I assume, however, that you are happy for me to keep working on my projects in my studio?'

'Yes indeed, comrade,' Fyodor replied, flushed with victory. 'That is something the whole commune will need to agree on, of course.'

'We agree,' I spoke up immediately. 'Or rather, let's vote. I agree – Marina, Volodya, Vera?'

'Yes, yes,' they nodded hurriedly. The atmosphere in the room was strained, only Fyodor was cheerful. Slavkin sat like a figure of stone.

'Well, good; to implement the efficiency measures, then . . .' began Fyodor.

As we turned to listen, out of the corner of my eye I saw Sonya's hand creeping into Nikita's. He enveloped it with his own.

No hierarchy – for goodness' sake, the phrase had become a cliché in our discussions on the structure of the commune! No specialisation – the regular reassignment of all roles, by timetable – so that no one becomes comfortable in a position of authority. We had deferred to Nikita precisely because he had presented us with a vision of egalitarianism; surely he understood that? I was enraged with all of us, including myself, but much more so with Nikita. If you can't adapt, can't control your pride, your emotions, how can you expect the same of the rest of us? Unsaid, my thoughts chased each other around my brain long into the night.

*

A new stage began in the IRT. We decided on measures to occupy and oversee every minute of a communard's day. I reproduce here a copy of the timetable that we painted up on the meeting-room wall, above the fireplace:

167

Daily Timetable
Comrades Please Note: All Activities Are Compulsory.

A Gong Will Be Struck For Each New Activity.

6 a.m. Wake up. Wash and dress

6.15   Model T exercises

6.35   Breakfast

7.00   Clear away breakfast

7.15   Clean teeth

7.25   Put on outdoor clothes

7.30   Leave for place of work

6 p.m. Dinner

6.30   Clear away dinner

6.40   Household chores as allotted by rota

8.30   Analysis of time cards

9.30   Other business

10.30   Retire to dormitories

11.00   Lights out

Full Punctuality, Full Rations!
Remember – Each Minute Wasted Is a Gift to Rockefeller!

Time cards were issued to each of us to record the events of our day, which we were meant to study each evening for possible savings. Every week, one member was given the responsibility of striking the gong to announce each new activity of the day.

There were some good points to the new regime. The mornings were dark and getting out of bed in the damp air of our dormitory was certainly made more bearable by the morning Model T exercises, which Nina had now expanded to include a series of Hungarian dances, very rhythmic and cheerful. Meanwhile Anna Vladimirovna was delighted by the timetable, which seemed to remind her of her childhood. 'That boy is just like my father,' she would hiss as Fyodor bustled about with a notebook. 'Terrible bossyboots!' Even the constant ringing of the gong, which infuriated all the other inhabitants of the house, pleased the old lady; apparently her father had ordered the church bells to be rung in the village each time he won at backgammon. It was hard, on the other hand, on poor Mamzelle, whose chest infection was worse and who longed only to be allowed to sleep.

We all became more punctual, particularly when poor Vera's ration was reduced after she took too long scouring the pots. It did seem harsh to leave her bowl empty while we munched away at our bean porridge on either side of her. Her eyes filled with water and she bit her lip. A little colour rose in Fyodor's cheeks and he chewed slowly and deliberately, looking everywhere but at her face.

Now the evening meetings began with our daily efficiency reports. Dr Marina, for example, might report an increase in the productivity of her ironing – she had ironed ten shirts in only twenty-five minutes, rather than the thirty-five it had taken her last time. Fyodor would sit on the edge of his seat, fidgeting with

169

excitement. 'Good! Now tell us, how did you achieve this? Did you have a different method? Perhaps you can demonstrate this method to us? Imagine if all over the world ironing speeds are increased by over 20 per cent!'

I imagined instead Pasha's likely response to this breakthrough and had to stare very hard at my lap not to laugh.

It was impossible to imagine how our minute increases in efficiency would ever make any difference in a world as utterly un-Taylorised as Moscow under War Communism. Most of my time cards reported two or three hours spent queuing for rations, reporting to empty classrooms on the off-chance of a bread delivery or walking to and fro across the city to give private English classes – a waste of time that would have been impossible to imagine before the Revolution.

This was the first problem with Fyodor's system; the second was that our meetings, under his guidance, had all the excitement of a railway timetable. Ivan and Nina lasted one week and then excused themselves on theatrical business. Not long afterwards, they moved out, into a hostel belonging to the Kamerny Theatre. We were left to practise the Model T without Nina's deep voice commanding us to 'Release the pancreas. Release . . . the spleen. Release . . . the duodenum.' Where *were* Pasha and Volodya? Without them, our evenings became almost funereal. We were all worried, and didn't want to talk about them. Slavkin would sit a little off to one side, tense, red-eyed, with a nervous twitch of the head that I hadn't noticed before. When it came to his turn, he said only, 'I have no increases in efficiency to report.'

'Come on, Nikita, stop sulking!' Dr Marina snapped after a week or so of this. 'Surely you've got some ideas. You've always been fascinated by time, in theory, at least?'

Slavkin glared at her. 'Yes, in fact I do have a suggestion,' he said at last. 'If I could spend these evening hours in my workshop I believe I could bring forward the completion of my Socialisation Capsule by as much as six months. This is certainly the greatest service I can do for the Revolution.'

'Fuck you!' Fyodor suddenly bellowed.

'Fyodor!' said Dr Marina, shocked.

'Yes, I mean it!' he rushed over to Nikita and shouted in his face. 'Fuck you! How dare you sabotage my attempts at progress, you bastard? How dare you treat me with this disrespect when we have gone through with all your half-baked idiotic whimsical "experiments", your narcotic counter-revolutionary fancies! You'll suffer for this, you cretin, I'll make sure you do!'

A pause while we all stared aghast at Fyodor, scarlet in the face and shiny with sweat. 'And fuck all of you too!' he screamed, his voice breaking, as he stormed out of the room.

The Red Guards upstairs broke into applause. Fyodor stamped downstairs and out of the front door, slamming it behind him.

Sonya was the first to speak up. 'I do understand what Fyodor means,' she murmured.

Nikita looked at her, and we all waited.

171

'I should probably apologise to him then, should I?' he asked.

'Yes, Nikita, well done,' said Dr Marina bossily. 'And by the way I think we can all agree that you'd be better off spending the time on the Capsule.'

'Perhaps these evening meetings have run their course, just for the moment?' I suggested. 'Could we have a holiday, so to speak, until Pasha and Volodya return?'

I immediately regretted having mentioned their names. Vera burst into tears and Sonya jumped up to comfort her.

'Oh, for goodness' sake,' Sonya rounded on me. 'Gerty, you are as bad as Fyodor. There's no need to say everything that pops into your head!'

*

As usual, Pelyagin had a few tasks to finish off when I arrived at his office. I sat down to wait for him and looked around. The room was warm and stuffy, and there was the usual faint smell of food from the canteen. His assistant was not there; I watched Pelyagin working methodically through his papers, scanning, signing, placing them on one pile or another. A delicious sensation of peace crept through me; I removed my coat and leant back in the chair, feeling the muscles in my back and legs relax, the tension in my forehead seep away. My eyes drifted shut . . .

'My apologies, Comrade Freely.' Pelyagin was standing over me and there was an expression on his face . . .

I gazed at him, trying to read it. 'I've kept you waiting,' he said. 'Why don't I fetch some coffee from the canteen, and something to eat?'

He left the room. Flustered, I struggled upright and tried to make myself tidy. I took the *Illustrated London News* out of my bag and bent over it as he entered, carrying a cup and a bag of rusks.

'Goodness, coffee!' I exclaimed. 'I haven't tasted it for months.'

'They call this coffee. I think it is made out of wood chippings.'

We both laughed, and for a moment I caught a glimpse of a younger Pelyagin, a boy with a loose, aimless grin.

'I'm sorry,' he said diffidently, sitting opposite me. 'I couldn't help with the housing compression. It is not my department, you know. I talked to my colleagues but they were not sympathetic. Are you managing to continue your communal work?'

'Oh, yes, we are managing – although things are not easy at the moment, we have some personality clashes – it is inevitable, it may even be a necessary part of the evolution of the commune.' Suddenly my loneliness came out in a wail. 'But it is hard . . .'

'I'm . . . I'm sure you will persevere.'

I leant forward and put my hand on his arm.

'I really am so grateful to you for doing what you could.'

He almost snatched his arm away. 'We must start work.'

'Yes, you're right. Please, read this passage for me.'
As he stumbled his way through an article on recent innovations in the Manchester textile industry, I drank the
rest of my coffee and tried to calm down. I was becoming morbidly sensitive. It was poor nutrition and lack of
sunshine, no doubt.

*

Summons to Nikolai Gavrilovich Slavkin to a Labour
Tribunal at the Centre for Revolutionary Research, 29
November 1918.

. . . Comrade Slavkin takes as his starting point ob-
scure and esoteric theories of 'quantisation' and develops
these theories erratically and with little evidence of
either mathematical or empirical backing for his work.
We cannot allow the limited resources of the Centre to
be wasted.

The tribunal will take place on 12 January 1918.

I don't think Nikita ever apologised to Fyodor. While
I was with Pelyagin – a strange little stage-lit excerpt
from winter – this summons to justify his working methods arrived from the workers of the Centre.

According to Sonya, he fell into a panic on reading
these words. 'He was shaking and gasping for breath,'
she told me. 'You know that funny little twitch he sometimes has? I think it's from the narcotic, he's been taking
it quite often. He wouldn't listen to anything I said –
he didn't seem to be able to hear me. He ran out into

the night and the only thing I could do was to go after him. He ran all the way to Bryansk station and I thought I'd lost him among the crowds. Then I found him just standing at the bottom of the main steps – in everyone's way – he didn't recognise me, Gerty. I stood with him and we were being pushed here and there by the crowds, but he wouldn't move a step, it was as though he was made of stone. At last a station guard shouted at him and dragged him out of the way, and that seemed to wake him up. He looked around as if he didn't know where he was and then he saw me, and I could see him wondering who I was, and then it dawned on him and he smiled . . .' She smiled too, at the memory.

'Romance, for Revolutionaries, is as horrid a perversion as anything the French Marquis dreamt of.' I said it aloud, without quite meaning to; Sonya frowned.

'What?'

'Oh, something Nikita once told me . . . I thought he meant it.'

Sonya stood up, turned away, her voice cold. 'Don't you need to get on with your chores? Fyodor will reduce your rations if you're not careful. I can manage him perfectly well . . .'

I glanced over to the mattress in the corner of his workshop. Nikita was sleeping now; I had arrived back to find Sonya struggling with him in the hall. He was refusing to go upstairs, shouting that he must work, that he didn't have any time to lose, and so on. He agreed to lie down only when we made up a bed next to his workbench.

In the centre of the workshop, on stands, were two

175

long metal pods the shape of canoes, lined with cotton wadding. On the outside they were encrusted with electrical circuits and batteries made out of the iron bars Volodya had successfully purloined from the railway station, copper wire from Marina's hospital, vinegar I had bartered for at the market.

'Why is he building two Capsules?' I asked.

'He wants me to test it with him. Just in case, you know . . .'

I swivelled towards her. 'In case of what?'

'I'd better not say – it's just a remote possibility . . .' But there was something about her smile, half suppressed, that filled me with miserable rage. I was shaking as I left. Anna Vladimirovna was calling me, but I stood for a while in the hall until I had gained control of myself. Then I heard Vera's voice calling too.

'Gerty! Please, Gerty, we need you! It's Mamzelle . . .'

*

Mademoiselle Bourget looked as if she were sleeping. Her small, wrinkled face was pale and calm, her eyebrows very slightly raised. My first thought was how very thin she had become. The bones in her skull were clearly visible through her wisps of grey hair. Her jawline was horribly sharp. That morning she had complained of the cold and when I set off to see Pelyagin I had wrapped her in my blankets as well as her own. In her faint voice she had thanked me.

'Fille sage, c'est-ce que tu es . . . très sage . . .'

176

Now it seemed that those were her last words. No one recalled her having said anything while I was out. She had always been shy; like the gentle little creature she was, she had left us at the quietest moment in the day, when all of us were out at work and even her old companion was taking a nap.

'I woke up and tried to speak to her, and she didn't answer!' Anna Vladimirovna kept repeating. 'It's most distressing! She's always been with me, ever since I came to live in this house!'

I persuaded the old lady to sit outside in the hall while Vera and I laid Mamzelle out. She was so light that we were able to lift her easily. There were no flowers, but we lit what candles we had and arranged them around her. When the others returned we sat quietly with her. There seemed little to say about her. I realised that I knew nothing about her childhood or her family; I'd never heard her mention anything about her life before she came to the Kobelevs. A lonely, unassuming soul, a governess through and through. I began to cry and suddenly I was sobbing noisily and burying my face in my apron. Yet even those tears, I reflected bitterly, were not for Mamzelle.

14

By December we had developed the habit of going straight to bed, fully dressed, the moment we arrived home – that way we preserved any heat we might have managed to create by walking. All of us were malnourished. Sonya had twice fainted in the street. I had been feeling dizzy and nauseous for some weeks; occasionally I had no desire even for our meagre rations. Now, of course, I'm an old lady and I need very little food. But I still feel the urge, now and again, to control hunger by embracing it; the strange pleasure of not eating.

The Centre had relieved Slavkin of his post due to his nervous collapse and articles began to appear in the papers accusing him of various Bolshevik taboos – 'spiritual tendencies', 'self-indulgent bourgeois experimentation'.

'This is to be expected,' Nikita said shortly. 'They don't understand particle physics. Before a great advance in science you will always find nay-sayers.' The Socialisation Capsules, he thought, would soon be ready for trials.

Instead of our evening meetings we chatted and read aloud – poetry, usually. Novels we avoided not for any political reason but for their unbearably detailed descriptions of meals. Blok's poem *The Twelve*, which had come out earlier that year, was strangely cheering, despite its subject matter – a prostitute murdered by an ex-lover. Its rollicking pace was as catchy as a marching song, and its slogans and red flag, starving dog, fear and hope felt entirely familiar to us. The last lines, in which one glimpses the shadowy figure leading the twelve Red Guards, always made the hairs on my neck stand on end:

> So they march with sovereign tread . . .
> Behind them limps the hungry dog,
> and wrapped in wild snow at their head
> carrying a blood-red flag –
> soft-footed where the blizzard swirls,
> invulnerable where bullets cross –
> crowned with a crown of snowflake pearls,
> a flowery diadem of frost,
> ahead of them goes Jesus Christ.

'I feel it, don't you?' said Nikita slowly, from the dark corner where he lay, 'the scouring out of the old. Almost everything will go, almost all of us, we will be hollow shells, baked clean and white, to receive the future. It is happening already – time itself is speeding up to allow for the transformation. Look at the children – a child of five is already an adult these days. Look at us – decades have passed in the last year.'

We glanced around at each other's pallid, wasted faces, at our old, tired bodies.

'Don't be afraid. This is all as it should be. This reality must cease to exist in order for the other to be imaginable.'

We shall all die here, like this, lying around this stove,

I thought to myself, and nausea rose up inside me again.

A knock at the door, and all of us froze for a long minute. A visit so late meant danger. Since the end of August the only vehicles in the streets at night time were the Cheka's Black Marias; sitting in the dark we had watched them in Starokonyushenny Street and on the Arbat, swinging their headlights into the courtyards, car doors banging, torchlight, shouting, making their way through the buildings, weeping voices, hurried steps down the stairs, slam, slam, engine gunning, and a black pool of silence behind them.

Door on the chain, Fyodor opened it cautiously. 'Who's there?'

'I've come from Mikhailovka,' muttered a small, dark figure. 'It's Golubukhin.'

'Golubukhin!' Sonya struggled upright. 'Good heavens! Come in . . .'

As she hurried him towards the stove, I recognised the head coachman from Mikhailovka, stooped, with a grimy, lined face and half-frozen fingers wrapped in rags. Formerly he had had a certain swagger – in charge of the busy stables and a renowned trainer of horses and dogs, a rogue who could be found in a drunken stupor at every horse market in the region.

'How are things at Mikhailovka? Look, we've some warm water, have a little tea – sit down and warm yourself.'

'Here . . .' With a sigh he swung the heavy bag off his back. 'It's only a little, all that we could spare this winter.' He untied the sack and to our amazement we saw that it was three-quarters full of millet.

'My dear,' said Sonya softly. 'You brought that all the way from Mikhailovka?'

He bowed slightly. 'Glad to do my bit, your honour,' he muttered.

He had put his life at risk several times over by this act. Carrying goods without the right documents on the train; crossing Moscow after the curfew; let alone removing a whole sack of corn from his village during a winter like this one – any of these could have earned him a bullet in the head.

'Well, you see, your brother comes to Mikhailovka,' Golubukhin began. He sat and accepted a cup of our brackish tea. 'He and Yakov's boy arrive in the night, oh, must have been four weeks ago – before All Souls', about the day of Our Lady in October – waking up half the village with their shouting and joking around, they haven't changed. So by the next morning the local Soviet hears that a former landlord is in the village and they're planning to come up and get him, and of course my wife's sister, you remember her, miss? Paulina, her name is, that helped in the nursery—'

'Yes, yes, of course . . .'

'Her man Alyosha Gumiltsev is a commissar now, Paulina goes in mortal fear of him, but anyway she ran up to us and told us, she was always fond of all of you, and so I went over to Yakov's to tell the boys to make themselves scarce. But I was too late, see, and I was just passing the church when Commissars Debryakov and Gumiltsev come riding in (they took Star and Rowan

181

for their own use, miss, you remember them? Beautiful beasts they were, it breaks my heart to see them now) and another Bolshevik with them, and so I stood back in the porch and I saw them dragging the boys out and taking them off. Paulina tried to find out what had become of them and it seems Gumiltsev said they were mixed up in some kind of counter-revolution.' He hesitated, glancing at the slack faces around him. 'Well—' He cleared his throat. 'Your family were good to me, your excellencies, I had nothing to complain of from your father and mother, so I thought I'd better come and let you know. It's not easy to travel these days as you know, took me several weeks to get away, but they can just throw you in prison and forget about you, this lot . . .'

Sonya was trembling. '*Bozhe moi*. How do we find them?'

Nikita went over to her and placed his hands on her shoulders. 'This will be a simple matter,' he said slowly, looking her in the eye. 'Tomorrow morning we go to Lunacharsky, and tell him that a worker in his own department and his colleague have been mistakenly placed under arrest. We'll get them out all right.'

'But . . . counter-revolution!' she blurted out, starting to cry.

I said nothing, but lay in bed fuming at her. Really, didn't she understand anything? These confusions were unfortunate, but there was no need to panic. Sonya was physically weak, and, I thought to myself, mentally unreliable as well. After some time I got up and went out into the dark hall, hoping some air would clear my head.

A rustle from the corner . . . I jumped aside.

'Vera, what are you doing there?'

She was slumped on the floor, hugging her knees. When she looked up I saw her face was red and swollen with tears. Of course . . . in all the drama I had not thought of Vera.

'Oh Vera, don't cry,' I murmured, placing my hand awkwardly on her back. 'We'll get Volodya back—'

'But I haven't even told him.'

'What?'

Her face crumpled and she wailed, 'Don't you see, I'm having his baby . . .'

Suddenly I could see, quite clearly – the greasy plumpness of her face, her breathless, saggy bosoms. 'What have you done?' I heard my voice as though it were someone else's. 'You deceived us, didn't you? You carried on with your . . . your entanglement. Oh Vera, how could you?'

*

That night in the dark dormitory, lit only by a smoky flicker from our stove, we listened as Golubukhin told us in his hoarse voice about affairs in Mikhailovka since the October Revolution. The last time I visited was in August 1917, with the little children and the usual entourage of staff. In my mind Mikhailovka was still white-columned, still standing in a haze of sunshine and green shade, the buzz of bluebottles and frogs croaking in the evening light.

'It was summer, a warm night with a big moon,' Golubukhin began diffidently. 'Word had been going round and there was a fair old crowd, led by the boys back from the Army, but they came from all over – everyone felt they had to join in, you see. Frielen, the steward, saw them coming and tried to run away with his family but he left it too late, they caught him and began to beat him, he screamed like a girl. He'd squeezed them for twenty years, after all. Anyway he wasn't too hot but his wife got him and the children away, he's in Moscow now, I hear. And then they carted out the furniture and passed it around, and the pictures and objects and that, "loot the looters", you know – some people have got all sorts in their huts now, carpets and china, but most of it was broken straight away – the pictures got a boot through them and the furniture was smashed up. They were drunk of course – the first place they went was the cellar – and crazy too. They were prancing around dressed up in the fine clothes, and shooting out the fireplaces and the windows. And then we smelt smoke and someone shouted '*Krasny Petukh!*' – the red cockerel, you know, fire – and I and my boys ran to let the horses out – I wasn't leaving them to be burnt. Most of them got rounded up later and sent off to the front. I told you already about Star and Rowan and, miss, your mare was grabbed by that fat old Pryanishnikov and he's beaten her half to death already. I tell you, it breaks my heart to think of the animals. But the fire fairly ripped through the house, I've never seen anything like it, the flames must have been fifty *arshin* high . . .' There was a ghost of a smile in his voice. 'We were drunk on it all for three days, like a wedding.'

*

In order to build the new, we must dismantle the old. So we believed. We must clear the wide world of this bourgeois clutter. We must throw Tsarist culture out of the steamer of modernism. We must smash, destroy, sweep away . . . until we are left with the pure white rooms of the future. The world around us was emptying. Possessions were lost to the four winds, and the Russian people themselves were cleared away. They were scattered by fear or need, abroad or to the countryside.

At the same time people disappeared within Moscow too. Typhus and dysentery and hunger gathered up many. But many vanished quietly into Cheka buildings: the garage on the Varsonofievsky, the sheds near the Church of the Resurrection and, most of all, the cellar of the Yakov company building on the Lubyanka, which became known as the 'Ship of Death'. Since the end of August, when the Red Terror was announced, these places had started to fill up and overflow. Shooting could be heard all night long in Petrovsky Park, and the labour brigades of former people who had previously been put to work clearing rubble from the streets or feeding the furnaces at the electricity station were now given the job of digging graves.

Many prisoners were genuine opponents of the regime, of course, and there were always rumours of plots.

185

At the Bolshoi Theatre someone took advantage of a power cut to scatter anti-Bolshevik leaflets from the balcony onto the stalls ... there was pandemonium. The Civil War was still pressing in on us from five sides – in Siberia and the north, on the Volga, in the south, and just outside the gates of Petrograd – and there was a view that many of these prisoners were hostages of war. But we also knew that others crowded into the cellar on the Lubyanka were just the flotsam and jetsam of events. We knew that many of the secret police officers were thugs, perhaps even insane, and they fuelled their nights with cocaine.

We knew these things, but we did not discuss them as we did every other aspect of the Revolution. When you are carrying a huge, delicate and precious thing between you – when your future, all your hopes depend on it – a certain concentration is needed. 'Don't be distracted,' Slavkin told us. Stray doubts, or too much emphasis on the problems of the Revolution, could distort the whole project. Unhelpful questions about the victims of the Cheka, for example, or the over-zealous actions of the Red Army in the villages, or the Bolsheviks' ban on workers' strikes, could poison the atmosphere and be fatal to the work of the commune. Self-control is a vital element in any communal activity; and although we failed in many areas to control ourselves sufficiently, on this topic, that of the Revolution's dark side, we were rather successful.

I have rarely discussed this aspect of our Revolution even after leaving Russia, throughout my life in London.

During my years of political activism, at my Socialist reading groups and women's groups and marches and demos, I've been asked endlessly about my experiences in Russia. I mentioned already that even my memories of the October Revolution used to upset people – they weren't the correct memories. The same went for other details of life in the Soviet Union, some of which I have never told until now. Socialists couldn't afford to listen, they couldn't afford to doubt. They had devoted too much already to the cause. Slavkin's remark came to mind: 'Revolution will redeem all these sacrifices.' If, however, one doubted the Revolution, none of our sacrifices made any sense at all.

Now I am finally laying down the burden of silence, I am confessing, and I find myself awake in the middle of the night, feeling like a traitor to the cause. Oh, I can see already that my husband was right – the truth will carry out its surgery on my ragged old heart. I can feel already the almost sensual relief of blurting everything out, even the most shameful parts that I've been terrified of revealing, all my weaknesses and petty inhumanities. But what about the people who are being told, the dedicated Socialists – what effect will it have on them? And what about Sophy? I am almost eighty now, alone, and my only daughter is my greatest comfort in the world. I am afraid that this story can only cause her pain and confusion. I dread the thought that it will take her from me.

*

We slept little enough that night and by six o'clock Sonya, Slavkin and I were already in the hall of Narkompros, where Pasha worked. Slavkin thought it might be useful to have me with them as a foreigner – perhaps thinking of the magical effect my British passport had had on the militia when, long before, they had come to search the house. I thought he also knew I was good in a crisis, whereas Sonya was shaky and close to tears.

At the Narkompros we waited in a crowd of petitioners hoping for a hearing. Lunacharsky had only just moved from Petrograd to Moscow and he was impossible to see. At any rate, I knew Slavkin would insist we wait our turn. He always used to say in these situations, 'How do we know what urgent business occupies these fellows?'

'Oh, Gerty,' Sonya kept whispering, 'please, convince him that we must hurry!'

I did no such thing. However, after a few minutes Sonya spotted a colleague of Pasha's called Bokin and flung herself on him.

'I'm just the person you need. I'll talk to the Commissar immediately,' he announced, leading us into his office. Slavkin to my surprise made no objection, and we followed in the wake of Sonya's grateful babble.

As always there was tremendous bustle and excitement at the Narkompros, people rushing in and out, banging of doors, posters laid out all over the floor, and so on. After an hour and a half of fidgeting about, I couldn't help wondering out loud whether we had been right to believe Bokin. 'After all, we might have been better off without pulling strings, just waiting in the queue like the other petitioners.'

Sonya jumped up, her face set. 'I'm not sitting here any longer.'

Bokin, we discovered, was standing in the corridor in the midst of a heated discussion about poster distribution.

'Comrade Bokin, forgive me for interrupting,' burst in Sonya, thrusting herself between him and his colleagues, 'but you said you could speak to the Commissar straight away! Comrade Kobelev has been wrongfully arrested by the Cheka – you know as well as I how hasty they can be in their judgements . . .'

Shame-faced, Bokin hurried us into another ante-room. 'Here, here, just a moment, I have mentioned it to him.'

'No! We won't wait another "just a moment"!' Sonya shouted. Tears were pouring down her face, she could barely speak.

'Shh, Sonya,' I tried to calm her, glancing at Slavkin for his approval. 'This behaviour won't help.'

She pushed my hand away and turned to Slavkin. 'Nikita, how can you let this happen? They'll shoot them!'

'Nonsense, Sonya, don't exaggerate,' I told her sharply.

'No,' Slavkin spoke up suddenly. 'Sonya's right. Bokin, you could have blood on your hands if you don't take us straight to the Commissar.'

I couldn't believe my ears. 'But . . . the other petitioners?' I couldn't help saying.

'The other petitioners can go to hell,' spat Sonya. 'And

why don't you go with them? You seem to care about them more than you do about Pasha . . .'

'Come on, Bokin, we're following you,' snapped Slavkin, taking Sonya's hand. 'Let's go!'

They hurried off through the warren of offices.

'Ugh, Bokin,' said his colleague, watching their backs disappear. 'Like a piece of puff pastry.'

'Why's that?'

'You know what he promised me last week? He'd have public-health posters up in Vladimir, Kostroma and Yaroslavl by Saturday. Now I've just found them still in boxes a week later.' He sighed gloomily. 'I don't know where Bokin is taking your friends. The Comrade Commissar isn't even here. He's gone back to Petrograd for a few days.'

I stared at him for a moment. An image sprang into my mind of Pasha, blindfolded, arms tied. Adrenalin gushed through my veins. Sonya was right . . .

Running through the streets, sweat trickling down my sides, gasping for breath. Where now was my principled belief in equal treatment for all? Involuntarily I let out a groan.

'All right, comrade?' said the guard on the door of the Hotel National, alarmed at the sight of me. 'Oh, it's you. Go in.'

I staggered past him and stopped to catch my breath in the entrance hall. To my horror I realised I was about to be sick and rushed outside again.

'Ugh,' said the guard, making a face like a little boy.

'I'm sorry,' I managed to blurt out.

'You go in and get warm,' he said nicely. 'I'll cover it up, don't worry.'

I took the stairs slowly, one at a time, and hung onto the banister. There – Pelyagin's door. His assistant opened it just as I got there.

'Comrade Freely!' she gasped. 'What's become of you? Here, sit down.'

'Oh,' said Pelyagin, fussing, 'a glass of tea, please, Rosa – warm yourself.'

'No, comrade, please, we mustn't waste time. I've come to beg for your help. Two of our commune members have been arrested by mistake.' Breathlessly I told as much as I knew: their names, the date and place of their arrest.

'Wait here,' he commanded. 'I will make enquiries.'

For a moment I was speechless. How strange, how comforting, to feel myself among friends here. In the next room Pelyagin was making telephone calls – I was too exhausted even to listen. He would tell me in a moment, I thought. With a vast sense of relief I relinquished myself to doing nothing – sipping the carrot tea that Rosa brought me and looking around me idly. Goodness, the realisation flashed into my mind, it's Rosa Gershtein – the daughter of an acquaintance of Mr Kobelev's. I had a sudden, vivid picture of her dressed as the Universe in Its Entirety for a New Year's Eve party at Gagarinsky Lane during the war. How had I not recognised her before? She had been a large, stout girl and was now thin, like everyone, but her hooded eyes were the same.

'Rosa Gershtein?' I whispered. 'Do you remember me – the Kobelevs' governess?'

191

Her eyes snapped on mine. 'Shhh. Of course.'

'Forgive me, I couldn't place you.'

'I'm Rosa Andreeva now,' she murmured, glancing nervously at the door. 'Best not to mention it . . .'

Pelyagin reappeared. 'I think we've found them,' he said shortly. 'They brought them up to Moscow and put them in a holding cell. There's a little confusion over their identities, however. I suggest you come with me, Comrade Freely, and identify them formally. They didn't have their identity cards when they were arrested, apparently – foolish.' He frowned. 'We're on a war footing, you understand, comrade. We have to take all precautions.'

As we left the building a car drew up in front of us and for a moment I gaped at Pelyagin, astonished. I had not been inside a car since the Kobelevs' was requisitioned; in the circumstances it seemed a bizarre, almost disgusting luxury to purr so gently and warmly along the bitter streets.

'A treat for you, eh?' Pelyagin said suddenly, genially, misreading my silence. 'Perhaps one of these days we'll go for a drive together?'

It was an ordinary day for him – I must have looked incredulous.

He frowned. 'You don't care to? I see . . .'

'Oh, no – yes, of course . . . I'm grateful to you, but I don't . . .' I stammered.

Pelyagin pursed his lips and looked out of the window. At the Lubyanka I followed him into the building. Pelyagin strode through the hall, past the duty sergeant, motioning me to follow him, and clattered down steps. 'Through there,' he said shortly, pointing out a door. He put a paper into my hand. 'Show this to the officer on duty, he will tell you what to do. They have been alerted to your arrival. Now I must be getting back to work.'

'Thank you, thank you so much,' I stammered. 'Comrade, I am so indebted to you – please . . .' I don't know quite what I was pleading with him for, but in any case he was not in the mood to grant it. He turned his back and was gone.

I looked at the paper. It was signed by Pelyagin himself, with his title: Deputy Administrator, Cheka, Krasnopresnensky District. Cheka? Hadn't he said he was in distribution? I pushed open the door cautiously. It opened onto a gallery with a bench, where two soldiers were sitting with their backs to me. 'Excuse me? I've been sent by Comrade Pelyagin . . .'

The soldiers looked at me dully. 'What do you want?'

I passed them the paper. 'I've been sent to identify two men that you are holding mistakenly.'

'Sez who?' one of them drawled. My hands were sweating; they were obviously illiterate.

'Says Comrade Emil Pelyagin.' I spoke in my most schoolmistressy tone. 'Would you like me to summon him and tell him that you don't believe me?'

The younger got up wearily. 'All right, all right. Come and have a look.'

I stepped onto the gallery and for the first time saw down into the cellar below. It was hot and smelt rotten, but it was so quiet my footsteps echoed. I looked down

and to my shock saw a large number of people below, unmoving, staring up at me.

'Gentlemen.' I cleared my throat. 'Comrades, please –
I'm looking for Pavel Aleksandrovich Kobelev and Vladimir Vladimirovich Yakov.'

Nothing. They seemed frozen.

'Pasha, Volodya, are you there?' It came out as a
scream, like a madwoman.

Suddenly a faint voice, 'We're here, we're here . . .'

Two old men were pushing through the crowd, thin,
ill – my eyes ran over them without stopping, then
flicked back onto their faces: it was Pasha, exhausted, but
smiling; Volodya behind him, bent over, gaunt.

'Get up here, lads,' said the guard. They came awkwardly up the stairs and stood before us, handcuffed.
'Can you identify these fellows, then, comrade?'

'Yes – Pavel Aleksandrovich Kobelev, Vladimir Vladimirovich Yakov. Pelyagin has vouched for them. You've
been holding them wrongly! It's a disgrace!'

'Quite a firebrand, isn't she, lads?' said the guard, raising his eyebrows at them, but to my amazement he was
leading them out of the room and up the stairs to the
duty sergeant. As we left the cellar a few voices called
out. Pasha and Volodya turned but the other soldier was
up on his feet, pointing his pistol over the balcony, shouting at them to be quiet.

There was paperwork, signing this and that in tripli-
cate. The handcuffs were removed, and they were free.

*

Back at Gagarinsky Lane the boys stripped off their clothes in the hallway to be fumigated and washed. Kolenka ran to fetch Sonya and Nikita from the Ministry. At last we were sitting around the stove preparing the best meal we could run to: slices of sausage, kasha with some onions and beetroot, rusks with raspberry jam and tea.

'We didn't know you were so well connected, Gerty,' said Sonya, rather stilted. 'I owe you an apology.'

I didn't meet her eye. 'No, no. It's me who should apologise to you. You were right.'

'You appeared like an angel in that stinking room,' said Pasha, grinning in the old way. 'I thought to myself, I know that accent, just like the Empress – she murders Russian like Gerty.'

I laughed, and suddenly caught Sonya's eye, and stopped. Then Vera, who had hardly said a word since they returned, burst into tears and ran out of the room.

'What's the matter with her?' asked Volodya.

'Perhaps you should go out and have a word with her.'

'You'll find things a little changed around here,' said Fyodor, into the silence. 'The IRT is now being run with strict attention to efficiency and punctuality. You will see, here, the members' time cards, which they have completed for yesterday; we had to speak to Vera yesterday about cutting down on the time she took to complete her chore, which was to dispose of the commune's waste . . .'

'Oh for God's sake, Fedya, do shut up,' snapped Nikita.

'Why can't you let him have his say?' demanded Marina fiercely.

195

'Well, you're cheerful, all of you,' said Pasha, after a pause. 'If we're not having meetings any more, then I think I'll get some rest. Takes it out of you, being rescued.'

There was a silence, and then Nikita and Sonya shuffled to their feet and announced that as there wasn't room for all of us to sleep in this room, they would make up beds in his workshop.

'Won't you freeze?' I said stupidly, but they shook their heads, Sonya looking at me a little contemptuously, I thought. Oh, I hated her then. 'Are you . . . are you keeping the rules, Sonya? You know it's in the commune's interest to be told.'

'Oh, it's in the commune's interest, is it?' mimicked Sonya.

I could barely get my words out. 'You have a duty to tell the truth! You can't hide it from us, you know! Are you . . . are you . . .'

'No, we are not,' said Sonya firmly, hands on hips. 'All right? We are keeping the rules. How dare you even suggest such a thing! You should do the Model T for your mean, suspicious thoughts, Gerty. Don't you trust anyone? Don't you even trust Nikita?'

15

In retrospect this moment has the feeling of a great vessel preparing for departure. Doors slam shut, one by one, and rotating locks swivel. Safety checks are carried out, one, two, three; navigation orders given and noted down. Each member of the team is in his or her position; they know what is expected of them; it is too late, now, to deviate from the chosen course. We do not know if doubts assailed the captain of the ship.

After Pasha's and Volodya's return, Nikita shut himself away in his workshop. Sonya came out once or twice a day to fetch food. 'We are hard at work,' she would only say to my queries. 'The Capsules are nearing completion.'

Since it had emerged that Vera was pregnant, she and Volodya had ceased to make any attempt to hide that they were a couple. I avoided them as much as possible.

I took one of our last pots of jam with me when I next went to Pelyagin's office. All the way I rehearsed my thanks. 'I think you mentioned a drive?' I saw myself murmuring. It was a windy, dreary day with sleet in the air, and I thought of Pelyagin's warm office as I walked, swinging my arms to ease a persistent ache in my stomach.

But when I reached the National, Rosa Gershtein was alone. 'He told me to say that he will not be having any more lessons,' she murmured.

'No? Did he say why?'

'He said it was no longer the best use of his time.'

'I brought him this, to thank him for helping us,' I said, leaving the jam on her desk. 'But did he . . . is he offended with me, do you think? Did he seem angry? Why does he suddenly not want lessons?'

'I don't know.'

I peered at her, trying to interpret her expression. 'When did he start working for the Cheka?'

'He always did. But he was only recently given this public job.'

'I liked him . . .'

'Yes . . .' She looked at me. 'I think he felt the same.'

*

In the half-dark yard back at Gagarinsky Lane stood a silent crowd. Inside, lights were moving about, muffled shouting and banging could just be heard. I found myself standing beside the metalworker from the Volga and his wife. The youngest children were hiding their heads under her skirt.

'What is it?' I whispered.

'Red Guards – they say your lot have been up to something,' he muttered out of the corner of his mouth. 'I'd stay out of the way if I were you.'

The lights were moving about in Slavkin's workshop; crashing metal, splintering glass. 'Oh no . . .'

I pushed through the crowd and into the house. Prig

was leaning against the doorway to the workshop and smoking a cigarette.

'Ah, Comrade Freely,' he said. 'Your friends thought you had deserted them.'

'Excuse me?'

'A report came through that there were valuable materials in this workshop, materials that had been illegally requisitioned,' said Prig. Behind him the Red Guards were methodically dismantling the room, throwing every book and file off the shelves onto the floor, kicking over his half-completed projects. The Socialisation Capsules were dented, wires wrenched out, batteries destroyed.

'Where is Slavkin?'

He jerked his head towards the end of the room. 'He's not being very cooperative.'

I caught sight of Nikita slumped in a chair at the other end of the room. He was so still that I had not registered him at first. 'Nikita,' I hurried over. 'Quick, you need to find the letter of permission from Lunacharsky.' I began searching through the papers on the floor. 'Where did you keep it?'

He gazed at me dully, slowly registering my presence; then a little light of venom crept into his eyes. 'Oh, you're back, are you? That letter's gone, I can't find it. They arrived just after you went out—'

'Shh,' said Sonya to him. She was on her hands and knees, picking up papers.

'Where have you been? To see your special contact?' said Slavkin and laughed mirthlessly. 'Perfidious Albion.'

'What can you *mean*?' The breath had been knocked out of me; my voice emerged as a croak.

Sonya stood up, swaying a little with exhaustion. 'I've got it,' she said. 'The requisition order. It was in the wrong file.' She stalked up to Prig and handed him the paper silently.

'Hmm, yes. Very well,' he said, stubbing out his cigarette on the floor. '*Rebyata!* Boys! I think you can stop that now.'

'What about the damage you have caused?' demanded Sonya furiously. 'You have set back our experiments by weeks.'

Prig raised his eyebrows. 'Well, you'll just have to work harder then, won't you? Make up for all the time you spent lying on the divan in the old days, eh, mademoiselle?'

They left, and the other inhabitants filed back indoors to their rooms. One of the factory workers spat on the floor as he passed our door. 'Scum,' he said. 'Sooner we put a full stop through you, the better.'

I went upstairs to the empty dormitory and lay down. My stomach was twisted up with cramp and I was shivering. I lay on my own as darkness fell and let the tears slide into my hair. After a while Pasha came to find me. 'What times,' he said softly, sitting by my bed. 'Now Nikita is accusing Fyodor of betraying him to the Cheka.'

'Really?'

Pasha nodded. 'Yes, and Fyodor produced his time card and started proving how it would have been impossible for him to denounce Nikita *and* preserve his productivity level of 84 per cent.'

Despite myself, I laughed. 'Pasha, you don't think I would have done such a thing, do you?'

'I think it would be constitutionally impossible for Miss Gerty to do anything of the sort. Now come on, come downstairs. Slavkin and Sonya are in the workshop. You must eat, and it's too cold in this room.'

I sat up. 'Was it just spite on Prig's part?'

'Maybe.'

Fyodor, Marina, Pasha and I ate potato soup and drank tea; slowly my stomach relaxed a little. After a while Volodya and Vera joined us. I marvelled at Vera, her prettiness, the delicate flush on her cheeks. Volodya puffed up his chest beside her and told tedious stories of the army.

'I've been talking to the people at Narkompros about an event for Slavkin,' mentioned Pasha after a while. 'A bigger hall, we're thinking of the Polytechnic. Mayakovsky has said he will introduce him. Nikita needs to put across his views more clearly, to get public opinion on his side.'

'The Camel's lost it, you know,' Volodya said.

I was shocked. 'Volodya, no . . . don't lose faith in him.'

'Shut up, Volodya,' interrupted Pasha coldly. 'Don't dismiss what you don't understand.'

'I'll speak if I want! Can you understand how that piece of trash is going to work? No! No one can! It's madness . . .'

Vera was tugging on his arm. 'Leave it, darling.'

'We're going, anyway,' he said, standing up. 'We've got ourselves registered to a place on Taganka. It'll be a bloody sight more harmonious than this place, I can tell you. Commune? It's a joke. You can't even bear to all be in one room together. Fyodor mincing around with his timetables, Pasha flopping about like a degenerate, Gerty giving the lovebirds in there the evil eye . . .'

'You've got yourselves re-registered?' I repeated. 'That doesn't happen overnight.'

'Yes, well, you are not the only one with special contacts, Gerty,' said Vera with a triumphant look.

Volodya reappeared, carrying their bags. 'Well, thanks for everything, lads.'

Insomnia was my companion yet again that night, as it has been so many nights since. Sometimes it feels as if I have lived a whole second life lying awake in the darkness, wondering if things could have turned out differently. Remembering, too, how just a few months before, Volodya had adored Nikita.

'The Camel – well, he uses a lot of complicated language, but underneath all of that, he's just like one of those calculating machines at the fairground. You feed in the question, whatever it might be, and out comes the answer . . .' Volodya used to laugh, full of pride. 'Come here!' He'd grab Nikita and put his head in an armlock, wrestle with him until Nikita was pink and tousled as a little boy, laughing helplessly. 'Ekh, Camel, you're a freak, you are, but I love you.'

*

Slavkin woke the IRT, and most of the rest of the house, at half past four the next morning by banging the gong.

I ran, my heart pounding. 'What is it, Nikita? What's the matter?'

'Come on, come on, get up, up, up!' His face was flushed, his eyes glittering with excitement. 'We need to print posters, you know what a business that is. If we want to get them around town today we'll have to be at the printer's before nine!'

One of the factory workers came crashing out in the hall, threatening to punch Slavkin. Pasha laughed and embraced him. 'This is about the talk at the Polytechnic, is it, you lunatic? Well, I'm glad you're enthusiastic about my idea—'

'Of course it's about the talk!' exclaimed Slavkin. 'What else would it be about? Forget breakfast, we've no time to eat. Gerty, dear, you've got such an eye for proof-reading, come with me to the printer's today, and we'll need Vova to borrow that handcart he got hold of before – where is he?'

'Er . . . he and Vera have gone away for a few days,' put in Pasha hastily.

'Oh?' Slavkin was disconcerted. 'Gone away? They didn't tell me.'

'No, it's her condition, you know,' improvised Marina. 'I advised her to stay overnight at the hospital.'

'Oh.' He looked at us dubiously for a moment, then, with an effort, put the subject aside.

'So! We must busy ourselves! This is a great opportunity, Pasha, I am much indebted to you. It'll give me a chance to set all those fools at the Centre right. I want you to go to Narkompros today and settle a date – next week would be best, Thursday or Friday.'

'It will be done, *mein lieber Kommandant*,' replied Pasha, grinning and patting his arm, and Sonya laughed and sang, '*Ach, du lieber Augustin, Augustin, Augustin . . .*' A favourite of Tatyana's Day, the students' drinking festival; the others immediately joined in, even Marina and Fyodor: '*Ach, du lieber Augustin, alles ist hin!* – Oh, my dear Augustine, all is lost!'

Slavkin jumped up. 'I must get back to the workshop. Sonya, come with me, I need you.'

Pasha, Marina and Fyodor hurried out to work together and I, after tidying up the breakfast, returned to my bed. Rather without my admitting it, the number of private pupils I taught had been dwindling, week by week. Pelyagin had been the most regular and much the most lucrative. Now I found myself at a loose end and, without my usual occupations to distract me, tiredness overwhelmed me. I had been feeling nauseous for a couple of months; now my stomach was tender and bloated. Nothing surprising, when one considered our diet; this week we had been reduced to eating linseed cakes – cattle feed – that burnt the throat as one swallowed; yet now I promised myself that I would go to the doctor. However that day, and the next, I felt too weak and lethargic to do anything but rest. No one seemed to notice, for which I was glad: I did not want time to be wasted on my weaknesses.

Slavkin whirled through the week in a frenzy of preparations. I wanted to talk to him privately, but he was always busy. The lecture was arranged for the following Saturday at the Polytechnic, a huge hall where Mayakovsky had recently given several popular lectures. Posters were printed (without my attendance at the printer's) and Sonya and Pasha stayed out late night after night, supervising a mob of street urchins whom they had employed to paste them up all over town. Marina lost her temper with Sonya. 'You are underweight and anaemic. Yet you haven't eaten for the past three nights! Don't you understand, you'll fall ill?'

'Well, I've only got to keep going for another month or so. After that it doesn't matter.'

'What are you talking about?' demanded Marina. 'What does that mean?'

But Sonya did not reply, only grinning mischievously.

'She's talking about their experiment,' said Pasha drily from a corner. 'Apparently they're going to disappear together – poof! – like a magic trick. Whisked away to a better place. Or something.'

'Pasha . . .' Sonya warned.

'They'll hear about it all at the talk, anyway, won't they? What's the secret?'

'Leave it until then.'

Fyodor cleared his throat. 'Incidentally, I'm moving out,' he said suddenly in a thin voice.

We swivelled to look at him. He was scarlet in the face, always a sign of high emotion. 'I've had enough of your childish secrets. Cliques and whispers.'

'OK, spare us the speech,' said Pasha. 'We're sick of

you too, Fedya. Go on, get out now, before I knock you down the stairs!' and Pasha leapt menacingly to his feet, fists ready, so Fedya jumped out of his way.

'I didn't think it of you, Pasha,' he spat as he left.

'Well, good riddance to you, you bureaucrat,' shouted Pasha out of the door after him. 'You bloody pencil sharpener! You . . . you tube of foot cream! You pallid mushroom, go and cover your nose with mud!'

We couldn't help it, we started laughing, as Pasha still stood by the door yelling more and more ridiculous insults. 'You rotten cucumber! You bulkhead! You plug!'

And at that, Sonya started to cry, and then we all did, half sobbing, half laughing at ourselves.

'It's pathetic,' sniffed Sonya. 'One by one, they disappeared . . .'

'Who's next? Gerty, is it you?' asked Marina.

'Gerty would never leave. She's loyalty personified,' said Pasha, with a certain dry tone that I couldn't interpret.

*

In the streets of Moscow was a wind, a sharp, cold, whirling wind that whipped around the piles of rubble and through the parks liberated of their railings. It tore the posters off the walls and rushed their messages through the streets:

> We strike them once
> and then again.

Again we hit,
And then they are broken!

It shredded, too, the smudgy posters that Sonya's band of street urchins had pasted up the week before: 'The Physicist–Inventor, Nikita Slavkin, will speak about his Ultimate Communist Futurist Technology at the Polytechnic University on 12 January 1919 at 6 p.m. Entrance free. All Hail to the October Revolution!'

I hurried, alone, towards Novaya square, and the exclamation marks flew past me like arrows in the darkness.

Half an hour early, there was already a crush. I waited, looking out for Slavkin and the others, while the auditorium filled with jostling, eager spectators. Seven o'clock came and went and the audience grew impatient. Catcalls and bellowing filled the hall and three sailors sat on the edge of the stage and began to sing Red Navy ditties.

Shambling, dazzled by the light and the noise, Slavkin appeared from the wings. Raising his long, pale hands as though in blessing, he arrived at the centre of the stage and waited. His skin was bluish-white, his cheeks tinged with the delicate flush of porcelain. At last the hall fell quiet and he began to speak, his voice shaking his whole body – an engine too powerful for its fragile chassis.

'What this Revolution really means is that we have made a promise to ourselves – that we will do everything we can to build Communism. We will not shirk, however hard the task may be. But there is one great obstacle that we have been ignoring. Who is it who grabs the best food for his own family? Who is it who shows pettiness and jealousy towards his fellow workers, who demands individual reward, who denounces others on the slightest evidence? Who, even under the dictatorship of the proletariat, deceives others, exploits others, demands his own needs be met before anyone else's?'

'The bourgeoisie!' yelled a woman near the front.

'No, it is not. We can no longer blame the bourgeoisie – they have left the country. Nor the aristocracy – they are sweeping our streets.' He spread his arms wide as he answered his own question. 'It is you. It is me. It is our own selves. We are now the obstruction. Before we achieve Communism, we must be wiped out – rewritten – changed.

'I can see that you feel apprehensive about this task. You are right, it's ambitious – by comparison everything that we have achieved so far for the Revolution is minimal. But let me reassure you. Its strength lies in the great evolutionary strength of mankind – our imagination. In your imagination – in the imagination of everyone in this room – lies the blueprint for our future. Think about it! You have the key, here, in your own mind. Here.' He turned to the blackboard behind him where there was a drawing of the long, pod-shaped Capsules. 'I will explain the process. This problem is in one sense merely the problem of time . . .'

The audience listened strangely quietly, as if stunned, to Slavkin's lecture. They applauded, politely, his historical analysis ('The battle is already won. It is only a matter of the slow march of time before the age of Communism dawns'); they were a little fidgety during his discourse on particle physics. As he developed the idea of multiple Universes, however, the heckling began.

'Among this infinity of Universes, there will be one in which Communism already exists. Even if . . . well, even if it is not possible in this universe, I suppose.'

An incredulous murmur arose.

'In my researches,' he continued, raising his voice, 'I have been forced to consider the possibility that a brain fully attuned to Communism cannot physically exist in this dimension. Planck's Law has shown us that there are some energy states that are impossible for particles in our reality. It may well be that Communism is one of those impossible states . . .'

The murmur swelled to a rumble. 'What the hell does that mean?' yelled someone.

'Therefore a brain attuned to Communism would instantly cease to exist in this dimension and begin to exist in the compatible dimension. The Socialised subject may just . . . vanish,' said Slavkin.

'Did he just say Communism is impossible?' said a girl near me.

'He's gone off his head, that's what,' said someone else. He turned and pushed through the crowd. 'Move, could you? I'm not sticking around to hear this.'

'Give him a chance,' a voice remonstrated. 'He's a scientist, they talk like this.'

But all around me, others were turning to leave, shoving each other out of the way. 'This is all wrong. Saying we're obstructing Communism – he's mad.'

'What about housing?' came a shout from the back. 'We need living space, not this nonsense!'

Slavkin ignored all of them. He came right to the front of the stage and raised his voice.

'You'll say, what are we to do, if our world is incompatible with Communism? But that is to misunderstand the nature of our quantum world – the nature of matter. You are still clinging to the Newtonian Universe, but this is an illusion – it has gone, just as the whole world of Tsarism has gone, the court and the Duma and the landowners and all those facts of the old life have turned out not to be facts of our new life. Now – listen to me! – now even matter is Revolutionary. We do not understand it all yet, there is a vast amount of work to be done, but let me tell you: even matter can be bent to our will, the world shall be rebuilt even as we are rebuilt.'

I clung onto my place by a desk, straining to hear him. By this time people were filing out of the door, chatting to each other as though they were at the market. Slavkin raised his voice to a shout.

'This has been known by the great prophets of all ages: even in the Bible, it talks of this moment. "Behold, I shew you a mystery; We shall not all sleep, but we shall all be changed, In a moment, in the twinkling of an eye, at the last trump: for the trumpet shall sound, and the dead shall be raised incorruptible, and we shall be changed."'

He stopped. 'Don't give up,' he said after the departing audience. 'Don't give up. Wait – don't give up!'

His shoulders drooped.

'Bravo!' I called, pushing forwards. 'Well said, Nikita!'

He didn't hear. Sonya came on from the wings. She spoke to him and I saw him look up at her, so tenderly. A voice beside me made me start.

'Well, I don't think the audience thought much of that.' It was Fyodor, pursing his lips. 'Quoting from the Bible!'

'Of course you're delighted about that, aren't you, Fedya? *Schadenfreude* – such a joy to the mean and narrow-minded.'

Fyodor flushed angrily. 'No, no, quite the opposite,' he said in his most measured voice. 'I wish Nikita all the best. In fact I'm taking some colleagues of mine to meet him – they have expressed an interest in working with him on his research.'

'Really?' I was taken aback. 'Who are they?'

'From the Ministry of Internal Affairs. They are serious people, cultured.'

Fyodor gestured to a pair of dark-suited men at the back of the hall; they did indeed look serious.

'Oh – forgive me, Fedya. I should have known you better . . .'

The men followed Fyodor up onto the stage. I watched as they introduced themselves. Slavkin's face lit up. Talking ceaselessly, gesturing and embracing the men, he led them away.

16

Without any warning, a week or so after Slavkin's last lecture, came the moment that sliced my life in two: before, after.

'Let us go up to the dormitory. I have something important to discuss with you,' Marina summoned me one night.

Feeling sluggish and low, I had found myself longing to leave Moscow. Unexpected details of Cornish life kept coming to mind — muddy aconites in January, bare trees against the skyline, low cloud lit up beneath by wintery afternoon sun.

I let out a sigh of exasperation. 'Oh, Marina, I'm worn out. Couldn't we talk here?'

Marina raised her eyebrows. 'I think you'd appreciate privacy for what I've got to say.'

'I've got no secrets. Talk away.'

'Very well, I will.' She looked at me. 'As your doctor, I'd like to give you a physical examination.'

'Really?' I was taken by surprise, although in my heart a little worm of doubt, long suppressed, suddenly wriggled to the surface. 'Why's that?'

'You have been nauseous for, I should say, several months. We've all heard you say how you have lost your appetite for various foods. You have lost a considerable amount of weight from your face, your arms, your legs, your ribcage. Yet I have noticed even in your clothes that you are filling out around the lower abdomen. Last night, in the *banya*, it was unmistakable; a distinct swelling. This could be evidence of a tumour, in which case one might expect some bleeding in addition to your normal menstrual discharge. Has there been any bleeding?'

My face flamed. I cleared my throat. 'No – no. No bleeding at all.'

'I see. For how many months?'

I was acutely aware of Pasha and Sonya, like statues, gazing at the floor. 'For . . . for perhaps four months. I assumed it was our poor diet. I didn't think . . . Vera told me she had the same situation, she said it was malnutrition—'

'Yes, it's quite true, Vera did have the same condition. Although Vera, as it turned out, was not malnourished.'

'No—'

'I'm so sorry,' said Sonya suddenly, her face blazing, 'but since you have chosen to hold this conversation in our presence I assume you want us to know. Gerty, can this be true, are you—'

I gulped, unable to speak.

'—pregnant?' interrupted Marina. 'Are you pregnant, Gerty? Is this possible? If one does not allow for the possibility of virgin birth, that is?'

'No, no, it's impossible,' I stammered. I was trembling so hard, my hands were shaking. 'I mean, I suppose it is *possible*, but . . . it can't be true—'

One, two, three, four, five months since August.

'Don't give us modesty now, Gerty,' snapped Marina.

213

'You didn't spare my sister when she found herself in the same position. When did it happen? Who have you been creeping around with behind our backs?'

'Our poor Gerty, who could have done this to you?' Sonya's face was full of concern. 'Has some beast mistreated you?'

Furious tears were suddenly running down my cheeks. 'Oh, Lord, Sonya, surely even you can't be as utterly self-centred as that? It was Nikita, of course – in the summer, before you came back from the south, before you and he began your silly little fling. Who else could it be?'

'Enough,' Pasha stood up. I'd never seen him so angry. 'Quiet, all of you. Marina, hadn't you better take Gerty away and look her over, or something? For God's sake, behave like a doctor and not a bitch. Gerty . . .' He looked at me for a moment, then turned away. 'I don't know.'

I went out with Marina and after she'd confirmed that I was indeed pregnant, and well past the time when miscarriage usually occurs, I simply lay in the cold dormitory gazing at the ceiling. How, how could this have happened, how could I not have realised . . . My face burned with shame in the icy room. I *had* had an inkling – all that nausea and cramp, the tiredness, the strange heaviness in my limbs – but I had suppressed it, I had refused to countenance it. I was so ignorant, I hardly knew how or when it was possible to become pregnant, and somehow what Nikita and I had done together seemed unthinkable now. August was another world from January. I must have thought any trace of our affair would vanish spontaneously, just as Nikita's affection for me had vanished. Although, of course, my own love for him had, if anything, solidified and taken shape during these months of secrecy. To the happy, uncomplicated affection I had felt during August I had now added layers of self-sacrifice, devotion to him and his cause, pride in his achievements – all shot through with bitter veins of jealousy, humiliation and pain.

Almost my first thought was that this might change what Nikita felt for me. I strained my ears for the sound of his voice downstairs. Did he know yet? Had they told him? Surely he would come up to see me if he knew. Surely he would feel something for me again . . . But night wore on and no footsteps came up the stairs. Of course it would not alter his Revolutionary ideals, what a fool I was to think otherwise. He had, after all, been honest with me from the beginning – he had never claimed to feel for me other than as a friend. He was an idealist, I told myself, and I would never try to persuade him to abandon his ideals. I could not admire and love him any other way. He did not have to pretend some kind of romantic love. He only had to decide to be a father, to be with me, to love our child . . . Still no footsteps came up the stairs. I was alone, and I was no longer alone. The unassuming governess, the unselfish wonder, was now – what? A 'ruined woman', a mother-to-be. A child was only the basis for bourgeois life with two parents. How would we survive?

Towards morning I cried – a storm of sobs that no one heard. I admitted at last what I had known for months

– that Nikita Slavkin had long ago betrayed his ideal of chastity in mind and body, but not on my account.

*

When I came down to the communal sitting room, shaky and weak after my sleepless night, the others had left me a small portion of millet porridge, *blondinka*, horribly congealed. I began to reheat it, but just the smell made me retch. How ridiculous you are, I thought; for five months you've been eating this for breakfast each morning, and now you suddenly have all the affectations of a pregnant woman . . . When Slavkin comes in, I thought furiously, I shall say everything to him. I shan't stop myself. We all tiptoe round him as if he were a child that needed protecting. Well, there'll be no more of that. You can't pick someone up like a toy, and then put them back in the cupboard when you are bored with them!

Pounding on the front door; a man's voice.

If it had been Nikita at the door, would this story have ended differently? In some parallel universe, I suppose that is what happens. Slavkin enters. What do I say to him? As I write this I sit alone in my empty house, nibbling little pieces of bread that I have rolled up into balls to make one slice last all evening. I have not talked to anyone for a day or two; Sophy rang, but I couldn't bear to speak to her. I rehearse this version of events over and over again, as if to force it into being. Sometimes, in my mind, I am cold and collected, sometimes screaming, throwing things at Slavkin. He attempts to calm me,

216

I push him away. He puts his arm around my sobbing shoulders, I shrug it off. I speak, and he listens, sadly. Afterwards there are no smiles or kisses between us. He nods to signal that he has understood. Then he walks thoughtfully back to his workshop without saying good-bye.

In this universe, however, on that day in January 1919, a largish, hefty man in a leather jacket pushed open the front door. He stepped in and looked around, and it was only then that I saw Pelyagin behind him, mild but busi-nesslike. 'Ah, Comrade Freely, just the person,' he said, hurrying up to me. 'Are you . . . are you not well? Sit down, sit down. Here.' He produced a hip flask. 'Have a nip of cognac, you look faint.'

He was always so unbearably solicitous. Burying my face in the divan, I broke down in tears.

'Oh,' said Pelyagin ineffectually. 'Oh . . .' The hefty type was sniffing around the room, inspecting things. Pelyagin signalled to him to leave. Then he sat down be-side me and patted me stiffly on the back.

That was all it took. I abandoned myself to my misery and began to speak. I had only ever had kindness and assistance from Pelyagin, after all. I was sobbing, inco-herent. 'These people, they don't care for equality, they don't really believe in Communism. I am just a governess to them, to be exploited as they see fit . . .'

And when Pelyagin asked, 'Which people?' I blurted out immediately, 'Well, Nikita Slavkin, of course, and . . . and Sonya Kobelev – it's just an old-fashioned hierarchy, or more than that, feudal! He's no better than a thief, he does just what he pleases. He has used us all. And now his aim is not even to build Communism in Russia, he says it isn't possible . . .'

Was this what I said? I have spent a lifetime trying to remember my exact words. I was full of vicious cathartic joy. I didn't want to stop – I remember that. At last Pelyagin stood up. The movement brought me back to myself.

'I'm . . . I'm sorry. Why did you come? Were you looking for me?'

'Yes,' said Pelyagin after a pause. 'I was looking for you.'

'Did you want more English lessons?' I sat up and tried to tidy myself, mortified.

'No. Comrade, you have done enough for me.' He bowed slightly. 'I was passing and I realised I hadn't thanked you for teaching me. My driver here will drop off a token of my gratitude later today. Now, please forgive me . . .'

Later that day, when half a sack of wheat flour arrived at our door, I explained that it was payment for some lessons; I was a little vague about which ones. Slavkin returned in the evening and went straight into his workshop; as far as I know, he still knew nothing about my condition. I meant to go in and talk to him, but my anger had now been replaced by a deep unease, almost terror, and although I approached his door several times, I did not have the courage to knock. No one else brought up the subject, for which I was grateful. How could I have known this was my last, my only chance? Despite the cold, I slept in the dormitory again, not downstairs with the others. I lay on my mattress and closed my eyes, dreading insomnia; but for once I was asleep instantly and did not dream.

That was the night Sonya fell ill.

When I came down the next morning, only Sonya was there, lying on the divan. She did not look at me or speak in response to my greeting. Of course I assumed she was still angry with me.

'Oh, Sonya, it's no use being offended. I'll explain – if this is to be the reality, we must find a way to understand each other,' I tried to speak gently.

Sonya murmured something, I couldn't hear what. I was suddenly so angry all over again that the blood was buzzing in my ears. 'You, of all people, you've got no right to judge me! I stuck to my principles. I'm not ashamed,' I began – then stopped. Her eyes were strangely blank, her cheeks were scarlet. 'Sonya?'

She was shivering, though her hair was wet with sweat. She was running a high fever.

The room was cold. I banged on the door of the workshop and shouted. No answer. Where was Slavkin? Pasha and Marina had no doubt left for work early, as always. Sonya must have been taken ill after they'd gone. I brought her water, and helped her to drink, sip by sip; I wiped her face with a damp towel, and built up the fire, and all the while a single thought ran round and around my head. Today I must tell him.

'Has Nikita been here?' I asked her. 'Did you talk to him?'

'I don't remember,' was all she could say.

With difficulty, I removed her clothes and put them to be fumigated, dressed her as best I could in what was available. She cried; I think she was in pain. I noticed that the light was agony to her and half closed the shutters. It was this that made me fairly sure she was suffering from typhus fever. God help me, as I stood and looked down at her, moaning and shivering, I felt nothing but coldness towards her. Good old Gerty will look after the poor delicate girl, the little bird . . . Gerty with her English phlegm; Gerty, the soul of loyalty . . .

In the fading light I went out into the yard, took the axe and chopped up what remained of the joists from the barn. A son of the metalworker volunteered to fetch Pasha and Marina back from their work. I boiled water, cooked up what vegetables we had and fed Sonya broth. I was ravenous, suddenly, and aching with tiredness. I ate my portion slowly, savouring each mouthful, while at the other side of the room Sonya seemed to be slipping in and out of consciousness.

'Nikita,' she kept saying. 'Where are you?'

I have since read up on typhus fever. Every detail of Moscow at that time could have been designed to breed the disease: the lice that transmit it thrived on the hordes of soldiers pouring back from the trenches, on the dirty hungry queues everywhere, in the crowded trains. Sonya could have picked up her louse in a dozen different places – at the market, or at the printer's, when she went to collect the posters, or from any of the dirty little boys she employed to paste them up around town. Her fever was progressing fast, no doubt because she was weak and underfed. After a few days a rash would appear and the crisis would come; four out of five did not survive. Twenty years later, antibiotics would have brought the disease under control quite quickly. I did all that I could for Sonya – gave her boiled water to drink, mopped her skin to reduce the fever. Yet I'm crying now as I write this, remembering how I sat across the room from her.

'I don't know where Nikita is,' I said. 'He has more important things to see to. He has the Revolution to arrange.'

'Why doesn't he come to me?' she kept whimpering.

'Don't ask me.'

'Hold my hand, Gerty,' she said once, weakly. 'Please, don't leave me alone.'

She couldn't help looking beautiful even then, flushed and bright-eyed.

'I'd better not,' I said from the other side of the room. 'Typhus is contagious, you know.'

At last the door opened and Pasha returned and then Marina, and the decision was made to take Sonya to the Golitsyn Hospital. There she would give Sonya an antipyretic to bring down the fever; also Marina insisted that Sonya should be nursed in the isolation ward at the hospital, rather than at Gagarinsky Lane, in a household of more than thirty adults and children who would be at risk of catching the disease.

Pasha was crying openly. 'But, Marina, isn't she safer here?'

'Better there, among professionals,' Marina repeated.

Pasha was gone for an hour or more searching for transport and it was only when he had returned with a peasant and a covered cart of some sort, and we were dressing Sonya for the journey, that Slavkin appeared. He came in, very pale, he looked . . . I'm not sure what that look meant, almost as if he didn't recognise us; he seemed not to understand what was happening. He staggered a little as he entered.

'She's very ill, we must go immediately.' Marina spoke gently. 'There's the curfew – if you've got anything at all to pay for medicine, we'll take it.'

Slowly he went to his workshop and filled a box with equipment, bottles of chemicals, wire. He held it out to Pasha without a word.

'What? Oh, to pay for medicine – yes. But you can bring it yourself. Come on, we must go now . . .'

Slavkin shook his head. 'I'll be gone before you return.'

'Gone? Where to?' My voice emerged squeakily, like a little girl.

He did glance at me then – he caught my eye for a moment, and afterwards it always seemed to me that there was pity in that look. 'Tonight I must begin the experiment,' he said.

Pasha shook him by the shoulders, 'For God's sake, can't you see how ill Sonya is? What the hell are you talking about, you bastard? Why now? Where's the timetable?'

'I'll stay with you,' I tried to say to him. 'I must talk to you—'

'No!' Slavkin blurted, shrinking away from me with a look of horror, and Pasha took me by the hand and led me away from him. I was crying as we went out to the cart, stumbling over the snowdrifts. As we left the yard I turned and saw him for the last time.

He started towards us, raising his hand and mouthing something, I didn't catch what; then he changed his mind and stopped, hand still raised, a shadow against the snow as we rounded the corner.

17

In the early hours of the morning, I left the others gathered around Sonya's hospital bed and set out across the dark city to Gagarinsky Lane. It was as though I were making my way through some long-abandoned ruin. The wind had dropped; it was long past curfew, the streets were deserted and thick with new snow. The bluish, luminous snowlight was my only guide. I stumbled into hidden craters in the road and heaps of rubble, terrified I would fall and hurt the baby.

The icicles strung along roofs and balconies were too menacing to use the pavements, so I kept to the middle of the road. I had never seen such icicles as that year, huge, tubular specimens like baroque organ-pipes now that no one had the job of knocking them down. Some grew to several metres, sharpened each freezing night. Stories circulated of people injured and killed by their sudden descent. As a Communist, the thought flashed through my mind, I do my best to be rational, to make sense of the world in scientific terms. Yet one person walks down the street safely, while the next is felled by an icicle: what sense can one make of that?

God forgive me, I was not planning to give Nikita the news about Sonya's health straight away. I pushed aside the image in my mind of her thin hands plucking at the blanket as I rehearsed my first remarks: 'Nikita – now we are alone, I have something to tell you, something that concerns us both . . .'

*

As I approached the house on Gagarinsky Lane my anxiety increased. The windows were unlit.

'Nikita, are you here?'

The door of his workshop stood ajar. In the dim light it was hard to make sense of what I saw – smashed and broken equipment, a lamp leaning drunkenly. The Socialisation Capsules were gone. Their stands lay overturned in the centre of the room.

A quavering voice in the hall: '*Gospodi pomilui* – Lord have mercy '

'Anna Vladimirovna.' I hurried to her. 'You're so cold, come and sit down.'

'It's all too unpleasant.' In the study she sat and glared at me, trembling.

'What is?' I sank to my knees before her and took a deep breath. 'What happened?'

'I was looking for you, where have you been? I was frozen, I wanted that boy to light the stove, so I looked into his room. I just peeped in, I didn't mean any harm by it, but he caught sight of me and started shouting to leave him alone – he raised his voice to me! So I left, I fell in the hall and bruised myself—' She sniffed, furiously. 'I dragged myself in here and hid, and he carried on shouting. I thought he was coming to murder me! And then I heard him start up his engine, and he left . . .'

'Oh dear.' I tucked a blanket around her; my hands were shaking. '*Bednyashka*, poor dear, I'm sorry. We'll try to get warm now. I'll put the kettle on, we'll drink tea. How did you know that Slavkin had left?'

'It all went quiet and when I came out to see, he'd gone.'

'What did the engine sound like?'

'*Bozhe moi*, it just sounded normal, noisy – then it faded into the distance.' She paused for a moment and added peevishly, 'I've never liked him, such an odd boy. It wasn't very kind of you to leave me with him . . .'

I stood up. 'Let me make the tea now.'

As I stepped out into the yard to fetch water, I gazed up at the dark sky, spread dustily with stars from one horizon to the other, galaxy upon galaxy – universe upon universe. For one cloudless, happy night, I knew exactly where Nikita had gone.

*

Then the fog rolled in, a swirl of conflicting accounts that continued for decades. *Pravda* ran an article on the 23rd:

> The inventor, Nikita Gavrilovich Slavkin, was reported missing last night from the commune that he founded, known as the Institute of Revolutionary Transformation. Fellow members of the Institute have not seen him for several days and attest that the inventions he was

working on are missing from his workshop. The probability is that he, like many of the Avant-Garde, has left for the capitalist West. Slavkin has already been reprimanded for the fanciful turn that his researches have been taking; there is a distinctly pessimistic element to his theories. It would be typical of this strain of false Communism that Slavkin should abandon his duties to the Soviet motherland and leave for some dusty, nostalgia-soaked café in Berlin or Paris. We expect to hear reports soon of his posturing for the benefit of the French and German bourgeoisie.

Sonya, I am glad to say, never read this piece of official venom. Towards the end she seemed to think Nikita was with her. She fell into a coma on the 22nd, and died on 24 January in the isolation ward of the Golitsyn Hospital. So quickly – that was how typhus took you. She was buried the same day in the temporary cemetery near the hospital; Pasha hoped that once the Civil War was over, he'd be able to transfer her remains to Mikhailovka, where his grandparents and great-grandparents were buried. The whole commune was at her funeral, apart from Nikita. Vera and Volodya had heard the news from Marina, and had tracked Fyodor down at work. The day was bitterly cold and windy, we had to haggle for a coffin with a vile fellow outside the hospital, and I couldn't believe the girl that I had known and lived with for almost six years was being laid in the ground. I didn't feel like crying. I was in a breathless panic at the thought that her smile was gone, her vain little way of pouting out her lips, her breathy laughter when Pasha teased her, the look of adoration she used to turn on Nikita that enraged me – all gone. Her poor, weak pleading right at the end.

Poor Pasha was distraught. 'She should have gone abroad with Mama and Papa. I persuaded her to come back.'

All I could say to comfort him was that it was her choice. 'We shouldn't deny her that.' She was brave, I thought. She was more honest with herself than any of us.

Afterwards we all went back to Gagarinsky Lane, where Volodya produced a copy of *Pravda*. We read the piece once, twice, three times.

'So has he? Has Slavkin gone abroad?' said Volodya at last.

'No—' Both Pasha and I answered together; then he bit his lip and looked away.

'No,' I repeated. 'He would never have left us like that, without telling us.'

'Surely he wouldn't have left Sonya in hospital,' murmured Marina.

There was a silence in the room.

'Apparently there's some sort of grant they are handing out to academics in Czechoslovakia,' said Fyodor. 'Quite a few Russians are receiving it. Perhaps he's gone to save the work – we know how close he felt he was.'

'Why would he not have told us?'

'Perhaps he couldn't bear to,' said Vera softly. 'He had to save himself, and his inventions—'

'Where did he go after the lecture?' Pasha asked Fyodor. 'Do you know where your colleagues took him?'

'No. They congratulated him, said how impressed they were, which I must say surprised me because I thought his talk very confused, didn't you? But they apparently approved of it, and they said that they wanted him to work for them. And Nikita got more and more excited, you know how he did, gabbling away, and they suggested they go to the Polytechnic café to discuss it further. I left them to it.'

'They were Russian, were they?'

'Yes, Russian, normal people – *kulturniye*, cultured.' This was always Fedya's highest praise.

'They could have planned his journey this week,' put in Vera.

'They'd be hard pushed to organise it in one week,' I objected. 'It takes people a month at least to get a passport, let alone a visa.'

'He could have been thinking about it for a while.' Volodya's voice was hard. 'After all, didn't he tell you? He said he wouldn't be here when you got back.'

'But he didn't mean a journey abroad, a train journey,' I whispered.

'What did he mean then?' Fyodor, matter of fact.

'He meant . . . I thought he meant . . . Pasha, you knew more about it than me. He said something like this might happen, didn't he?'

'You mean his idea that his Capsule might transport people into another dimension? I didn't know how seriously he meant that. It was a theoretical possibility, but . . .

I said, "Nikita, are you telling me you've invented a Time Machine?" He loved that, he couldn't stop laughing about it. "That's very well said," he kept repeating. "A Time Machine." He came back to the idea a couple of times. "Of course my Time Machine is an improvement on most, because it uses so little fuel, and it's so simple to make the return journey – one merely needs to set the Capsule back to the original frequencies." "Yes, H. G. Wells would be jealous," I told him, and we laughed together . . . He was in high spirits those days before the lecture, wasn't he? I was just pleased to see him so cheerful.'

'Sonya believed it,' I said slowly. 'That's why he built two Capsules, so that they could go together. But what I don't understand, in that case, is why would he go without her?'

'Oh, for goodness' sake,' snapped Volodya, getting up. 'You people will believe anything! What, you think his machine whisked him away to a better place? With Father Christmas and the Snow Maiden? Leaving behind his girlfriend dying in hospital and, so I hear, a baby on the way. Congratulations, Miss Gerty,' he added spitefully. 'How does it feel to be in Vera's shoes? Except you're not, are you – the father seems to have run away. The sooner you realise that the only thought that man ever had was for himself, the better.'

*

I gathered up the courage to go and see Pelyagin the following day. Surely, I kept thinking, if Nikita had simply been arrested, we would have been informed by now – his name would have appeared in the papers. But my last conversation with Pelyagin was all I could think of. Had Slavkin's disappearance anything to do with my tirade? I was not sleeping. Adrenalin fizzed and popped horribly in my veins. It was all I could do not to blurt out my fears twenty times a day. But I kept them to myself.

'Comrade, I'm afraid . . .' Rosa Gershtein half rose from her desk at the sight of me as if to bar my path, but Pelyagin had already looked up.

'Comrade Pelyagin,' I called past her. 'Please, may I come in?'

He looked a little annoyed. 'Comrade, I thought we understood each other. I don't need any more lessons, thank you. I hope you received my gift?'

'Yes, of course, I quite understand. Your English has already made such progress I don't believe I had a great deal more to teach you!' My laugh came out as a hideous, artificial sort of trill.

He considered me, and turned back to his papers. I flushed deep red. What I had said and done the last time we met was obviously as distasteful for him to recall as it was for me, and he wanted nothing more to do with me. But still I had to know – what exactly had he understood by it?

'I've come on another matter, comrade. You have perhaps heard that since we last spoke, our friend Nikita Slavkin has gone missing. We've heard no word from him now for over a week.'

'I really don't have time,' he said, not looking up.

231

'Please—' As a gift I had brought him a copy of Dickens's *Dombey and Son*; this I now thrust towards him clumsily. 'I beg you. You helped us before, and we were so grateful. I came here to try to thank you in person then, but was sent away.' I sat in front of his desk and looked him straight in the eye. 'I know you quite well from our lessons, comrade. You are an honest person, a man of integrity. Last time we met I was not myself, and you kindly offered me comfort. Now, I beg you, tell me – have the Cheka had any dealings with Slavkin? The things I said – you didn't misinterpret them, did you, for I never meant . . .'

'Goodness me, that's enough!' broke in Pelyagin, jumping up and walking over to the window. 'What's all this about? What makes you think I'd have the least interest in what you say about Slavkin? You must have realised that his type doesn't appeal to me, these weird avant-garde sorts with all sorts of wild ideas—' There was a pause, and he spoke simply. 'Comrade Freely, I hope I would always try to assist you in any way that I could. But in this case, I'm sorry to say, I can't help. As it happens, for your sake I have made my own enquiries. If I had discovered anything I would have come to you myself. But I heard nothing.'

'So the Cheka . . .'

'He's not being held by the Cheka, that I can assure you.'

I leaned forward, wanting to shake his hand; I was so grateful for this effort on his part. 'Oh, thank you!'

He gaped at me then with a new expression,

something close to revulsion. I stepped back. 'Forgive me.'

'That's all I have to tell you on the matter.' Pelyagin sat back down at his desk. 'Goodbye.'

As I hurried home, full of relief and hope, a glimpse of myself in a shop window stopped me in my tracks. The wind blew my wrapper against my body and I suddenly realised the cause of Pelaygin's repelled look. My pregnancy was clearly visible. My poor little one, what a reaction to provoke.

*

In February the frost dipped down to minus 27 and then kept falling, into the thirties. The house on Gagarinsky Lane, which had been crumbling long before the Revolution, now began to crack up in earnest. In the early part of the winter we burnt the beams and doors from the stables. Now we moved on to the panelling, the shutters and even the floorboards in some rooms. Chunks of plaster fell from the walls, revealing the brickwork underneath.

After Sonya's death Marina moved into accommodation for doctors near Chistiye Prudi. She was distraught, blamed herself for insisting on taking Sonya to hospital. Anna Vladimirovna also moved out to live with Vera and Volodya; she had developed a fear of the Kobelevs' house, her home for so many years, ever since the night Slavkin disappeared. 'I can't be expected to live here now that strange one has ruined it — now he's driven everyone away.'

Only Pasha and I were left of the members of the IRT. When Nikita returned, I wanted to be there to meet him.

My pregnancy began to slow me down. I was out of breath after the slightest exertion; I was worn out, and yet could not sleep for more than a few hours at a time. Just recently I had felt my baby move inside me for the first time — usually such a cause for joy for prospective mothers. Instead I was terrified. I willed away the time with work, a medical translation job that Marina had found for me.

The hope I'd felt on leaving Pelyagin's office had not entirely faded. The longer we didn't hear from Slavkin, the more certain I was that he hadn't gone abroad. We had made enquiries of everyone we knew, but there was no breath of a rumour that he was in Europe. Anna Vladimirovna still insisted that he and his machine had left together — 'Just like that! The engine started up, and . . . poof!' Pasha and I moved into Slavkin's workshop, giving up the other rooms in the house to new inhabitants. I insisted on keeping the stands for the Capsules exactly where they had been, not moving them by so much as an inch.

Then a colleague of Pasha's, on the condition of strict secrecy, showed him a confidential publication by the Department of Mobilisation of Sciences, a division of Narkompros, dated 18 February 1919, that listed current research by Soviet scientists in government facilities. Among the list, the following phrase appeared: 'N. G.

Slavkin, study into Transformational Science'. In the column that listed the research faculty, there was only a line of stars. What could this mean? Could it simply be a typing error – some tired secretary copying out last year's list without checking? In which case, surely his area of study would have been 'Possible Applications of Iridium Alloys'? And what of the line of stars?

Everyone had heard rumours of secret State-run institutions where Soviet scientists were creating astonishing new technologies. This was the first sign either of us had come across that they might exist. Pasha and I went immediately to Lunacharsky. He had been supportive of Slavkin's research, even if he had dismissed the Propaganda Machine. Waiting outside his office, I felt almost faint, suddenly, with relief. Surely at last we were to hear the truth.

'Come in, come in!' Lunacharsky stood to greet us, shook both our hands warmly. He read the list slowly. 'I rather think you need not worry,' he said at last.

'Not worry? Why's that? Is he working in a government laboratory?'

He said nothing, simply looking at us both kindly. 'I am not at liberty to tell you,' he murmured at last. 'We are at war; certain freedoms are not available to us as they would be during peacetime. Can you, foot soldiers, simply accept what I, your commanding officer, tell you? Slavkin is putting his talents to work for the future of our country. That is all you can know.'

Darkness had fallen by the time we emerged onto Ostozhenka Street. By the door we gathered up two or three sharp stones and set off towards home. If the dogs got too close we threw them, not very accurately, but as hard as we could. On one occasion there was a sharp crack and an anguished yelping retreat. Hurrying, breathless, keeping to the shadows, I found myself grinning like a madwoman in the dark.

He hadn't abandoned us. It was just that they wanted Slavkin to pursue his experiments in peace and quiet. I still had to talk to him, of course; for the baby's sake, I would not be warned off, however hard Lunacharsky tried. But at least I didn't need to worry about his safety.

18

On 14 March, the *Moskovsky Komsomolets* – a new paper for Party youth – ran with a simple banner headline: 'The Vanishing Futurist!' Slavkin had been awarded the title he would bear for the next fifty years. The piece began: 'Scientist who claims to be creating the New Soviet Man disappears ... is this the result of his Ground-Breaking Discoveries?' *Pravda* picked up the story as well: 'We have to transform ourselves, claims Slavkin. Has the brilliant inventor made the greatest sacrifice for the Revolution?' The majority of both articles could have come from his last lecture; some sentences were quoted word for word. Yet there were a couple of details in the *Pravda* article – for example, I remember that the Capsule was described as 'darkish silver, coated with iridium alloy' and 'about seven foot long' – which seemed to suggest either that the author had seen it himself, or that Slavkin had described it to him.

Pasha and I together identified four main possibilities:

1) Slavkin, as a result of his experiments, had disappeared from Gargarinsky Lane on 19 January with the knowledge of the authorities; they had therefore registered him as working in a secret location for Soviet science. (This tallied with Anna Vladimirovna's account.)

2) Slavkin had moved to the secret laboratory on the night of the 19th and had disappeared, as a result of his experiments, from within the secret laboratory.

3) Slavkin was still working in the secret laboratory and the Party was keen, for some reason, to promote the mystery of his disappearance.

4) Slavkin was somewhere else entirely, perhaps without the knowledge of the authorities, and again they were simply promoting the mystery of his disappearance.

A young man came to interview us for a newspaper article about the IRT. I began to describe to him our programme. After a few minutes he stopped me, frowning. 'He sounds like an avant-gardist!'

'Well, yes, I suppose he is.'

'Hmm.'

Into his uncertain pause I inserted a question of my own. 'May I ask, why the sudden fascination with Slavkin? Who had the idea for this article, for example?'

'Well.' He looked confused. 'Why the fascination? I should think that would be obvious. He's vanished, hasn't he? He's given his life to the cause of Soviet science – he deserves to be celebrated!'

'But we don't know he's given his life. We don't know if he is dead or alive, or anything about where he is or what he is doing . . .'

'I think you'll find there are people who know exactly what he is doing, and that's where the orders are coming from.' He smiled at me a little condescendingly. 'Perhaps because you're a foreigner, you find it hard to understand his action. But trust me, for a Soviet citizen there could be no more glorious fate.'

That evening Pasha and I quarrelled. Lunacharsky had made it clear that we should cease all our efforts to find Slavkin, and Pasha was concerned that we might make things difficult for him if we disobeyed. But I was now almost seven months pregnant and his words of caution meant nothing to me. 'I have to see him, Pasha, just once, do you see? If only I'd known in that last week; if only I'd talked to him then – but think of this poor child. When he or she grows up, at the very least I'd like to be able to say that his father knew of his existence and was glad.'

Pasha went very pale. 'Don't cry, Gerty. I can't bear it if you cry. I have thought of something ... just a faint possibility, it might lead to nothing. Look, the list of research projects.' He hurried to find it. 'Look at these other names: Beloborodov, do you see, Yu. M. – isn't that Miss Clegg's old employer? Or is it his brother? He also seems to have been working in a secret facility until February, he has a line of stars by his name. I wondered if it was worth going to see them – he would know something about the system, wouldn't he?'

*

There was no answer to my knock on the door of Miss Clegg's apartment, but to my surprise, it opened to a gentle push.

'Miss Clegg? Are you at home? Please forgive the intrusion—'

A voice came from the sitting room. 'Enter!'

The room was dark and painfully cold. I found Miss Clegg sitting up in her bed, dressed in an overcoat and hat. She turned her head as I entered and seemed to be searching for me in the gloom.

'Here I am, Miss Clegg, it's Gertrude Freely, do you remember me?' I said gently.

'Of course I remember you, Gerty,' she said. 'I haven't lost my wits. But my eyesight, I'm afraid, is not what it was.'

Coming up close to her I was shocked, not by her thinness – everyone was thin – or even her filmy eyes, but by the fusty, neglected smell of her room, the stains down her overcoat and her long, dirty nails, so unlike Miss Clegg. She looked in my direction and I couldn't help a flash of uncharitable gladness at her affliction; if she could have seen my stomach, she would no doubt have had a great deal to say about it.

'Well, Gerty, are you still living in that madhouse? You've ruined your reputation, you know, no good family will touch you now.'

I paused for a moment, then offered her the small parcel of bread I had brought for her. 'I'm afraid this is all I had.'

'I'm no charity case, you know,' she snapped, but she reached into the bag immediately and began to eat, trying to hide her mouth with her hands. I looked away, moved almost to tears. 'I'm still teaching, I receive my pupils like this too.' She suddenly cackled. 'Imagine that! I sit up in bed and my young men come and sit on the other end! That wouldn't have done in the old days, would it?'

I laughed too. 'No, our manners are very simple these days.'

'Light me a fire, would you? There's a few sticks of wood in that corner. I manage very well on my own, always have done, but if you're here . . .'

Of course she'd been alone before the war too, in the days when I found her so infuriating, with her half-martyred, half-condescending air. She'd been surviving on her inexhaustible willpower even then.

'Miss Clegg, I've come to ask you for your help,' I said as I tried to get the fire going. 'I'm searching for a friend of mine who's disappeared. I wondered if you were still in contact with the Beloborodov family? I think they may know something.'

'Gracious me, you plan to bother them about it, do you?' Her voice drifted off. 'The Beloborodovs are still living in their old home on Vozdvizhenka. They have suffered at the hands of the Bolsheviks, and they're surrounded by informers, of course, so be careful how you speak to them.'

'What were the names and patronymics of your employer, Miss Clegg, I can't remember? And what was his specialisation – was he a scientist, like his cousin?'

'Elizaveta Igorevna and Yuri Maksimovich. He was trained as an engineer, it was thought that the training would come in useful when he took over the family business – railways, as you remember. Now the poor man is a wreck. He was in prison for several months – it almost killed him.'

'I'm so sorry.'

'How they are surviving now, I cannot imagine,' went on Miss Clegg. 'Elizaveta Igorevna was such an impractical woman. She could hardly dress herself, and she had certainly never brushed her own hair. Send them my regards. They don't visit me any more. No doubt they are too busy, but if they had the time . . .'

Once the fire was lit I left Miss Clegg, promising to do my best to come and see her soon. I wondered if I would find her alive at my next visit.

Down Vozdvizhenka one had to negotiate great heaps of filthy slush and rubbish. It was getting late, yet I was so close to the Beloborodovs', I could not resist visiting, even if only for a few minutes. My mind was full of that snowy day in November 1917 when we had taken refuge in their apartment from the sight of a dead man on the street. Now the door swung open on a hallway like a railway station, humming with the activities of the fifteen or so families crammed into the Beloborodovs' spacious rooms. A large woman in a soldier's jacket wanted to know my business there.

'Comrade Beloborodov? What do you want with him?'

I hesitated. 'It's his wife I'm looking for,' I said quietly, hoping she wouldn't query my accent.

'His wife, eh?' she nodded towards the right door. 'She's quite the good-time girl these days' – she winked coarsely – 'but he doesn't have much to say.'

'He's at home, is he?'

'Oh yes, he's always at home. Doesn't go out at all these days.'

I found Madame Beloborodov, her husband, and three young children living in two small rooms. The children looked fed, and fairly well dressed. She was very thin and her beautiful hair had gone completely white. Superficially, her husband was little changed since before the Revolution, yet there was something odd in the way that he gazed at me so blankly. Before I could say a word, Madame Beloborodov hushed me fiercely, took out a coffee grinder and began to grind beechnuts. The children watched her.

'Miss Clegg sent me to you, she'd so like it if you had time to visit her. I'm afraid she is almost blind now, and very weak,' I began. 'Please, forgive me for coming to see you,' I murmured hurriedly under cover of the crunching of the grinder. 'I am trying to find out the whereabouts of our friend, Nikita Slavkin — you remember — he was involved with the sale of the Svyatinsky's minerals.'

Monsieur Beloborodov did not respond; he was gazing at the dark window panes as though he was hardly aware of what was going on around him, but Madame fixed me with an icy look. I felt myself flush — why should these people help Slavkin? — and gabbled on.

'He has disappeared, Madame; perhaps you have seen it reported in the papers. Please, forgive me for raising his name with you. I understand that you do not feel any warmth towards him. But we have been led to believe he may be working in a secret laboratory run by the

Ispolkom, and perhaps – it's a long shot, I know – your husband may have been working in the same, or a similar establishment. I wonder, would Monsieur Beloborodov agree to talk to me?'

She almost spat. 'My husband does not talk about such matters.'

I turned to her husband. 'Please, I – I am Slavkin's wife,' I found myself saying. 'I beg you to take pity on me . . .'

She pushed past me and said nothing. Heavily, I turned to leave. 'Forgive me for disturbing you – it was ridiculous of me to think—'

'Who told you I was working at a secret laboratory?'

My eyes snapped towards Beloborodov's. It was his low, amused tone, so at odds with his earlier manner, that was so unexpected. I smiled at him involuntarily. His wife seized the coffee grinder and began to turn furiously.

'We were shown a list of current research projects and your name was there, as was Slavkin's. But next to each of your names, instead of an institute or a university department, there was only a line of stars,' I murmured. 'Lunacharsky hinted to us that Slavkin was working on some kind of secret research organised by the State, so I thought perhaps you were too.'

He nodded slowly. 'Yes, I think that's right, he is working in a scientific establishment. I, on the other hand, only got as far as the Cheka prison at the Lubyanka. But I did come across your friend there.'

'At the prison?' Involuntarily my voice had risen.

Madame hushed me sharply.

'Yes – Nikita Gavrilovich Slavkin, that's right, isn't it? He was only there for a night or two, I believe. I never saw him, just heard him talked of. Of course I remembered him.' He grimaced. 'Then they took him to some kind of a laboratory. I never heard of anyone else going there.'

I was so shocked to hear he had been in prison, I could hardly get my words out. 'D-Did they say anything more?'

He leaned forward and whispered in my ear. 'Lab 37, they called it. Don't ask me anything more – that's all I know. *Laboratoria* 37.'

One of his children began to cry. He glanced at the boy and back at me. Then he shook his head. 'Well, good luck,' he said in a normal voice. From outside their door came unashamed scuffling noises and creaking of floorboards. 'Thank you for telling us about Miss Clegg. We'll do what we can for her.'

'Thank you—'

'Our pleasure,' snapped Madame Beloborodov, without looking at me.

Distracted, I turned the wrong way out of the courtyard. I was exhausted and chilled, my boots were soaking, and I soon realised I had no idea how to find my way out of this maze of unlit alleyways. I couldn't make sense of the idea that Slavkin had been held by the Cheka, even if only for a few days. With a rising sense of panic I wandered until I finally came out on the bank of the river. I was near Narkompros, I realised, and had to take a deep breath for a moment to calm myself. When I arrived at his office, Pasha took one look at me, frowned and broke off from the report he was writing.

'Sit down.'

'No — I mean, I am tired, but would you mind if we went straight home?'

'Wouldn't you like to rest?'

'No . . . Please . . .'

Outside in the silent streets I told him what Monsieur Beloborodov had said. Pasha nodded, holding my arm against his, and was quiet for a long time. The temperature had risen and it began to snow in the darkness. Soft, unhurried cascades of snow fell all around us, obscuring the whole world except for the few feet immediately before us. Large flakes melted on my padded coat, now frayed and threadbare. I regretted the loss of its cosy astrakhan collar — too bourgeois to wear safely in the street, so I had bartered it, like everything. All was gone, scattered, broken. Again tears were prickling at my eyes, and I wiped them away furiously. I turned, and caught Pasha looking at me, such a sad expression on his face.

'Much though it pains me to say it,' he murmured, hesitating, 'I think the time has come for you to go home.'

'What? Go home, now? Are you mad? I can't go anywhere until we've found him. You see, I talked to Pelyagin. I'm — I'm terrified I said something that might have harmed Nikita . . .'

I suppose that was the closest I ever came to a confession, until I began to write this.

Pasha dismissed it. 'Yes, yes, but where do you intend to look now? You think your Cheka friend will show you the way to Lab 37? This isn't nice tidy England, you know. There aren't necessarily answers to questions in Russia.'

'You're giving up!' I stopped in the middle of the road and turned to face him. 'You're surrendering! I can't believe it!' I was so enraged that I took him by the arms and shook him, shouting in his face. 'Pasha, you can't give up!'

'I'm not.' He spoke very quietly. 'But this isn't your quarrel. It isn't your fate. Why sacrifice yourself for no reason? You have a baby to think of now. You should go back to England and raise your child in peace.'

I gazed at him. How he had changed. I remembered him in the garden at Gagarinsky Lane reading Khlebnikov – 'O laugh it out, you laughsters!' So light, he was then, like a beacon, warming us all.

'And what about you?'

'I'll carry on. I'll work for the Revolution. I suppose I'll –' he gave me a twisted smile – 'I'll find someone else to love.'

'What?'

I was aware suddenly that he was trembling. We stopped in the cart-tracks and the warm, wet snow fell on us both. It highlighted every fold in Pasha's coat, his hat, his eyebrows.

'What . . . what do you mean?'

'*Milaya moya*, don't tell me you didn't know . . . I love you. I've always loved you. I fell in love with you from the

247

moment you arrived in our house – you gave me a look, a sort of considering look, and you laughed, and I'd never heard a woman laugh like that before. I've been trying to make you laugh ever since.'

I felt rather than heard him say it – a physical jolt, as though all the cells in my body were realigning themselves. I opened my mouth and only a stammer emerged.

'I know what you feel for Slavkin,' he went on. 'I'm not a fool. When we returned from the south and I saw how you glanced at him, I could have slit my throat. How many times have I wished I didn't go with my parents? I've seen you suffer from his treatment of you. I've suffered with you. When I heard about the child, I felt so angry – so furious with him. Then I tried to put my ego aside and think only of you and the child. I've done my best to look after you both – but now I beg you, go back to England. There's been so much unnecessary death already. You're a foreigner here, and these people hate foreigners. Please, Gerty, do it for me.'

'Pasha—' I reached forward, unthinking, and touched his cheek. He caught my hand and suddenly we were kissing in the middle of the street, and I was crying, and so was he. All alone in the darkness, with a curtain of huge dirty snowflakes to shield us, we kissed each other. And it was as though a great river had overflowed inside me and I was carried along on the surge and suddenly all the struggle, all the hard, dry slog of life dissolved and it was easy, and warm, and irresistible.

19

I woke in the night, as though someone had tapped me on the shoulder. Pasha lay on his pallet beside me. A sentence was running through my mind. 'He's not being held by the Cheka.' I knew what to do. I thought it through again, trying to fix it in my mind. Then I slept.

At six in the morning I got up and packed a small bundle. I took the last few coins from underneath the floorboard in the corner – the remains of the valuables that in the summer of 1918 Sonya and I had sewn into the hem of her coat. I removed a stone from the back of the fireplace and took out the Mauser that Monsieur Kobelev had left in my care. Dubiously, I blew the dust off it. I had no idea how to fire it, or even if it was loaded, but it hardly mattered.

'Busy?'

I jumped. 'Lord, Pasha, don't frighten me like that! Not when I'm holding this thing!'

'Yes, what the hell are you doing with it, may I ask?'

'I've thought of something. I mean, I've remembered something that I think might help Nikita. Meet me in a couple of hours in front of the National—'

But Pasha grabbed my arm. 'No. I'm coming with you now.' He was already pulling on his coat and boots. 'How dare you try to leave me here, you bloody . . . Galliffet.'

Despite myself I laughed and he smiled slightly.

'What is your plan then?'

'You don't have to come in the building with me – there's no need for both of us to be implicated. Wait outside, I'll need you when I get out. I'm going to see Pelyagin. Just show me how to use this thing, would you?'

'Don't be ridiculous! What good will a gun do you? If you fire it, they'll arrest you immediately. And even if you don't, you'll be searched at the door of the National and that's the end of you as well as any chance of saving Nikita.'

I grimaced at him and put it back. 'I suppose you're right. It was just to give me courage. I'll tell you the plan as we walk, shall I? On one condition – you promise not to try to stop me.'

I explained as we trudged through the deep snow towards the centre. Every few moments I had to stop and catch my breath. The moment I stopped, the baby began to turn inside me. Be calm, I willed it. This is for you.

The first pinkish tinge of dawn was in the sky by the time we reached the National. Pasha took both my hands and gave me a serious look. I knew what it meant. We could still turn around and go on with our lives. 'Are you sure?' he whispered.

I leant my forehead against his for a long moment. 'I'm sure.'

'So – I'll wait for you here. I'll do what I can about transport. If you don't appear within an hour, I'm coming in to find you.'

Sweat was running down the back of my neck as I approached the main entrance. I had no pass to get me into the building. The baby kicked me sharply, so hard I saw the bulge through my coat.

'Pass,' said the guard. 'Oh, it's you.'

I smiled at him. 'Yes, just me – here to see Pelyagin as usual. I brought you something to thank you for clearing up after me that other time.' I pushed a lump of barley sugar that I had miraculously discovered at the back of the cupboard into his hands. The boy's eyes lit up.

'Wait.' He stopped me suddenly. 'He told me you weren't giving him lessons any more.'

'Oh – er, yes. But unfortunately he still has to pay me. These high-ups, you know, they forget we all have to live.' I took a step past him.

He grinned. 'Too right.'

I was across the hall before he could change his mind. Out of his sight, I climbed the stairs slowly to the third floor. What if my supposition was wrong, and Pelyagin simply didn't know? There was no turning back now. I stopped for a moment to regain my breath, and slipped into his office. Rosa Gershtein, just arrived at work, was unwinding her scarf.

'Rosa,' I said hurriedly and in an undertone. 'Please forgive me, but you must leave us alone now. Go, and do not come back until this afternoon. I don't want to put you in any danger. And I must warn you, if you alert the guards I shall have to tell Pelyagin your real identity.'

'Wha—' She looked at me in horror.

'Go now, don't make a sound. I'll tell Pelyagin you'll be back at four o'clock. Not before, do you understand?'

She nodded, then took her hat and left. I glimpsed

Pelyagin's black shiny head bent over his desk in the next room.

'Rosa!' he called without looking up.

'Rosa has been called away,' I said as I entered. 'Good morning, Comrade Pelyagin.'

He half rose from his chair as if to bar me from the room. 'I've nothing to say to you.'

'But if you don't mind, I have something to say to you.' I took a deep breath and tried to speak calmly. 'You should know that I am a spy for the British government and you have been passing information to me about the activities of the Bolsheviks for six months.'

His expression was almost comical. 'You're a spy?'

'Am I or not? I know what I would believe if I was the guard in the entrance hall downstairs. Please sit down.'

He fell into his chair, staring fixedly at me. 'What do you want?'

'Where is Nikita Slavkin?'

Pelyagin's face worked. 'I don't know, I swear to you – I don't know.'

'But you did know where he was taken, didn't you? Last time I saw you, you told me as much. "The Cheka aren't holding him," you said. It took me all this time to realise you meant "They aren't holding him *now*."'

He said nothing, looking at me coldly. Was I right? Or was he weighing up what I might do, what his best option was? Backing away from him, I opened the door into the corridor and called, 'Comrade?'

Pelyagin jumped up. 'What are you doing?'

'You seem unconvinced. So I'm calling the guard up

from the hall to tell him about our lessons. All the information I've gathered from your office. All right?'

'No!' He was ashen. 'Wait—'

The young guard was coming up the stairs. 'Did you need me?'

I raised my eyebrows at Pelyagin. 'Do we?'

'No, no – I'll tell you what I know. For God's sake—'

'Oh, I'm sorry to bother you, comrade. We don't need you after all. Thank you so much.'

'Oh,' said the guard, a little disconcerted. 'All right then.' His footsteps turned and receded down the stairs again.

'You'd better be quick,' I said to Pelyagin. 'If I have to keep calling him up and down the stairs he'll be in an even worse mood to hear what I've got to say.'

He swallowed. 'All right. I don't know much – only that our boys arrested him that night. He knew they were coming. They'd been questioning him that day, then they let him go, idiots. They were sent more or less straight back to pick him up. He was taken first to the Lubyanka. But after a few days they transferred him. He went to a special place, a laboratory . . .'

'Lab 37.'

Pelyagin looked amazed. 'You knew?'

'Where is it?'

'It's . . .' He gulped. 'It's in the Church of the Ascension at Kolomenskoye.'

'How do you know all this?'

'I – I—'

'You put together a case against him, didn't you?' I

said slowly. Hatred boiled in me. 'You said – let me think – that his experiments were counter-Revolutionary? That he was plotting against the State? Why?' With my huge belly, standing before him, I suddenly felt my rage was invincible. '*Why?* Was it because he humiliated you, that time at the Futurist performance? Or was it because you were offended I didn't want to go out for a drive with you?'

Pelyagin frowned. 'No,' he said.

'Yes, it was, it was some little pettiness like that, wasn't it?'

He looked at me oddly. 'No, that wasn't it,' he said quietly. He sat up. 'Of course his line about "Communism can't exist in this version of the universe" was enough to get him thrown into jail alone. But have you forgotten that you denounced him yourself?'

Ice down my spine. 'I told you – I said I was mistaken, don't take it seriously, I said.'

'It was too late by then. Why did you think I came to the house that day? I had the warrant in my pocket.' He had recovered his sangfroid. 'By then you'd all denounced him, one after the other. We could have arrested him ten times over. Marina Getler spoke to an agent of ours at the hospital; Volodya Yakov shopped him to the Cheka; Fyodor Kuzmin came to us not long afterwards to tell us that Slavkin was making anti-Soviet statements; it seems as though it was one of the few things that commune of yours managed to agree on—'

'*Stop.*'

Pelyagin stopped with his mouth still open.

I began to improvise. 'How many hours have I spent here, in this room? You've left me here on my own several times, do you remember? When I fell asleep, for example? A spy doesn't fall asleep like that. I've got so much good information from you, Pelyagin. The British Foreign Office are very happy with you.'

'What information?'

'Numbers in Cheka prisons, methods of interrogation, conditions in prisons, arbitrary arrests ... It'll cause quite a scandal, you know.'

He sat down. 'What do you want?'

'I just ... I just want you to leave me alone. All right? I'll leave now, and you won't send anyone after me. You won't mention this conversation to anyone, you'll forget it entirely. Otherwise you'll soon be at the mercy of those Cheka officers of yours.'

He stared at me for a moment, and then he nodded. 'All right.'

'I'll need your ID card, and those spectacles, too.'

He gave them to me reluctantly.

'Just one last thing. When you first asked me to come and give you lessons, was Slavkin already under investigation?'

He smirked. 'You were a useful source from our first lesson.'

I slipped out of his office and down the back staircase. I could barely feel my feet on the floor. With shaking hands I pulled my shawl over my head and walked the long way around the building to the Aleksandrovsky Gardens.

20

'Here, *dyevushka* – girl, over here!'

From the other side of the gardens a gnomish figure was gesturing to me. Behind him stood a cart pulled by an ancient donkey. As I drew closer I saw Pasha in the back.

'Where to, then?' sang out the old fellow.

'Where to? My God, Pasha, what on earth are you doing?' I hissed. 'We need to get to Kolomenskoye! Dobbins here won't get there before nightfall!'

I calculated that Kolomenskoye was eight or nine miles from the centre of Moscow. At a walk that would take us three hours . . .

'Kolomenskoye? *Chort vosmi*, I thought we wouldn't be going so far . . . but this is all there is, and the old man tells me she trots. She might do it in a couple of hours.' Pasha pulled me in. '*Poekhali, golubchik!* Let's go, whip her up, as fast as she can go!'

'We might not have a couple of hours!' I snapped at him, but he fastened up the back of the cart and we set off, the old man whispering a commentary to the donkey. 'Yes-s-s, that's a good leg, and the other one's good, and that back one, pick it up nice and smart, yes, my beauty! Oh, you're a fine old lady, twenty years and you trot like a schoolgirl . . .'

The tension twisted my insides as I watched the

National slowly, slowly dwindling behind us.

'Perhaps we'll be able to catch a lift on a lorry if we see one,' murmured Pasha. 'And we're resting here. If we have to get out and run, we'll be faster than if we'd already walked five miles.'

We were at least inconspicuous on the cart. Huddled down and covered with a blanket, it looked as though the old fellow was simply returning home with an empty load.

In whispers under the blanket I told Pasha all of it – almost all of it, all that I could bear. At the end he was silent for a moment.

'Don't think you are going into the church alone,' he remarked.

'No, I need you with me. You're going to use Pelyagin's papers.'

'What, me, impersonate that evil slug?'

'Don't be so vain.'

Pasha laughed and fell quiet again. 'So Nikita had spent a day being interrogated when we saw him.'

'Yes.'

'He wanted us all to go to the hospital with Sonya, didn't he?'

'I think he did. He wanted to be alone when they came. That's why he shouted at Anna Vladimirovna, and maybe why he didn't want me to stay behind.'

'They would have arrested all of us, I presume. Why didn't they come back for us?'

'Perhaps we'll find out now.'

The last time we had seen him was over two months

ago – when Sonya was still alive, when the IRT still existed. I had thought about him every hour, every minute since, obsessively going over the possible reasons for his disappearance. Every other feeling, I realised, had been pushed aside in order to concentrate on my hunt for Slavkin. With a grimace I remembered poor Sonya crying helplessly in the hospital, her thin, pale hands plucking at the blanket. 'Where is he, where is he?' Even while she was dying I burned with jealousy. Pasha was sobbing, trying to make her drink water, until Marina stopped him gently. 'It's no use, Pasha, the little bird has flown away.'

I had watched it all as if from a distance, and slipped away to find him. I had been determined to be the one to tell him she was so ill. I had wanted to see his pain, and then, no doubt, to comfort him myself, the loyal Gerty who can always be counted on, strong, capable – so different from the flighty little bird. Who needs a little bird in a Revolution!

And yet Nikita had loved her, despite himself – despite our ridiculous insistence that love was no longer relevant. What fools we had been. At least he and Sonya had found a few moments of happiness together – the night they walked together, the days and nights they spent in his workshop, while Pasha had watched me twisting and torturing myself with Revolutionary ideals.

And now, what of Pasha and me? Last night we had comforted each other. I had felt something astonishing, a sense of basking in another's warmth that I had no memory of ever feeling before. Yet what did it really mean? Slavkin had carved himself into my heart so power-fully. The habit of placing him first in all my thoughts was deeply engrained. But I couldn't tell whether it was love – or some kind of bitter longing for suffering, a poisonous egotism masquerading as devotion.

*

I tried to eat after writing this last chapter, but I couldn't keep it down; every mouthful seems to smell like *blondinka*. Even a whole slice of bread is too much for me now. I've been welcoming in my hunger for so long that now I seem to have forgotten how to swallow. I'm a little dizzy when I stand, but if I sit and keep writing, I feel fine. Sophy rang, but I couldn't speak to her. She'll read this soon enough, and then . . . then we'll see what she wants. Whether she's willing to talk to me then.

*

At midday we finally trotted up to the Gate of the Saviour at Kolomenskoye. Pasha and I clambered out of the cart, aching and chilled, and blinked in astonishment. Since the morning the sky had cleared. The Church of the Ascension stood out, white as a swan against a cobalt-blue sky, on a high bank of the Moscow river. Behind it the snowy Russian countryside glittered and perfectly still columns of feathery smoke rose here and there.

The old man seemed agitated, and took our payment

without demur. 'Got to get my girl home,' he muttered. 'No good waiting around here.' And he whipped up the old donkey and disappeared.

Neither of us particularly looked the part, but Pelyagin's photograph was over-exposed and printed on poor paper – all that could really be made out was a man with a moustache and spectacles. Pasha put on Pelyagin's glasses and grinned at me.

'You see, the moustache turns out to be necessary after all.'

I laughed shakily.

'*Nu shto*. Are you ready?'

I took a breath of the sharp, clean air, leant forward and kissed him. 'Ready.'

We made our way to the main door of the church.

'Open up, comrades!' called Pasha.

A long pause. In the distance we could hear footsteps.

'Open up!'

A young man, dishevelled and pale, looked out. 'Forgive me, comrades, I was just . . . Oh,' he looked at us in surprise, 'I thought you were . . .'

'You've kept us waiting,' snapped Pasha, stepping inside. 'Commissar Emil Pelyagin, from the Moscow Special Commission. Where is your commander?'

'Oh, yes, well – he's out, Comrade Commissar, he's on a mission. They went during the night and they're not back yet—'

'Didn't you get my telegram?'

'T-telegram?'

'I sent a telegram to say I would be coming this morning to inspect your set-up. I have heard poor reports of this outfit.'

'Yes, no, comrade . . . They won't be long. Perhaps the Comrade Commissar would like to drink a cup of tea?' The poor fellow was shaking with fear.

'Drink a cup of tea!' bellowed Pasha. 'I don't have time to sit about and drink tea like a debutante! You'd better show us around. Come on.'

'Yes, certainly.' He led us into the aisle of the church, which was being used as a barracks. Shafts of red, blue and golden light, spinning with dust, fell on filthy piles of rags, broken bottles and ground-out *papirosy*. A girl was sleeping in a corner, bare feet sticking out from a blanket. 'We use this as the mess room—'

'Express yourself properly!' barked Pasha. 'Who's "we"?'

'First patrol, fifth division, South-East Moscow Region, Comrade Commissar!' he shot back sharply, drawing himself up.

'That's better. You live like pigs, comrade. We need discipline to win this war.'

This was not what we were expecting. It was an ordinary Red Army post. I noticed the door to the vestry and moved towards it.

'What's through that door?'

'Right away, Comrade Commissar . . . we have an office here . . . and a storeroom.' He showed us through the empty rooms. 'We keep ammunition in here—'

'We were informed that there was a laboratory on the premises,' said Pasha.

'A laboratory? Well—'

A thin, high sound echoed suddenly through the walls. Pasha turned silently to the young man, his eyebrows raised.

'Yes, sir, comrade, I was just going to take you,' he stammered. 'Through here, in the back courtyard – I have no authority, but of course you do—'

He unlocked a small door at the back of the vestry and led us out into the courtyard and a huddle of wooden sheds. We heard it again, more animal than mechanical. My stomach turned over. We crossed the snowy courtyard while the young soldier said over his shoulder. 'They can't control them, that's the problem, Comrade Commissar.' He pushed open the door and yelled, 'Serafima! The Special Commission are here!' He turned to us again and said, bizarrely I thought, 'They should really just settle their accounts, there's no place for them in our Revolution.'

He fell quiet when a tall figure appeared, dressed in black. Her face gave me a jolt – the ancient shrunken look of a woman decades older than her upright posture suggested. After a moment she nodded slightly. 'Yes, comrades? How may I assist you?'

I had the uneasy feeling that she had seen straight through us.

'Lieutenant Emil Pelyagin, Special Commission. I believe you have a scientific establishment here,' Pasha shot back at her.

She studied him for a moment. 'This is a closed facility. I am required to inspect all documents before admitting visitors.'

'Good, comrade. I am glad to see you take security measures seriously.' Pasha handed her Pelyagin's documents. 'What are you researching here? Are you a physicist?'

She looked at him a little strangely. 'A physicist? No.'

'Introduce yourself, comrade. Name and rank.'

'My name is Sister Serafima. As to rank, I have none.'

'Sister?' repeated Pasha.

'Nuns, aren't they,' interrupted the young soldier. 'They moved in here from some convent or other.'

'But what on earth are you doing running a research laboratory?'

Sister Serafima handed the papers back. 'Follow me.'

On the door of the first shed was a scribbled notice: '*Laboratoria* 36'. My heart was pounding. Sister Serafima pushed open the door and we were hit by the stench. It was dark inside, and for a moment I read the smell as something chemical.

I stepped inside the shed and saw – people. Half-naked, gaunt bodies jostled together, and eyes staring out at us, huge blank dirty eyes. Bile rose in my mouth. Some were sitting or lying on the earth floor – ageless and sexless, barely animate. Some shrank back at the sight of us. A few pressed forward, murmuring.

'I don't understand,' Pasha stammered.

'They call it a laboratory,' Sister Serafima said impassively. 'Perhaps in the future they plan some sort of research.' She paused. 'For now, these people and those in the two rooms beyond are my charges, a total of eighty-five souls. They are lunatics.'

A murmuring started up. An old man stumbled towards us; his face was horribly swollen and bruised. '*Barishnya*,' he said, and giggled. 'I haven't seen you before, miss.' He reached out and took my hand, and everything in me wanted to shrink away from him. With an effort I controlled myself, but Pasha pushed him away, snapping, 'Don't touch her!'

Sister Serafima watched. 'In this hut they are on the whole peaceable. In the neighbouring hut we keep the difficult ones. You heard them earlier.'

'How did this man get so bruised, then?' I asked.

'Sometimes there are problems in this hut too. Have you seen everything you wanted?'

'No – no. We were looking for a scientific establishment, a workshop,' burst out Pasha in fury.

'What?'

'Lab 37. We believe that a certain prisoner was brought here – Nikita Slavkin was his name.'

For the first time Sister Serafima's expressionless mask slipped. 'Slavkin?' she repeated.

'Yes. We believe he was brought to Laboratory 37 in January of this year, from the Lubyanka. Do you know anything about this?'

She turned to the young soldier. 'You may leave us now, Kurotov. I think I hear your comrades returning. You'd better let them in.'

When he'd gone she turned back to us and her face was suddenly animated. 'Now – you answer some questions for me. You're not Chekists, for a start. The Cheka visited me last week, a very different kettle of fish. What do you know about Lab 37, or Slavkin? Tell me the truth or Kurotov's comrades will get their hands on you, and they are not as meek as he is, I'll tell you that.'

The inmates seemed to pick up on her tone and they began to talk excitedly, gathering around us. A woman touched my arm and someone pressed themselves against my back. I took a deep breath and spoke.

'Sister Serafima, we are not from the Cheka, you are right. Please understand. We are friends of Slavkin's. We have been hunting for him all over Moscow since he disappeared in January. We were told he was working in a laboratory here, in the Church of the Ascension.'

Sister Serafima looked at us and I was amazed to see tears in her eyes. She turned swiftly to the people around us. 'Go to your places!' she barked. They fell back. 'They don't understand, they could hurt you without realising. So . . . you are Slavkin's friends. The IRT, wasn't it?'

I nodded. 'He told you?'

'Yes.'

Her charges had taken up their places on wooden bunks around the walls, four or five to each bunk. Those that did not fit sat on the earthen floor. They were silent and watchful. I gazed at them, trying to take this in. 'So is *this* where they brought Slavkin after the Lubyanka?'

She nodded.

The baby suddenly began to twist violently inside me, the nausea in me was so strong I felt myself stumble. Pasha caught my arm and held me. I saw he was crying. 'But' – it came out in a wail – '*why?*'

Sister Serafima took a deep breath. 'When he came

265

here, he was ... I thought he might not survive the night. As they dragged him out of the van he was having a fit. He lay frothing at the mouth and convulsing for almost half an hour. He didn't speak for days.' She put her hands on my shoulders. 'I fed him like a baby, spoon by spoon. Those brutes at the church there, they make sport of my poor charges. Oh my God, the suffering! But I didn't let them near Slavkin. He was so weak ...

'Come with me, I'll show you. This is the room I kept him in' – a bare little cell with a tiny window – 'not comfortable, but clean. And safe. After a week I was washing him and he suddenly looked at me and smiled. "Dear one," he said, "how tired you look." I couldn't believe my ears. His eyes were clear, his speech was a little blurred because he'd bitten his tongue so badly in the fits, but it was calm, reasonable. He had forgotten a great deal, but slowly he began to remember, and to tell me, little by little.'

'Did he tell you about his machine?'

'More than that, he began to build it again. As soon as he could get about, he went out by day and gathered materials – bits of scrap metal, this and that. I thought at first he was still crazed, but then I saw him at work, shaping, hammering. He took a broken engine from one of the Army trucks here and fixed it – even those brutes of soldiers were impressed then. I found tools for him in one of the old stores. What he needed was a furnace, but that was impossible. "It doesn't matter," he kept saying. "Victory will be ours." He worked constantly, eighteen hours a day – I couldn't stop him. He said, "Thank goodness they arrested me. I had no idea before how much there is to do." He talked to my poor patients. He explained to them about the machine that he was building, and how it would transport us all far away from today into another world, where Communism is possible.

'I have lived all my life as a nun, but God forgive me, I believe that Communism will come one day . . . and I believed him that his machine could make it possible. Why not? Why not? God will not stand by and watch us all suffer for ever . . .

'But I worried that he was exhausting himself. I was dreading another attack. Sometimes his mind would wander, and he'd start talking gibberish. All of us are starving, every one of us, but he was so thin   his wrists, his shoulders – and yet he burned with energy. I don't know. He seemed to have some kind of superhuman strength, just for those weeks. I used to look at his bony back, the shoulderblades that stuck right out through his shirt like wings, and I used to think . . .' She looked away. 'Never mind what I thought.

'He told me about the IRT, about all of you. He was terrified that you had been arrested. He hunted the streets for the papers to check for your names on the lists. He felt that if he made contact with you it would endanger you. They arrested him on charges of plotting counter-Revolution, but he must have had his first fit almost as soon as they took him in, because he couldn't remember anything about the prison at all. So presumably they dropped the case. Once he went to watch you –

to spy on the building from some doorway or other. He came back so sad. I think he was hoping to see someone – perhaps someone who wasn't there?'

'Sonya.' My voice came out strangely. 'He was hoping to see Sonya. But she died of typhus the week after he was arrested.'

'Sonya. Yes, he did mention that name when he was ill.'

'But where is he now, Sister? Our . . . our informer said he didn't know.'

'He was telling the truth. We don't know.'

'*What?*'

'I don't know where he is. At the end of March I had to make a trip out to the countryside to try to collect food for my patients. We are starving here, I've already said. What food I grew last summer ran out and we receive only third-class rations. I left my patients here in Slavkin's charge; he was not entirely well, I knew, but still – he was the only person I could trust.

'I came back . . . Oh, forgive me. I came back and that Red Army *filth* had wreaked havoc. They claimed there was trouble and they had to come in to sort it out. I'm willing to bet that any trouble before they arrived was nothing to what they left behind. And Slavkin had gone. He *and* his machine – disappeared.'

'And . . . and you don't know where he went?' I said stupidly.

Without a word, Sister Serafima led us out of the cell and through a dank corridor. At the end was a heavy door with two bolts. 'Be very calm and quiet,' she said over her shoulder. 'These patients are anxious about people they don't know.'

The sign on the door read 'Laboratory No. 37'.

'Good morning,' said Serafima politely as she swung open the door. 'I hope we are not disturbing you.'

We stepped inside another long, dark hut. There were many fewer people in here – perhaps a couple of dozen – each sitting on their own, bare pallet. At first the greater order and space seemed to contrast favourably with Lab 36. Then I realised that they were manacled. Many lay motionless, as if barely alive. One man was curled up in the corner, groaning. One, who looked young and strong, was straining at the end of his chain, tugging on it and grunting.

'Grisha, calm yourself. These patients are chained because they have consistently harmed themselves and others. It is unpleasant to see, but it is the only possible course of action.' Sister Serafima shrugged. 'If she is able to talk, one of the patients told me something about Slavkin's disappearance that perhaps would interest you.'

She led us up to a powerfully built young woman who was sitting on her pallet and gazing blankly out of the window. Very gently, she took the woman's hand in hers and spoke to her almost in a whisper. 'Anna, my dear, don't be afraid.' The woman looked at her blankly. 'These are good people, friends of our dear Nikita Gavrilovich. They want to hear about the day he went away. When I was not here. You remember, don't you, Anna? Be brave and tell.'

Anna's eyes swivelled and she caught sight of us. She began to whimper and sidle backwards on her bed. Her face had been horribly burnt and was covered in red scar tissue. I could hardly bear her expression of terror. 'Hush,' murmured Sister Serafima. 'Calm yourself.' And over her shoulder, to us, 'It's best not to look at her – look away.'

Pasha and I turned away and gazed down the hut. After a moment a croaky whisper emerged. 'Are they truly his friends?'

'Yes. They are searching for him. They love him.'

'I remember what happened,' she said hoarsely. 'I'll tell them, shall I?'

And so the story of Nikita's last journey was told, in Anna's poor, painful voice, while the inmates gazed dully at the ceiling and Grisha grunted and pulled at his chains.

'It was the day that evil men came in and made misery for us. They said they were coming to help us but then they laughed and hit us and they frightened everyone and they took our food. They took my cloak and laughed and they beat Misha and they—'

'Shh – you needn't remember all of that.'

'Nikita tried to stop the bad men. He stood in front of them and he spoke a long time to them, lots of words, all about his machine and the world and everything. He thought they were friends, but they weren't friends. They were laughing at him and one of them hit him and he fell over. And then they made fun of him and pushed him and he banged against the wall, and they made him walk about and prodded him with their bayonets. And they said show us this machine then and he took them outside and I heard them say get in and he lay down in it and they did more laughing. And then . . .' She sat up straight and turned towards us, and very cautiously I looked back at her, keeping my head bowed in case I frightened her again. 'Then there was a very loud noise, it hurt my ears so much' – she covered her ears to show us – 'and shouting. And we didn't see our Nikita again.'

'What did the noise sound like?'

'It – it sounded like the air splitting in two, crack! – and crack in my ears – like . . . like thunder right here in the room, like a gun . . .'

There was a pause.

'And then you talked to the bad men, didn't you, Anna?' prompted Serafima.

'Yes, and they said straight out to me, they said, "He's gone away in his machine." That's the words they said. They didn't say anything else, because they didn't know about it like we do, do they, Sister? Nikita didn't tell them everything that he told us.'

'No, that's right, he didn't tell them what he told us.'

'They didn't say that he was coming back, because only we know about that. But they said he had gone away and that was just what Nikita told us they would say.' For the first time she looked at me full in the face with her big blue child's eyes, wide and clear and triumphant. 'He's gone away in his machine, they said so, in those words. And he told us, if that happens, it means we've won. So we've won, haven't we, Sister Serafima?

We've won the future, and they don't even know it.'

'Yes,' said Sister Serafima, and her voice was a little hoarse, 'I believe we've won. Somewhere in the future, we've won.'

21

'Anna.' I leant forward. 'Thank you.' Without thinking I reached my hand out towards hers.

'No!'

Serafima tugged hard on Anna's chain. She screeched and fell back.

'Move away, please – go to the door.' Serafima hurried us out, tight-lipped. 'You don't understand. They can't help it.'

As we came out into the corridor men's voices could be heard in Lab 36. Serafima stopped. 'That's the Red Guard. I think it best if you leave by this door. Take the path down to the river and wait for me there – I will come as soon as I can . . .'

She bundled us through a small door and we found ourselves outside again, blinded by the sun.

'Oh, Pasha, I don't know if I can—'

'Come,' muttered Pasha, taking my arm. 'Little by little.'

We slipped and staggered together like drunks down the steep, narrow footpath to the river. No one seemed to have seen us go; if they had, I doubt either of us would have been able to run. Within a few moments we were out of sight of Serafima's huts. A few more and we were in a little copse leading down to the river. The trees were like huge swaddled peasant women beneath their layers of snow. We crept beneath the skirts of one and pushed ourselves in among the brushwood. From this place we looked out onto the glittering river and waited. Slowly, slowly, I felt my heart calm and the dizzy, sick sensation seep away. We didn't talk.

I don't know if it was hours, or minutes before Sister Serafima appeared quietly on the path, leading an old donkey with a blanket on its back.

'The Cheka seem to be on their way. I suggest you keep away from the road. At the edge of the park, by those firs, there is a path running north. It will take you back to the river – we are in a huge curve here, do you understand? Follow the river until you see the railway bridge. There you can climb up to Kotly station, on the Moscow Circular railroad. Let Dusya go when you get there – she will come home by herself. Here, this is all I can give you.' She pressed a little parcel wrapped in a cloth into my hands. 'Forgive me if I ask you one thing.' She looked hard at me. 'Is it his child?'

'Yes.'

'Oh, I'm glad. Very glad. Go with God, my children . . .'

Dusya waited while I mounted her in an awkward side-saddle and Pasha took the rope; and then she slowly, carefully stepped out along the path. Her neat little hooves made no sound on the narrow animal tracks. Light sparkled and snapped around us and the air tasted like iced leaves. Apart from one deserted road, there was no sign of human life, no building, no chimney – just the blank curves of the snowy forest. I had not been out of the city for over a year – a year and a half, since we were at Mikhailovka in the summer of 1917, and we played blind man's buff in the twilight . . . Dusya's warm, comforting back moved beneath me and the baby was calm. Pelyagin was obviously after us, but all I could feel was weariness. The sun was sinking in the sky when we finally saw the railway bridge. I dismounted Dusya and we let her go: we didn't want anyone to see her at the station. She looked at us for a slow moment, blinked, and turned for home.

'Just a moment,' murmured Pasha. 'Before we enter the station, I think we should decide on our plans. We may not be able to talk openly there.'

After the warmth of the day, the woods were full of dripping and the occasional 'flump' of melted snow sliding from the branches. We turned our faces to the last sunshine.

'The only course for you now is to go abroad. I've heard the Estonian border is open at Narva. We must get to Petrograd and then find out how to make the rest of the journey.'

'And you? What about you?'

'I will accompany you as far as you wish me to, of course. Then I suppose I'll continue my work at Narkompros.'

I stared at him. 'But you've impersonated a Cheka official – you're in danger too.'

'I doubt Sister Serafima would identify me.'

His expression was stony, a look that I would not have recognised on him a couple of years ago. Weakly, I changed the subject.

'How will we get tickets to Petrograd? People wait for weeks to get them . . .'

'Volodya might be able to help us. But we shouldn't spend a minute more than we need at Gagarinsky Lane. I'm willing to bet Pelyagin's men will have been round to tell the neighbours to report our return.'

We waited in the woods for the next train, a goods vehicle that we managed to scramble aboard. We sat on the running plate until it arrived just outside Paveletsky station in Moscow at six in the evening. I was very cold, very tired and my belly seemed to be growing heavier and more uncomfortable each moment. Until then I had given little thought to the birth, but now it suddenly filled my mind. I had little more than a month left. I wanted to beg Pasha to promise he would stay with me at least until the baby was born, but he looked so grim I didn't have the courage to raise the subject.

'Perhaps we can rest somewhere?'

'If you want.' Outside the station we found an old woman with a little card saying simply 'Bed'. She took us to her room, in the basement of an old apartment building, and showed us the bed she meant – her own. We lay down and covered ourselves with our coats and she sat on a chair, keeping a close eye on us. At some point I woke in the night and found her trying to undo my shoelaces. I pushed her away but she clung on for a while, glaring at me reproachfully. Finally she let go and sat back down again.

During the hours of night Slavkin's hands, with their long, pallid, Orthodox fingers, appeared in my dream.

His gentle manner with the old ladies, his smile. 'Guardian angels', he remarked once to me, 'are a scientific fact.'

'Oh, don't be so ridiculous,' I said, laughing.

'Yes, a fact! They are the electric current that guides us, unknowing, through our lives . . . towards one decision, away from another. On what do we base our decisions? Most of them spring from an instinctive response, very few are based on logic. And yet we make good decisions much of the time. Like animals, we have a natural instinct for the electromagnetic currents of the Universe.'

We left before dawn and walked up to Gagarinsky Lane to collect our passports and a few belongings. I shoved the surviving IRT papers into a couple of boxes and, in return for the last of our food supplies, the metalworker's wife agreed to deliver them to the British Embassy. Volodya, miraculously, managed to obtain tickets for us that evening, to travel under false papers as a Communist Party member and his wife, going to take up a post in Petrograd. Once in Petrograd, we took turns all day to queue for tickets to Narva. The train left the following morning on a twenty-four-hour journey, much of which was spent stopping, starting and crawling into sidings for hours at a time. Around midnight, our compartment fell silent and I finally plucked up the courage to speak to Pasha.

I put my lips up against his ear and whispered as quietly as I could.

'I wanted to ask . . . I mean, I don't want to press you

. . . but I wondered if you would mind very much if I asked you to marry me?'

A pause.

'I didn't know whether I should ask you, what with the – the matter of the baby, and of course marriage itself is utterly bourgeois, against both our principles. I quite understand if you refuse . . .'

He still said nothing but I could feel him pulling away from me.

'No, I've started this all wrong. Wait, please, it's nothing to do with Revolutionary principles. You're right, of course I loved Nikita – we both love Nikita, we will never stop loving him. But I made a mistake. I misunderstood what love felt like, do you see? For whatever reason – I don't know why – I thought of love as something difficult, something I should suffer for.' I swallowed hard, floundering. 'I – I didn't realise I loved you, because it was just so easy, and warm, and good . . .'

He tried to speak, but I was determined not to be interrupted. 'The fact is, now I know that I love you, I have to say so. I can't let you disappear, and I'm terrified that when we get to the border they might not let you through, or they might take me off somewhere separate, or . . . or who knows what they might do to you, don't you understand?' I was gabbling by this time and my voice was rising. Suddenly I felt his finger on my lips.

'Sh. No – no.'

'No?' My voice rose to a squeak.

'No, I don't mind marrying you, my darling love. You absolute idiot. And also no, I don't care about the matter

278

of the baby, and it's not against my principles. And no, I am not going to disappear. I didn't think you wanted me to come with you . . .'

'Oh . . . Good.'

We started laughing weakly in the dark, and trying to stifle our laughter, which had the result of mild hysteria.

'Oh, shut your gobs!' snapped the market trader squashed beside us. 'You're shaking the bed up like a bloody blancmange!'

That didn't help. It was some moments before I could compose myself. Then Pasha whispered in my ear, 'Let's do it now, then, shall we?'

'What?'

'Get married.'

'Oh! How?'

'We each say our vows to the other. I, Pavel Aleksandrovich Kobelev, take you, Getrude Freely—'

'Gertrude Adelaide.'

'Really? I didn't know. How delightful. Gertrude Adelaide Freely, as my beloved wife. I vow to love you, care for you, kiss you, and always tell you the truth, till death us do part.'

'And not to disappear.'

'And not to disappear. Now you.'

'I, Gertrude Adelaide Freely, take you, Pavel Aleksandrovich Kobelev, as my beloved husband. I vow to love you, care for you, and always be truthful, till death us do part.'

'And to kiss me. You can start that now.'

We kissed, in the darkness, all the way to the border.

Finally we were told to disembark. At the checkpoint they kept us waiting for hours, searching through the mound of luggage that our fellow travellers were carrying. My stomach began to ache so painfully that I was convinced that labour had begun. I begged them to let me get to the hospital in Reval. The young customs officer looked alarmed, and went to consult his superior.

'Go on,' snapped the senior officer, jerking his head. 'Get out of here. We're not a crèche!'

Holding hands, Pasha and I walked across the bridge over the muddy, turgid Narva river and into Estonia.

*

We were married for the second time in Reval (or Tallinn, as it had just been renamed). The city was battered by civil war itself, but to us it seemed the epitome of peace. Its shops were magically stuffed with goods, and in the streets people strolled about and appeared not to be thinking about food at all. With our last funds we bought ourselves clothes and visited the barber. I remember the delicious luxury of lying back in the barber's chair, only the snippety-snip of the scissors breaking the silence, the previous months falling away from me as each long curl landed on the floor. We bathed ourselves carefully in the digs we had taken near the station and dressed in our new clothes, like children going to First Communion. Outside the Guild Hall we bought a bunch of snowdrops from an old woman. Half an hour later, we emerged with a marriage certificate.

The Kobelevs had friends, perhaps even distant cousins, the Rauds, who had an estate south of Tallinn. I hadn't met them, but before the war they had been frequent visitors in Moscow and Pasha had visited their estate as a child. We sent a telegram on our arrival, and the next we knew, several days after our wedding, was Mark Raud himself arriving at our door in a pony-trap, embracing us both, and insisting we eat the picnic he had brought with him from the estate. A big, stern figure, he stood over us, hushing us while we ate.

'Now get in the trap,' he ordered, 'and you can tell me the news of the family while we travel. I want to get you back to Jarvekula straight away. I am sorry to say such a thing, but you look terrible, my children. Never mind, thank God the war is over in Estonia, at least. You will have your baby here, my dear.'

The year was just tipping over into spring; every day the ground dried out a little more and the buds swelled. The Rauds, kind, generous people that they were, housed us for almost six months. Like all women waiting for their first baby to be born, I could not quite believe that an entirely new person was about to arrive in the world. I was scared – not so much that our living conditions might have affected her (I could sense how healthy she was inside me), nor of the birth itself, but of the great burden of sorrow that she would immediately have to shoulder. Yet when, in the middle of April, she emerged – *you* emerged – tiny and hairy-eared as a little wood sprite, with large, serene, dark eyes, I saw that my fears were quite irrelevant. We called you Sophia – for Sonya, and also for the calm wisdom that you seemed to exude. You immediately knew what to do, eating, sleeping and looking about you with lovely solemnity. I was tired, of course, in the first months, but now my little Sophy was here, the terrible events of the past year seemed somehow to make more sense.

In September we packed up and sailed for Paris, after exacting a promise from the Rauds that they would visit us soon. You were by then a solid baby with creases on your wrists and a throaty little laugh and Pasha had, at last, tracked down his parents. We had heard nothing from them more recently than November 1918, when they had left Russia for Marseilles. As a last resort, Pasha wrote to put an advertisement in the *Figaro*. A week later, to our amazement, a boy came up the track to Jarvekula with not one but three telegrams in his hand, all from Mr Kobelev. The first: 'Dearest children we are in Paris stop your mother Liza Dima all well stop send news.' The second: 'Dears come immediately I will wire funds Bank of Estonia.' The third, simply: 'All to meet boat Calais.'

Before we left, we decided to tell Pasha's father about Sonya by telegram. We felt it was better that he break the news to the others gently, before we arrived. There was a part of me that dreaded seeing them; again and again I saw poor Sonya lying on the divan in the study, glassy-eyed, while I tried to feed her broth.

The thought also struck me now, as it had signally failed to do when Pasha and I were signing our marriage certificate at the Guild Hall, that the Kobelevs might be less than pleased at their new daughter-in-law and their not-quite-granddaughter. Pasha and I agreed on an official line: we had had a Communist wedding in Russia, but having lost our papers in our hurried exit from Russia we'd decided to formalise our situation in Tallinn. It went without saying that you were his daughter.

My beloved Sophy, you've already learnt so many shocking and terrifying facts about your birth in these pages that perhaps the date of your birth will hardly matter to you; yet all these years, you know, I have held a little private celebration for you in mid-April, a private thanksgiving for my daughter accompanied by a plea for your forgiveness at having deceived you. All your life you have celebrated your birthday a month late, in mid-May; this began when we sailed out of Estonia. We could not risk his parents counting up the months and wondering how you could have been conceived when Pasha was still in the Crimea.

We came down the gangplank at Calais into a sea of waiting, anxious faces. I was carrying you, Pasha was heaving our suitcases; he was shaking with emotion. Where were they? And then – Liza. I saw her before she saw us, a tall, pale girl of sixteen, her expression reserved, chewing her lip – and suddenly she caught sight of her brother. She let out a piercing scream, and jumped in the air, blazing with joy. Beside her Dima began to wave and shout – 'Over here! Over here!' And pushing forward, Mr Kobelev, barely taller than his son, grey-haired, beaming and crinkling up his eyes which were already full of tears and his wife beside him . . . It was more than we could do to say anything at all; we embraced each other, round and round, and you smiled so sweetly at your grandparents, your aunt and uncle, and as your grandmother laid her cheek against your silken baby head, she let out a terrible sob, and said, 'Sonya.'

We stayed with them in Paris for some weeks, until everything that could be said had been said; we told them everything, only keeping from them the truth about your father for your sake as well as for my own. The story of my ideals and my actions seemed too strange and confused for them to understand; maybe I couldn't make sense of them to myself, either. It was a relief for me to edit out those months when I loved Nikita and when I would have done anything to make him love me.

This set the pattern for Pasha's and my life together. In every other detail than biological Pasha was your father, as you know; he was devoted to you. I never managed to have another child; and once I asked Pasha if he was sad not to have more children. 'Why on earth would I be,' he said, hugging you to him, 'when I have my own angel?'

We set up home in London, it being easier for both of us to find work here, and after a couple of years your grandparents joined us. Mr Kobelev was taken on by the Ethnography department at London University and Mrs Kobelev, who had, through some extraordinary strength of character, cured herself during their exile, now set up a small dressmaking business in the East End. She employed several other Russian women and proved an effective businesswoman. Liza went to veterinary college – I was so proud of her – she was one of only five female students accepted in 1923; and although she married before she qualified, she has practised as a veterinary assistant to her husband for many years. Dima grew into one of those English schoolboys, mighty in their cricket whites, whose charm and good looks waft them through life on golden wings. He started up endless business ventures and different careers, none of which led to a great deal, but no matter – his friends always came to his rescue with a new proposal. He seemed more English than any of us, although of course his faint accent and his name bequeathed him the lifelong nickname 'Cossack'.

My parents did their duty and came to pay their respects to their new son-in-law and their granddaughter, but they made no bones about their discomfort and returned to Truro as soon as they could. My mother's remark when (in a weak moment) I asked her what she thought of Pasha – Paul since we arrived in England – passed into family lore.

'Well,' she said, giving it some consideration, 'he's a little too *interesting* for you, dear.'

And so he was. We spent a good life together, with you, and later your boys, our grandchildren; his work in publishing, mine in the library; our political lives – both lifelong Socialists. We were an ordinary family, bourgeois by the IRT's reckoning, although over the years it seemed to me that the daily demands of being a parent and attempting to hold onto one's principles were a far more effective and gruelling programme of transformation than we ever envisaged in the commune. We grew old; our lives were not marked by any exceptional achievements, if you discount the raising of one clever, serious daughter who from the age of five had a tendency to dismantle every machine she ever came across, who – despite her parents' lack of scientific ability – became a mineralogist and studied for a PhD in rare earth metals, who brought up her two sons to dream of social justice.

*

Yet still I couldn't shake off my fear. Mothers love daughters – but do daughters love mothers? My mother and I were never close. I have always dreaded the day, which seemed to me inevitable, when the world would somehow force the truth about your father upon you. I knew I didn't deserve you. The longer I kept all this from you, the more convinced I was of it.

Since I began this account, without quite admitting it to myself, I have been reducing my rations. I have had this tendency throughout my life; the greater the store of tins under my stairs, the less I can bring myself to eat. I've never given this cycle much thought, but I notice now that the details which cause the nausea to rise in me are to do with shame. The endless self-deceptions that I've been acting and re-enacting all these years – it's reminders of these that make me long for the acid rush in my throat, the clean, scoured emptiness afterwards.

At first the lies were such well-intentioned, small sprouts, necessary for the cause, but over the years they grew up into forests, blocking out the light. Since Paul died things have looked pretty dark.

And yet I write these words, in fact I've written the last chapter, in your sitting room, after I fell and injured myself in my kitchen. I lay there unconscious for some hours, apparently, before you found me and called an ambulance. For some reason, when I came round in hospital I did not wake up woozily but was alert the moment I opened my eyes. You were sitting by my bed and I watched your worried face for perhaps a full minute. Then you looked around and noticed that my eyes were open. I watched as your dear face lit up, tears in your eyes. 'Mama . . .'

It struck me then that, at the very least, I owe you the respect not to pre-judge you. Otherwise how can history fail to repeat itself? Paul had been trying to convince me of this for years, but I suppose I needed to find my own way to the realisation. This account is, on a minuscule scale, my plan for a better future for us both. You still have to read these pages. I dread how they might hurt you. Yet I turn them over to you now in the certainty of your open heart and your powerful, generous imagination – the legacies of both your fathers – and in the hope, one day, of your understanding.

22

And so, at last, to the reappearance of the Vanishing Futurist.

With each year that passed, Nikita Slavkin became more celebrated. His scientific achievements were recognised in several ways: he was named a 'Hero of the Soviet Union' for his contributions to science in several areas including particle physics, and in the 1950s his pioneering experiments with iridium electroplating led to its use in the Soviet rocketry programme.

His fame, however, bore little relation to his work. In November 1919 Lenin sealed his status as a Soviet icon by mentioning him in his speech on the Second Anniversary of the Revolution as 'Nikita Slavkin . . . known as the Vanishing Futurist . . . To labour unstintingly, to seek knowledge, and to give one's life for science – this is a true Revolutionary hero,' Lenin declared. The following year the first, short book appeared about Slavkin's life. In Moscow in 1924 one of the floats in the May Day procession was dedicated to his memory, consisting of a large silver pod in which an unconscious Slavkin lay in a tangle of wires attached to outsize clocks and a huge dial marked 'To Communism!' When the arrow reached its Communist zenith, a bell rang and Slavkin leapt to his feet and performed a series of acrobatics. As the arrow ticked around to the beginning, he flopped back down again.

From 1928 and through the 1930s, the depiction of Slavkin moved away from a prone body to a more dynamic image. 'Nikita Slavkin Breaking the Boundaries of Human Knowledge' appeared in several further Soviet anniversaries. It showed Slavkin as a beefy fellow in white overalls slamming his fist through the outstretched page of a huge book. Soviet boys took this image to heart and came in their thousands to dressing-up days at school as little musclemen. I could imagine the scenes in the playground as they gave the boundaries of human knowledge what they deserved. 'Take that! Hurr!'

Further books and a feature-length film (*The Vanishing Futurist*, 1952) came out, and several physics departments were named in his honour. A street and a monument were dedicated to him in Sverdlovsk (formerly Ekaterinburg), where he went to school, and a plaque was put up on the house on Gagarinsky Lane. Yet no one has ever managed to replicate his experiment with the Socialisation Capsule, and fifty years of advances in quantum physics cannot explain how his machine could have resulted in his disappearance.

During Khrushchev's time in power, when so many injustices came to light, Pasha told me he wanted to try to discover the truth about Nikita's – about your father's – death. I was still reluctant; we argued over it, and Pasha didn't bring the subject up again. When you first brought these boxes of papers down from the attic, however, I opened them to find an envelope with a Russian postmark that I'd never seen before. Inside it was a printed slip in Russian: 'In response to your request.'

Pasha obviously wrote for information despite my resistance, and then left the results for me. He knew that when I looked through the IRT papers again – when I was ready to tell you this story – I would find it. It was a last act of love for you, Sophy, as well as for his friend.

The printed slip had a header, blurrily stamped in the pale green favoured by Soviet bureaucracy, which announced it originated in the Ministry of Internal Affairs of the USSR. Behind it was a photograph of some kind of form. My heart was racing horribly. Half of me wanted to put the envelope back in the box and pretend I had never seen it. It was hard to decipher; the photograph was not entirely clear, the Russian cursive script was typically fluid, one letter running on to the next with little attempt at legibility. Stamped in large red letters over the form were the words: 'Restricted Information'.

Beneath them I read:

CERTIFICATE OF DEATH

SLAVKIN, Nikolai Gavrilovich

Age: 25 years

Died: 15 February 1919

Place of death: Moscow, Kolomenskoye Barracks, Southern Region (formerly the Church of Ascension)

Cause of death: Shot to the head

This information is registered on 18 March 1919, at the Registration Bureau of the Emergency Commission (the Cheka)

*

Earlier on in this account, I suggested that the real cause
for astonishment did not lie in the failures of the IRT,
but in the extent of our success. Some may wonder which
success I am referring to. It is true that in material
terms one would be hard pressed to point to any evidence of transformation. Our commune was split apart
by jealousy and self-interest, while all around us Russia's
experiment with social justice became a vast agar plate
for the cultivation of corruption and cynicism.

In the years since, an abyss has opened up between
the left and the right, millions of lives have vanished
into it, and the ideals behind our Revolution have been
swamped by tragedy. As the 1960s recede and the cynical
1970s wear on, the demands of the market are the only
signposts through the modern desert. On the right wing
they dismiss social justice as facile and dangerous, while
on the left, loyal Socialists – like myself for many years
– believe they support the cause by closing their eyes
to the reality of the Soviet Union, by blaming Stalin, or
Lenin's illness, or 'errors'. Yet the truth is that in January 1919 Nikita Slavkin died of a bullet to the head in the
filthy backyard of a lunatic asylum.

And yet ... and yet ... don't give up. History may
not advance in the swift straight lines that the early
Soviet artists envisaged. But surely the cynics who
claim it moves in circles are just as foolish. If it does
seem to repeat itself, if we do seem to arrive back at
the same place again and again – the outbreak of war,

the counter-Revolution – we are still in a slightly better position each time. We have the experience of our previous passes.

As I see it, the IRT's achievement was to embody, just for a fleeting moment, Slavkin's greatest insight. His concept of Atomic Communism describes the fundamental nature of reality in our universe, in which with every conscious thought, every action, each individual influences the world around him or her. If we give up on this future, in this intricately connected world, we stand to lose everything. Yet even the most powerless and insignificant among us can trigger vast transfomations. A poor boy from Galilee imagined a society in which outcasts and prostitutes were the equals of kings, and set in motion a social revolution that is still playing out today. The Constructivists in the dark winters of War Communism envisaged the design of the modern world. Now a defenceless scientist and his wife, Andrei Sakharov and Yelena Bonner, are shaking the foundations of the Soviet Union with their simple demands for cooperation and freedom of thought.

'Fortunately,' as Andrei Sakharov has written, 'the future is unpredictable and also – because of quantum effects – uncertain.'

Despite or, rather, because of the fact that the future is unknowable, each of us bears a responsibility towards it. If all that our imagination can summon up is some limp, apathetic, cynical vision of a world just like the one in which we now live, then frankly that's all we deserve.

An image floats back to me: the first weeks of the IRT,

and all of us are lying together on the lawn at Gagarin-sky Lane, gazing at the first stars, and the smell of dry grass is in the air – the end of summer – and Nikita is speaking:

'For better or worse, we are creating the future here, in our minds. Each time we allow ourselves to imagine a harmonious world, we bring it closer. Just share your thoughts with us . . . You know the answer, if only you can discover it within yourself. Inside your imagination lies the blueprint for the future. How, why, what you will into being – this is the choice that confronts you, and all of us.'

Acknowledgements

This book has taken me years to write and the patience of saints has been put to the test. Very many thanks and a deep bow to Neil Belton, Georgia Garrett, Hannah Griffiths, Sarah Savitt, Samantha Matthews, Alex Russell, Will Hobson, Emma O'Bryen, Jonathan Tetley, Roland Chambers, Clem Cecil, Emily Irwin, Victoria Millar, Anna Benn, Julian Reilly, Bojana Mojsova, Sophie Poklewski-Koziell, Wim Peers, Alexander Hoare, Jessica and Charles Thomas, Leslie Hewitt, Peter France, Anna Gunin, Alexander Gunin, and above all to my dearest Philip.

The Alchemy of Art

If Gerty's family was anxious about her decision to work for the Kobelevs, she could at least reassure them that she would not be the only Miss in Moscow. A steady trickle of enterprising girls set off to Russia before the war, drawn by high wages and generous treatment from their Anglophile employers, as well as the promise of adventure. Russia was after all one of the fastest-growing economies in Europe at the time, as well as Britain's ally in the Triple Entente – while the Tsar, the very twin of his cousin George V, had at last taken the first steps towards constitutional reform. A century on, we look back at 1914 and see a country on the brink of inevitable disintegration, yet many more experienced political commentators than Gerty missed the signs of the coming upheavals. Before the war, an alternative future did perhaps still exist for the Russian Empire.

It's quite possible, however, that Gerty's family would have been alarmed by reports of another Russian revolution, in the arts rather than in politics, which was already shocking audiences all over the world. Since the 1890s Russia had been experiencing a kind of Modernist Renaissance. As its industrial development drew it into the economy of Europe, so its cultural life became more and more closely linked with that of the West, both influenced by and increasingly influencing European culture. Artists of every discipline threw themselves into the modern experiment with form, coupled with an almost ecstatic belief in human creativity and the unity of all the arts. Diaghilev, Nijinsky, Prokofiev, Stravinsky, Vrubel, Bakst, Malevich, Kandinsky, Bely, Blok, Akhmatova, Mandelstam, Pasternak, Eisenstein, Stanislavsky, Meyerhold are just a few of the brilliant and wildly varied talents of this period, whose work – one thinks of Malevich's *Black Square* (1915) or Nijinsky's *L'Après-midi d'un faune* (1912), the birth of modern dance, in which a faun masturbates over a scarf – still looks challenging today.

The Futurists crashed onto the literary stage in 1912, with a manifesto called 'A Slap in the Face of Public Taste', which joyfully abused and rejected all previous Russian literature. They were a group of art students turned rock-star poets – swaggering, glamorous, publicity-hungry, their every pose designed for maximum shock value. In their firmly materialist world view there was one attitude which amounted almost to a religion – a belief in the power of art not just to depict, but to *transform*. The avant-garde's answer to the problems of Russia was Art itself, with its capacity to unite mankind and to transmute the base metals of our flawed world. Their creations were their contribution to the Revolution; by imagining the future they were performing the alchemy that would transform the present.

Vladimir Mayakovsky, probably the most famous of the Futurists, poured his poetic genius into the direct, funny, vulgar language of the streets. Cocky barrow boy crossed with tragic poet, he made himself the hero of his poetry and his life – a supersized 'handsome twenty-two-year-old' with 'no senile tenderness', who straddled the universe – chatted to the sun, man to man, walked a tiny Napoleon on a leash and marched up to heaven to threaten a mouldering old God (who, of course, was nowhere to be found). He was, his poetry suggested, a representative of a Promethean new breed of men, typical of the age, who with modern technology would crush nature and build Utopia.

If Mayakovsky was the pin-up of the group, the gentle, ascetic Velimir Khlebnikov was considered by his contemporaries to be the most brilliant. At a Futurist carnival in Petrograd in 1917 he was borne through the streets on a throne with the inscription 'Chairman of the World'. His 'transrational' poetry is a kaleidoscope of neologisms, arcane words and esoteric references – his own attempt at 'the language of the birds', an ancient, ideal language that was capable of expressing the pure essence of meaning.

While a political Revolution was still remote, nihilism was the literary avant-garde's default position. As Mayakovsky later summed up in his first long poem, the idea was: 'Down with your Love! Down with your Art! Down with your system! Down with your religion!' Yet before 1917, apart from the brawls that often con- cluded their readings, the Futurists' idea of bringing down the system was entirely artistic and performative. They talked of fusing Art and Life, dragging the artist out of his garret and placing him in the midst of people's ordinary working lives; but at this stage little more than token gestures were possible – dressing eccentrically, for example, in a yellow blouse instead of a jacket and tie, wearing spoons or radishes in their buttonholes, and painting on unframed panels rather than old-fashioned canvases.

And then came 1917. The Tsarist regime fell in March, but it was the Bolshevik coup in October that swept away the entire bourgeois system. The avant-garde was jubilant: its demands had been granted with incredible speed and thoroughness, and anti-Establishment artists and writers had all at once become the mouthpiece of the new state. One can only wonder at how extraordinary this must have felt, although with typical brass-nosery they affected no surprise. Anything, suddenly, was possible. In art as in politics, all the talk might have dwelt ad nauseam on rationality, utility and a scientific approach – but beneath all that lay a limitless utopia, released from pragmatism by the dreamlike chaos of the moment.

The Futurists had long since changed their name: in the visual arts, the 'Last Futurist Exhibition' had taken place back in January 1916, after which it was partially succeeded by Suprematism, and in 1917 by Constructivism, which rejected painting altogether for production art – art with a social meaning and a practical purpose. Nonetheless, under the banner of Constructivist 'labour', extraordinary works of utopian art were conceived, even if they were never built, nor the necessary technology ever developed. Tatlin's Monument to the Third International, designed in 1919–20, is perhaps its emblematic creation: a magical object conceived by a soaring, original imagination that aimed to enlighten and transform the world around it not by representation or depiction, but by the simple fact of its existence ... even though it did not and *could* not exist, because the very essence of its transformative power (materials, technology, organisation) was unavailable or had not yet been invented. In this alchemical spirit, the students of Vkhutemas created their extraordinary designs for flying, floating and dangling buildings, and El Lissitzky produced his *prounen*, architectonic drawings that hovered somewhere between the second and third dimension. 'This was one of those epochs,' the writer Darko Suvin later commented, 'when new Heavens touch the old Earth, when the future actively overpowers the present.' The inspirations of the avant-garde were as much guidelines to future creators as designs in themselves.

The Party's dream had many of the features of the hyper-controlled, draconian utopias otherwise confined to SF novels – although, fortunately enough, its political and administrative weakness prevented too thorough an implementation. War Communism, the system adopted by the Bolsheviks during the Civil War, was at least partially conceived as a prefigurative stage on the route to Communism. The most striking move was perhaps Trotsky's unilateral declaration of peace, which was followed the next day by a German invasion along the entire defenceless Russian border from the Baltic to the Black Sea. Internal policy was equally radical. All private enterprise was banned, industries and banks were nationalised and rations were distributed according to class, with workers, the Red Army and Party members being awarded the best rations, while 'former people' were given, in Trotsky's unpleasant phrase, 'only just enough bread so that they don't forget the smell of it'. Obligatory labour was introduced as well as conscription, in a ferocious version of the workers' paradise, while the 'old world' of the villages was treated ruthlessly. Under this system, even Party members and their loyal supporters could barely keep body and materialist soul together. The artist Olga Rozanova died of diphtheria in 1918; Khlebnikov, weakened by malnourishment, in 1922.

Despite these hardships the avant-garde pushed ahead as far as they could with the task of remaking the world. The Old was ritually cleansed with new street names and new, hurriedly built monuments; the walls of the Moscow Manège, for example, were painted with a list of Great People of History – Spartacus, Marx, Rosa Luxembourg. Mass theatrical events were organised to celebrate Revolutionary anniversaries, including a vast re-enactment of the storming of the Winter Palace with a cast of more than eight thousand. Avant-garde agit-prop posters were displayed throughout Bolshevik-held areas. Mayakovsky's plan to paint the trees outside the Kremlin red was typical of their witty conceptual approach to uniting art and life in one almost destitute but Revolutionary reality.

By 1921 War Communism had more or less brought the Bolshevik state to a standstill. Industrial production was minimal, the cities were half empty, starvation and disease were widespread. Lenin had no alternative but to reintroduce a certain level of market economics, the New Economic Policy, into the system, upon which his endlessly resourceful compatriots immediately set to work rebuilding their country.

For the next eight years or so Russians enjoyed something of a respite from the depredations of the State, and the avant-garde were able to carry themes from the pre-Revolutionary period to their conclusions. Despite their victory over the old order, the nihilistic tendency still persisted. The monochrome replaced colour, silence replaced music, nudity replaced fashion (the 'Evenings of the Denuded Body' which Pasha anachronistically wished he could attend, took place in 1922, with marches and the occupation of trolley buses), and a universal monosyllabic language called 'Ao' was proposed. The *nichevoki*, Russian Dadaists, made a single vow: 'to read nothing, write nothing, publish nothing'. There were even darker negations too, unsurprising perhaps after seven years of war: robotism, antiverbalism, suicidalism.

Yet at the same time a spirit of joyful optimism in Revolutionary man's capabilities possessed the avant-garde. The quest for egalitarianism took them in multiple directions – in the theatre, in dance, in music. One of the most successful was the famous orchestra without a conductor, Persimfans, which survived for a decade and inspired orchestras in New York and Germany. The artists Stepanova and Tatlin turned their attention to clothing – genderless, practical uniforms for different professions – which was never produced, although it has inspired later fashion brands such as Miu Miu and Chanel; disposable paper clothes were another suggestion ahead of their time.

Perhaps the most extreme and characteristic preoccupation of the age, however, was a fascination with man as a machine. Building on the Futurists' Promethean image of themselves, many in the avant-garde imagined a new type of Soviet man who could function with the precision and efficiency of a piece of industrial equipment. In theatre this idea was visited and re-visited, with Meyerhold's system of physical training for actors, *Biomekhanika*, which he described as 'organised movement' to create the 'high-velocity man', Foregger's *Machine Dances* and Nijinska's analogies between dance and mechanised motion.

At the same time the twenties saw a craze for the American efficiency gurus Henry Ford and F. W. Taylor, who seemed to offer a means of transforming the unpunctual and dangerously lyrical Russian people into effective factory workers. The League of Time, a mass movement, denounced 'tardy embezzlers of time' and carried out time-and-motion studies into every area of Soviet life. Like the Fyodor of these pages, they attempted to impose schedules and 'chronocards' on their long-suffering fellow-workers and communards – without huge success.

The idea of creating a new type of character, a Soviet man who had the capacity for Communism, was explored in dozens of different ways. Out of the work of Vkhutemas, the design studios, came the theory of 'rationalism' in architecture and in city planning: that the correct, functional, yet aesthetically designed living, work and public spaces could encourage good citizenship. Their suggestions may seem rather uninviting to us now – vast concrete blocks with a single laundry to service 25,000 inhabitants, or endless rows of identical dwellings arranged alongside motorways – but the theory itself, developed over the decades, has been vastly influential.

Communal living was one of the simplest yet most radical of these transformative methods. Under War Communism thousands of small cooperative rural communes (as distinct from traditional peasant communes) sprang up all over Soviet Russia; by 1921 there were 865 house-communes in Moscow (*dom-kommuny* in Russian – not to be confused with the archetypal *kommunalka*, communal flat, created when apartments were resettled by peasant and worker families, and famous for its squalor and ill-will).

Both rural and urban communes varied hugely, of course; some had little ideological content and were simply a way of stretching scant supplies, while others were a conscious effort to mould the 'new personality' and to influence wider society. Some were women-only; some were made up of groups of veterans, or employees of one factory, or university friends. Several accounts exist of communes in the twenties, to which the Institute of Revolutionary Transformation owes quite a debt: to the Muscovite librarians who collectivised their underwear, for example, and the Automotive Works of

Moscow Commune who appointed a string ensemble to entertain the other communards while they were doing the ironing.

As one might expect, sex, disagreements over money and petty domestic disputes emerge as the major challenges to harmony. Each commune had a different approach to the divisive issue of sex; some aimed for celibacy, while others allowed members to bring partners with them. A Moscow youth commune is reported as outlawing sex for two years until its members rebelled. The League of Time fiends seem to have been the most fundamentalist of all; they apparently disapproved of any close relationships between individuals, even platonic, and insisted on the commune spending all their leisure time together.

Discussions and 'confessions' of negative feelings were a fairly universal approach to solving disputes, while a charismatic leader was one of the factors that could bind a group together. There was a high turnover in most urban communes, particularly as many members objected to the communal raising of children. The collective life was in any case often seen as a temporary state for students or young workers, rather than a lifelong model. In the twenties a number of 'rational' communal apartment blocks were built, with shared living spaces and services, children's areas and so on. Some of these allowed a little privacy for couples and families; others provided conjoining rooms that could be locked in the case of divorce. The state also subsidised rural communes, even producing some pro-commune propaganda

– a leaflet entitled 'Come On, Live Communally!'

By the end of the twenties, however, the tide had turned against the avant-garde and all their experiments, including communal living. The two revolutions, which had run on parallel rails for a decade, now parted ways. State support was withdrawn and pressure was applied to individuals and institutions to end their search for new ways of living. Artists and writers were urged to adopt the simpler, drearier imagery and concerns of Socialist Realism, including, of course, the deification of the leader.

A century after the event, however, the extraordinary creativity and open-minded questioning of the avant-garde still amazes and inspires audiences across the world. 'The period of the Revolution and the twenties,' writes Richard Stites, 'was one of those rare moments when a large number of people actually tried to break the mould of social thinking that sets limits to mankind's aspirations, that defines "human nature" in a certain unchangeable way, that speaks in realistic, prudent, and ultimately pessimistic tones to the enthusiasts of this world in order to curb their energies and their fancies.' One of the irresistible aspects of early Soviet Art is its unusual optimism about humanity. The avant-garde's transformative art may have fallen short of its intentions, but like medieval alchemy it inspired new investigations and ultimately new understanding. Its creations – naïve to some, original and intuitive to others – have become an integral part of the fabric of Western culture. Dreamers then, but essential dreamers.

BIBLIOGRAPHY

Baer, Nancy Van Norman, *Theatre in Revolution: Russian Avant-Garde Stage Design 1913–35* (New York/London: Thames and Hudson, 1991)

Billington, James H., *The Icon and the Axe: An Interpretative History of Russian Culture* (New York: Vintage, 1970) (for the expression 'the alchemy of art')

Gray, Camilla, *The Russian Experiment in Art 1863–1922* (London: Thames and Hudson, 1962)

Stites, Richard, *Revolutionary Dreams: Utopian Vision and Experimental Life in the Russian Revolution* (Oxford: OUP, 1989)